GW00792915

Written
in Blood

Written in Blood

Robert A. Carter

**PIATKUS
CRIME**

Copyright © 1992 by Robert A. Carter

This edition first published in
Great Britain 1993 by
Judy Piatkus (Publishers) Ltd of
5 Windmill Street, London W1

**The moral right of the author
has been asserted**

*A catalogue record for this book is available
from the British Library*

ISBN 0–7499–0188–8

Printed and bound in Great Britain by
Butler & Tanner Ltd, Frome and London

HORATIO: And let me speak to the yet unknowing world
How these things came about. So shall you hear
Of carnal, bloody, and unnatural acts,
Of accidental judgments, casual slaughters,
Of deaths put on by cunning and forced cause,
And, in this upshot, purposes mistook
Fall'n on the inventors' heads. All this can I
Truly deliver.

Hamlet, V, ii

1

On Friday morning, the fourteenth of April, the movie rights to Jordan Walker's forthcoming book were sold to Talent Associates in Hollywood for three-quarters of a million dollars. On Friday evening, while attending a Book-of-the-Month Club party at the Waldorf-Astoria, I was hauled in to the city morgue on East 30th Street to identify Jordan's body.

Although I had never set foot in the place, I had a pretty good idea what the morgue would be like, from publishing—and reading—so many mysteries. Not only am I a fan of the genre, I consider myself a connoisseur. As the wine lover glories in discovering a rare and wonderful vintage, so do I cherish my ability to spot the vintage puzzlers and true crime yarns—the pride and joy of my firm, Barlow & Company, the best in the publishing business, if I do say so myself.

Yet the morgue was even worse than my crime-novel acquaintance with it led me to expect. The gray tiles on the walls and ceiling of the autopsy room, about forty by fifty feet in size, gave the look of an enormous operating room. Except that the steel tables under the glaring fluorescent lights were linked by pipes to the morgue's drainage system to carry away the blood—and covered with wire mesh like the stalls in a fish market. And the bodies brought here were beyond the reach of the surgeon's healing art. People in bloody aprons were working away at the tables, washing body parts. One of the corpses had bullet wounds; another had been crushed as though by the wheels of a bus. The body of one woman had a very private part cut out with a hacksaw. Another, so help me, had been beheaded. I shuddered.

The cop in charge led me along the tables until he found the one he was looking for, and drew back the sheet covering the body. I took a deep breath and looked down.

There lay the author of *Starlet*, of *My Life and Times on the Casting Couch*, of *Hairdresser to the Stars*, and half a dozen other show-business biographies.

"Recognize him?"

"It's him, all right," I said, with another shudder.

Poor Jordan. He was naked, his skin a cold greenish-white. He hadn't just been stabbed, he'd been carved up like a flounder. The upper part of his body, where the blood had dried, looked marbled. I'm not normally squeamish at the sight of blood, but I'll admit that Jordan's condition left me feeling slightly sick to my stomach. I must have swayed or blanched, for the officer with me—a remarkably cheerful young man, considering his duties—reached out to steady me.

"Better get you out of here," he said.

"I'll be fine," I said, but as soon as he closed the door to the autopsy room behind me, I bolted for the nearest john. There I did penance for a dinner far too rich in animal fats and starches.

When I emerged, still feeling light-headed, the young cop said, "If you're up to it, Homicide has some questions to ask you."

"I'm all right, Officer. Let's get to it."

•   •   •

I was led to an older plainclothesman seated behind a scruffy wooden desk half-buried under a small mountain of paper. A hand-lettered poster was Scotch-taped to the front of the desk: "If a Cluttered Desk Is the Sign of a Cluttered Mind, Then What Is an Empty Desk the Sign Of?"

The officer-in-charge looked up at me, unsmiling.

"I'm Detective-Sergeant Snyder. Homicide." He motioned me to a battered wooden chair beside the desk.

"Thanks."

I sat. We stared at each other for a moment. What I saw was a chunky, sallow face, heavily lined—probably by years of chain-smoking, disappointment, anger, and an understandable loss of faith in the human race's ability to police itself. His hair was silver and quite thick. He wore a neatly pressed if rather shiny blue worsted suit. His nails were cut to the quick, and he had shaved his chin so close it looked slightly raw. I put him in his late fifties.

He looked at me with eyes that took in everything and gave away nothing, but I could imagine what he thought of me. I was wearing my evening clothes: white tie and tails, a black silk opera cape, and a Borsalino hat. Moreover, I was carrying an ebony cane with a silver wolf's head, jaws ajar, at its handle. And as if that weren't intimidating enough, I am bearded, over six feet tall, and weigh in at 250 pounds, give or take a few.

In fact, I looked as I chose to look, like a cross between Orson Welles playing Falstaff, and Edward VII at his coronation. I was sporting all this regalia because I'd been at the Waldorf-Astoria attending the Sixty-fifth-anniversary dinner of the Book-of-the-Month Club when the patrolman came to summon me to the morgue. He'd been discreet, sent a message into the Grand Ballroom that I was wanted out in the foyer. There was no chance of anyone's thinking I'd been arrested, a prospect that any number of the authors and agents present on that festive occasion might have found appealing.

Let me digress a moment. I am seldom ruffled by unseemly behavior. Nor am I ever surprised by human frailty or venality, or disappointed by the daily instances I see of human folly. I have no great hope for the future of civilization, ours or any other, and no sentimental nostalgia for our appalling past. I don't forget an injury any more easily than I succumb to enthusiasm. I am as honest as the highly ambitious and sometimes insatiably greedy folk I deal with will allow me to be. What does all that make me, inevitably?

A successful book publisher, of course.

And in book publishing, that cottage industry with traces of glamour and pretensions of being Big Business, I am something of a personage—the head of my family's firm, founded not long after the Book-of-the-Month Club.

"I'm Nicholas Barlow," I said.

Snyder shrugged and lit a fat, dark cigar. Obviously not a subscriber to *Publishers Weekly*.

"I can give you coffee," he said. "Or booze. We've got that, too." He pulled a half-full bottle of VO from the desk drawer and pushed it toward me.

"Thanks, but I'd prefer just to get this over with."

He nodded. "I know how you must feel. So . . ."

He exhaled a cloud of cigar smoke that brought tears to my eyes. In self-defense I took an Uppmann from the gold case in my pocket, eased out the corona, and put the cigar into service, hoping I wouldn't feel sick again and spoil its heady savor. Soon I was enveloped in my own fragrant cloud.

"You knew the deceased well?" Snyder said. Now I felt at home. We were in that world I knew so well from police procedurals, where dead men are "deceased" and criminals are "perpetrators"—or, worse, "*alleged* perpetrators," sometimes even "perps." Indeed.

"I've been his publisher for about three years altogether," I said, "but he's been published by at least three other houses."

"Is that usual?"

"There was a time, Sergeant, when authors remained stubbornly attached to their publishers, and publishers could refer to *my* author and feel confident the possessive was accurate. Charles Dickens and Chapman and Hall is a good case in point. Ernest Hemingway and Charles Scribner is another. Not any longer. They come and they go. They go and they may come back—but not always."

"No loyalty, I take it."

"Loyalty," I said, "is not as important to most authors as royalty. Forgive the rhyme, it was intentional. In any case, there was another factor at work in Walker's case."

"Which was?"

"Jordan Walker was prolific, so prolific that no one publishing house could keep up with his output."

"I see."

"May I ask *you* a question, Sergeant? Because I don't think I can tell you much."

Snyder shrugged. "You never know what might be useful, Mr. Barlow. Anyhow, ask away."

"How ... where did it happen?"

"In his apartment." Snyder burrowed into the midden of paper on his desk and came up with a typewritten form. "Madison and Sixty-fifth, new luxury apartment house, all condos. Twenty-four-hour doormen, TV monitors, Thompson signal devices, the works. Victim was found just inside the door of his own apartment, stabbed repeatedly in the chest and abdomen"—Snyder hit the second syllable of that last word—"a classic break-in and felony murder, except—"

"What?"

"There's no sign of a forcible entry—none."

"Which means he probably let the killer in himself." *How many times have I run across* that *line*? I thought.

"Would you say Walker had any particular enemies?" Snyder asked.

"Only book reviewers with high standards."

"Nobody who would have wanted him dead? An ex-wife, maybe?"

"Four of them extant. But he treated them well. With all the alimony they had coming in, they'd hardly be likely to kill the Great Provider."

"We'll have to talk to them anyway," Snyder said. "Our motto in the PD is 'nearest and dearest.' Can you tell us where to find them?"

"Three of them, yes. He signed over some of his royalties to numbers one through three. Actually, he may have treated one of them less than well."

"Oh? Which one?"

"The next to the last one. Her name was ... let me think. Lavinia."

"Last name?" said Snyder.

"Her last name?" I mused a moment. "It has something to do with cats . . . something Latin. Oh, yes! Her last name was Felix. Lavinia Felix."

Snyder looked straight at me from under a pair of bristling black eyebrows and sighed, then scribbled in his notebook.

"You think maybe he was mixed up in a racket of some kind?"

"I'm not sure I know what you mean."

"A hustle? Something crooked?"

"Jordan Walker? I highly doubt it."

"Did he ever do anything criminal? That you know of, I mean."

Jordan's worst offense, in my view, was the way he dangled participles right and left, for all the world to see. Still, I didn't think such sins worth bringing up in this context. I shook my head.

"Hey, Gomez!" Snyder called out.

The young cop who had escorted me to the morgue snapped to attention.

"Yes, Sergeant?"

"Bring in Walker's clothes, will ya?"

Patrolman Gomez disappeared into another room.

"Do we have to?" I said.

"We found a letter from you in Walker's coat pocket, which is how we got your name in the first place, and why you were called in. Yes, we have to."

He located the letter in one of his folders and handed it over. I made no move to take it. I saw a long rip in it and dark stains I didn't need to see up close to recognize.

"It's an inquiry about his latest manuscript, right?"

Snyder didn't reply.

"That must be it," I said. "I remember writing him earlier this week. He's behind in delivering his next book."

"So?"

"You must understand, Sergeant, Jordan Walker was never late in delivering a manuscript. In fact, he was almost always early. He wanted his money, you see. The last installment of his advance was payable on delivery."

6

Gomez reappeared carrying a coat hanger with a suit and shirt draped over it, dark stains all over the suit—and a good many slashes in the fabric. I glanced at the clothes, then turned my head away.

"Are you satisfied?" I said to Snyder as calmly as I could.

"Just doing my job, Mr. Barlow."

"I hardly see why it was necessary for me to identify Jordan's clothes as well as his corpse."

"Recognize the suit, do you?"

"No. But then, Jordan must have owned a suit for every week of the year. He loved clothes. Expensive clothes." Remarkable how easily I had slipped into the past tense. It was only an hour since I'd learned that Jordan was dead.

"A dude, huh?" said Snyder.

He had shown me Jordan Walker's torn, bloody clothing because he wanted to shock me into blurting out something I would rather keep to myself. Wasn't that what the cops always did in police procedurals? Well, I'll grant him this: he had succeeded in shocking me. I got up.

Snyder rose to his feet along with me.

"I've got more questions to ask," he said.

"Then you'll have to take a rain check."

"You'll be hearing from us."

"I expect so. But for now—well, I've had enough."

He shrugged. "Anyway, we'll run you home."

"You needn't bother, I'll just grab a cab."

"We dragged you down here, didn't we? So you're still a guest of the city."

•　　•　　•

It was a short but dreary ride home. Gomez and a slim, light-skinned black cop sat up front, not saying a word to me and very little to each other. It began to pour shortly after we started: spattering volleys of something halfway between rain and sleet. We hit some gut-wrenching potholes near Gramercy Park and narrowly avoided colliding with a crosstown bus, a sanitation truck, and a bag lady. Naturally the traffic lights were all red, and naturally we ran them all with

7

sirens blaring. I spent half the time wanting the car to slow down and the other half wanting it to speed up, so I could get out of it all the faster.

I kept thinking of Jordan Walker lying on that cold steel table like so much meat. "Grossly, full of bread. With all his crimes broad blown, as flush as May." So Hamlet described his father's death. No human being should have to die that way, no matter how broad-blown his offenses, no matter how stupid or shallow his life. There was one thing that I was glad about: Jordan had undoubtedly known about the Hollywood sale of his new book. As I was deposited in front of number 2 Gramercy Park, I found myself wishing I had called to congratulate him about it. He'd have been pleased. There was nothing—not even gossip—that gave him more pleasure than money.

Which is only to say that Jordan Walker was put together the way most people are, whether they write books or not.

2

I love my weekends: I like to think they "knit up the ravelled sleave of care," to quote the bard once more. Not, however, the weekend after Jordan's death. Saturday started off routinely enough. I roused myself out of a sleep that felt like anesthesia to find a tray containing a moist blue cheese omelette surrounded by a ring of tiny broiled sausages, a pot of freshly brewed coffee, croissants with sweet butter and honey, the *Daily News* and the *Times* (for the crossword), and a red carnation in a bud vase, all organized by Pepita, my houseman Oscar's wife.

But I had hardly tucked my napkin inside my pajamas when the telephone rang. And rang again, and again. I decided to let Oscar take the call, which he evidently did, but a few minutes later the phone rang again. This time I shut off the bell, wondering who among my friends and acquaintances would call me at such an unseemly hour as ten o'clock on a Saturday morning—and on my private number at that.

I could hear the phone ringing away downstairs. It had no sooner stopped then the doorbell started.

I buzzed for Oscar.

"Noospepper pipple," he said.

"What are you telling them?"

"You not up yet."

"How about the doorbell?"

"Same thing."

"Next time anyone calls, say I'm out, OK?"

" 'K."

He took away my tray, the food half-eaten and already cold. Instead of tackling the crossword, I reached for the phone and dialed my attorney's home phone number. A woman answered. I heard a muffled conversation in the background, then the voice of Alex Margolies.

"What impels you to call me on *Shabbes?*" he said.

"Glad I found you in, Alex. I expected you to be out on the golf course."

"If you'd look out the window—"

"Can't. Curtains are drawn."

"—you'd know that it's raining."

"Listen, Alex. I need your advice." At one hundred fifty dollars an hour or any part thereof. I told him about Jordan.

"Is it in the papers yet?" he asked.

"In the Saturday edition? They wouldn't have had the time."

"Then my suggestion is that you hold a press conference, Nick."

"Oh, shit. Is that really necessary?"

"It's probably a hell of a lot better than being pestered all day by phone calls and doorbells. They won't let up, I assure you."

"But I don't know anything about the damned business— except that Jordan is dead and that he was probably mugged."

"Then you can talk about his books. Or his love life. And you should certainly express outrage at this vicious crime."

"You sound more like my publicity manager than my lawyer. Anyhow, I *do* feel outraged. I don't need any prompting on that score, thank you."

"Sorry if I took your feelings for granted. No offense meant."

"None taken, Alex."

"Fine. Then I'll look for you on the six o'clock news."

I swore at him, he laughed and hung up. Probably in bed getting his jollies off. I wished I was too.

Which reminded me that I had a dinner date with my former wife, Margo. I have been attempting, without conspicuous success, to talk her back into bed with me. I have no intention of marrying her again, nor would she be likely to consider it, but we're still good—if wary—friends, and she remains uncommonly attractive. I know I ought to look for somebody new to enhance my life, but I've been just too damned busy to get around to it.

I picked up the phone again and punched her number. A sleepy but surpassingly sultry voice answered. Except for an occasional lapse, such as the use of the hard *o* in *orange* or the flat *a* in *wash*, Margo has come a hell of a long way from her native Wayzata, Minnesota.

"Margo," I said.

"Yes?"

"It's me. Nick."

"I know the voice. You're growling at me."

"With good reason."

I told her what had happened. She was silent for a beat or two, then said, "Oh, God, that's dreadful. Just dreadful. Poor man."

"I know we'd planned to have dinner here tonight, but would you mind dining out instead?"

"Not at all, Nick. What is it, the cook's night out?"

"No, I'm going to be holding a press conference today, and I just don't know when I'll be free. I'll call you when it's over and pick you up at your place. Probably around seven."

"What are you planning to tell the press?"

"Oh, the usual things. How it's getting harder and harder to feel safe in New York. It would appear that we have enough thieves, muggers, and vandals here to populate a city the size of Cincinnati."

"Hadn't you better wait to see who or what is responsible for this?" she said.

"Who else could it be?"

She hesitated. "I don't know, anybody, I suppose. You, for example."

11

"Me?" My voice rose a register. "You've always said the easiest author to publish is a dead one."

"Don't be preposterous," I said. "Even in jest."

Anybody. The word stuck in my mind after we hung up. Anybody? Could that be possible? I finally shook the thought off. Still and all, I no longer felt quite so certain that it was—how had that cop Snyder described it?—"a classic felony murder."

The conference went about as I expected: a bunch of nosy reporters of both sexes, a couple of photographers, and cluttering up the place and getting in the way of the working press, the TV cameramen with all their gear. *"Yes, I consider the death of Jordan Walker to be a loss to American letters, at least to one subspecies of it, the celebrity tell-all. . . ." "No, I have no theories as to why he might have been murdered or who had done it. A vicious case of assault on an innocent citizen in his own home. . . ." "Walker was working on the memoirs of Graham Farrar, the Academy Award–winning stage and screen star. . . ." "No, the book was not quite finished. . . ." "Yes, Mr. Farrar is a personal friend of mine. . . ." "No, I have not yet spoken to him about Jordan Walker's death."* And so on and so forth.

When it was over, I invited everyone to stick around for a while and join me for a drink—certainly I'm no novice at handling the press. I blended myself a perfect Rob Roy and offered a silent toast to Jordan. His sales reports, like his books, always made entertaining reading.

Margo and I had dinner at La Caravelle, one of the obligatory eating and watering places for the book publishing trade. I don't remember what I ate, probably because I only toyed with my food. I couldn't get Jordan off my mind.

"How was the Book-of-the-Month Club dinner?" she asked.

"Do you know, I forgot all about it. Anyway, I never got back there. I'll have to ask Sidney how it went on Monday." Sidney is Sidney Leopold, my editor-in-chief at Barlow & Company. "And what's going on down on Wall Street?"

Margo, an executive for a high-priced downtown law

firm, spends most of her time shepherding young associates around, teaching them the ropes. She was a legal secretary before our marriage. While we were married, she earned an M.B.A. at Baruch; after the divorce I kept encouraging her to go back to law school and become a full-fledged lawyer.

"I wonder sometimes if I'm cut out for corporate law," she said.

"Too cutthroat for you?"

"That's not it necessarily. It's still such a closed corporation, a male enclave if you will—much like a private club."

"I'd thought that was changing as more and more women get law degrees. That's what Alex Margolies tells me."

"Oh, Alex. He's more enlightened than most. It just isn't changing fast enough for me."

"Then get *your* degree. Join the club. Make a difference."

"All good advice, but sometimes I think I'd rather ..."

"What?"

"No matter."

I had always thought of Margo as a transitional woman, one of those whose mothers had implanted in them traditional goals—marriage and family, *Kinder und Küche*—that were now options rather than categorical imperatives. Margo had remained a career woman during our marriage, although I certainly could have supported us both in a style some people would find luxurious. It wasn't, of course, her career that led us to the divorce court; it was the hours I kept at the office. I still insist on editing as well as acquiring books, you see— especially the thrillers and the whodunits—and I no more than any other editor can get any editing done during business hours.

I smiled. "I was remembering some of those marvelous fights we had."

"Like the night I locked you out on the terrace? And you had to climb in through the bedroom window?"

"Oh, yes. Along with the time you cut the telephone cord with a carving knife you then threatened to use on me. You wouldn't have, would you?"

"That was the night you were talking so long on the phone to that bitch, whatever her name was."

"That *author*, as I told you at the time."

"At the time I didn't believe you. But now I'll bet you were telling the truth—you workaholic sex fiend."

"That's a contradiction in terms," I said. "We could hardly have lasted as long as we did if we hadn't laughed a lot *and* loved a lot. Wasn't it V. S. Pritchett who said that sex is the laughter of two bodies?"

"Pretty words, Nick. But just words."

"We could have what's behind them again, you know. Still."

"Let's not and say we did, Nick. I like you but I don't trust you any further than the next room—especially if the next room has a bed in it."

"That's a hell of a thing to say."

She reached out and patted my hand. "Come on, Nick. Grow up. Take a look at yourself. You're good-looking, in a wolfish sort of way. You have a splendid set of teeth—"

I bared them, in what I hoped was a wolfish grin.

"You're perhaps a tad paunchy these days—"

I winced.

"—but you obviously patronize the right tailor. For a man you have beautiful hands, long, graceful fingers, a pianist's hands. I forget what your feet look like. You're intelligent, you can be witty and charming, but after one marriage and I don't know how many love affairs, you're a grumpy, somewhat misogynous middle-aged bachelor with hardly a selfless bone in your body."

"Ouch," I said. "You haven't got a particularly high opinion of me, have you?"

"On the contrary. I think you're a wonderful publisher. You have taste and integrity, yet you're a pretty good businessman as well. You're devoted to your authors, generous and caring to your family and friends. You're a reader, you really *love* books. In a society as avaricious as ours, you're practically a philanthropist. Moreover, you are a model employer, considerate and courteous to the people who work for you."

"I subscribe," I said, "to the George Bernard Shaw school of manners. A gentleman, if I remember it right, treats a serving-maid like a countess, and a countess like a serving-maid."

"Right."

"If I'm such a paragon, then . . . ?" I left the question unspoken.

"It's just that I have an equally high opinion of myself."

"So I'll keep on being a nuisance. . . ."

"And I'll keep on saying no."

Which is how the evening ended. At the entrance to her apartment building, Margo kissed me on both cheeks and said, "Don't hold it against me, Nick, I just don't want an ex-husband for a lover. But I do value your friendship, and your company. You have—what is that Spanish word, *duende?*—style. But you've got too much on your mind to play Casanova, your thoughts are weighing you down, and I don't want them weighing me down too. I love you, Nick, I really do—and good night. Call me again soon."

I phoned Margo on Sunday morning and suggested that since she was not only my Saturday friend but my Sunday friend as well, she might enjoy looking at forsythia buds and whatever crocuses had reared their heads in Connecticut. She thanked me but pleaded a prior engagement. I felt a twinge of disappointment, but only a twinge. Margo is right about me. I have too many things on my mind, and while she is certainly high on the list, Jordan's murder had taken pride of place.

So I tucked the newspapers and a couple of manuscripts under my arm and headed for the country. Oscar got the Mercedes out of the garage and drove me to Grand Central.

Along the way, I gazed reflectively at the pink furrows on the back of Oscar's neck, hair neatly trimmed, cap planted squarely on his head. I had told him when he was first hired that he needn't wear a uniform if he didn't want to (God knows I hated mine in my air force days), but he'd insisted. "Is more better" was the way he'd put it, clearly relishing his role as chauffeur. I was reminded of Wallace Stevens's line: "One is not duchess a hundred yards from a carriage."

"You've read about Mr. Walker's murder, Oscar?" I said at one point.

"Ya."

"What do you think?"

Without taking his eyes off the traffic, he waved toward the street with his left hand.

"No good pipple," he said. "Ever'where. Is murder, murder, murder, ever' day."

I looked out the window where he pointed, but saw no one more menacing than one of New York's mad bikers, pedaling furiously along against traffic, like a salmon darting upstream.

"But you're happy here, aren't you, Oscar?"

"It's good here for Oscar and Pepita, Meester Barlow," he said. "Where I come from in Latvia, is nawthing, you know? No mawney, no jobs, no bathtub, no nawthing. So maybe I get keeled, yes?" He shrugged. "I die happy."

We pulled up in front of Grand Central and I got out. As I was about to close the car door, Oscar leaned toward me and beckoned.

"Yes, Oscar, what is it?"

"Is good," he said softly. "Is *wery* good."

As he drove off, I mulled over Oscar's parting words. What, I wondered, did he consider good? America? New York City? My Mercedes-Benz? Or was it life itself he found good? I settled on life itself, and on a sunlit, almost-spring day, how could I think otherwise?

·   ·   ·

During the hour-long train ride I leafed through the papers, skipping over less vital matters such as the latest snags in the Mideast peace negotiations and the current *faux pas* of the administration, going straight to the reports of Jordan's death. Much of what I read I already knew. No suspects had turned up. I was quoted as having said that a memorial service for the late author would be held within the week, details to be announced. The burial would be private. Other, juicier details—what the French call *faits divers*—were supplied by the *New York Post* reporter.

Both dailies included the stock photograph my company's publicity department sends out: Jordan wearing a sport shirt open at the throat, a wispy patch of chest hair, his mouth open to project a grin worthy of the village idiot. We were never able to get him to strike a serious pose in front of a camera.

One item in the *Times* story caught my eye.

> The doorman of the victim's apartment building reported to police that when Walker entered, he was carrying an attaché case. The case was not found in his apartment and was presumably stolen by the murderer. A police department spokesman said that the victim's wallet was also missing and that various dresser drawers had been emptied of their contents. It was not known what other valuable items may have been taken.

I dumped the newspapers on the empty seat beside me and shut my eyes, hoping to catch a catnap. It wasn't to be. I kept picturing Jordan Walker's attaché case. What if it had contained the manuscript of his book? Somehow I had to get hold of that manuscript. Good lord, I was beginning to sound like Nancy Drew.

"Westport . . . *Westport!*"

Looking out the train window, I saw a familiar long black Cadillac limousine, my mother's chauffeur standing protectively beside it. Harry Dennehy had been around when the family car was a 1931 Packard Cabriolet. I suspect his was one of the first driver's licenses ever issued in Connecticut. Yet he's the best driver I've ever met, including one or two Indy 500 winners. Harry at the wheel is a modern centaur, half man, half machine. He is also a man of blessedly few words.

"Stayin' long?" he asked.

"Just overnight, Harry."

"Pity."

"Hiding out, you might say."

"Can't blame you."

Harry, I knew, read the newspapers. The daily paper was probably the only thing he *did* read.

Still, I knew I hadn't come out to Westport just to escape the phone and the doorbell. It was more that I needed to touch base, so to speak. Antaeus coming to earth so he might renew his strength. And I needed to visit the brightest man I know, my brother, Tim.

3

Home for my mother consists of an eighteenth-century Colonial house, a barn, and various small outbuildings on fifteen acres of prime Connecticut real estate. It used to be a working farm, with livestock, a truck garden, a flower garden, and a tobacco field. These—all but the flowers, now blooming in a greenhouse—have given way to a swimming pool, a tennis court, a paddle court, and a sculpture garden. There is also a small stream running through the property and flowing into the Saugatuck River. Shortly after the house was built, a dam was put in, along with a millrace and a wheel. My parents bought the land and rebuilt the main house several years before I was born—bought it for what in Depression times was a princely sum and today would be considered adequate, perhaps, for the down payment on a thirty-year mortgage.

Mother was on the telephone in the living room when I arrived. She waved at me and went right on talking, ordering up a supply of oats for the horses and complaining about the last delivery. I shuffled aimlessly around the room, staring at pictures I know by heart. She nodded at me, beckoning me closer with her free hand. I walked over to her and planted a kiss on top of her head, taking care not to disarrange the coils of faintly blue hair. At last, with a final sigh that resembled a snort, she put down the phone.

"You cannot buy good value these days," she announced.

"Is that so, Mother?"

"In *my* day, tradesmen were grateful for one's business. They did not whine and fuss and make pathetic excuses. If a customer was dissatisfied, they made good."

"Yes, Mother."

In *her* day they probably also tugged at their forelocks when spoken to. But no use trying to bring Mother up to date. Not only was she of the old school, she was its headmistress.

"Does *anyone* care about quality?" she asked me.

"If that's not a rhetorical question, Mother, the answer is yes, a few of us do. If you're talking about your grain and feed merchant—"

"But even you, Nicholas, are not above publishing trash from time to time. Books I wouldn't give houseroom to, yet *our* name is on them."

We were always on uncertain ground when talking about the firm. My mother and father founded Barlow & Company back in the thirties, when it was possible for two youngsters to start a publishing house with a five-thousand-dollar inheritance, one manuscript, and an underpaid staff of two. The printers waited for their payments until money came in from the booksellers and wholesalers; my father sold the first list to the stores himself, and it wasn't until they got a line of credit from the First Bank of Manhattan that the Barlows of Barlow & Company could even pay themselves salaries. They were equal partners. Both of them edited, and my father ran the business side.

Most of their early books were European, a good many of them British. They chose well: a couple of Nobel Prize winners, several Prix Goncourt novels. But it wasn't all caviar; they also published mysteries and what used to be known as ladies' rental library fiction. And so in the fullness of time the company thrived, and as they were the primary—at first the only—stockholders, they became increasingly prosperous. Moreover, to ice the cake, a doting aunt of Mother's died and left her another million dollars or so. Like so many of her class, Mother does not believe in talking about her assets, only in accumulating them.

"Well, Mother," I said, "that's really neither here nor there. After all, Alfred Knopf was happy to publish Kahlil Gibran, even though he never read *The Prophet* himself and couldn't understand why anyone would want to."

"You know perfectly well that I'm not referring to literate juvenile poetry collections but to books like that Jordan Walker's . . . nothing more than gossip columns writ large."

"Which is precisely why people want to read them," I said, "and aren't they better off reading books—at least, we call them books—than *The National Enquirer?*" Far be it from me to prescribe what people read. I'm glad they read anything at all.

She snorted, took a deep breath, filling her impressive chest with air that smelled of fresh lilac. In her embroidered housecoat, with her lacquered fingernails, powdered cheeks, and gold-rimmed spectacles, she resembled nothing so much as a Romanov princess in exile.

There's another reason I always tread softly when the firm comes up in my conversations with Mother. The truth is, *she* controls the purse strings. My father named me president and publisher of Barlow & Company before his death, but he left the fiduciary responsibility in her still-forceful hands. She doesn't do much kibbitzing editorially, if I may put it that way, but she surely knows how to read a balance sheet.

"You're worried, aren't you, Nicholas?" she said, breaking into my revery.

"About what, Mother?" A half a million dollars riding on a deal for a book I'd scheduled for the fall list and hadn't seen yet. Why would I worry?

"About that murder, of course. It's written all over you. When I mentioned that man's name, you blinked your eyes open and shut three times."

"That transparent, am I?"

"And I saw you on the television news. You looked rather dissipated, by the way, those awful circles under your eyes— are you sure you're getting enough rest?"

"Mother, there's no such thing as enough rest."

"You've always needed your eight hours, Nicholas. And an afternoon nap as well."

I sighed and wished she'd change the subject. When she did, I wished she hadn't.

"I hope you haven't gone and gotten yourself involved with another woman," she said.

"Good God, no."

"Because when I don't hear from you for over a week, I'm always afraid you're . . . mixed up with somebody."

"No, no, don't worry about that. If there's anything I'm mixed up with, as you put it, it's Jordan Walker's murder. Naturally I welcome your thoughts on this matter, Mother. Always."

"Though it's really Tim you've come to see, isn't it?"

"Well, I—"

"No matter," she said. "I understand. You want the benefit of his insights. All the same, I'll tell you my opinion. I think that your Mr. Walker was probably a homosexual—"

"Jordan? Oh, *come*, Mother."

"—and that he was probably murdered by some young man he picked up on the street. All those women in his life were only window dressing. He's just the type to prefer men, so catty and prying and vulgar underneath. . . ."

"Mother!"

"They do say that men who are promiscuous with women are often concealing their homosexual desires. It's called overcompensation, or something like that. Casanova for one. And Don Juan, and Lord Byron, of course! Didn't Sigmund Freud have something to say about it? Yes, I'm sure he did, somewhere in one of those peculiar books of his. Well, Nicholas, can you deny it?"

"I don't think I need to. I've spent enough time with Jordan Walker to have some idea of what he was like. I assure you that if he was homosexual, I never saw the slightest sign of it."

She looked so crestfallen that I added: "Not that I have any clearer idea than you of what might have happened, Mother."

"Then you aren't dismissing my theory out of hand?" she said, brightening.

"Not at all."

She nodded, as though weighing the strange behavior of a man who could spend all his life in thrall to women and, in his final days, turn gay.

"I'll go up and see Tim now," I said.

"I wish you would."

"Is he any better?"

"Let's say—no worse."

"Oh, Lord." Not swearing, but a form of prayer, if an agnostic like me can ever be said to pray. Do I believe? Yes and no. To quote St. Mark's Gospel: "Lord, I believe; help thou mine unbelief." And I'm not even so sure of *that*.

I rose, kissed her again, this time lightly on the cheek, and left the room.

•   •   •

Mounting the stairs to Tim's suite, I was so overcome by the presence of memory in this house that I had to stop at the landing for breath before I could go on. Playing hide-and-seek through the upstairs corridors and attic. My mother as a young matron. My father, vigorous and elegant and lordly in his Savile Row suits, freshly barbered and smelling of cologne. And Tim, riding bareback in our meadow and doing the butterfly stroke in our pool. The past was all around me; I inhabited it now in a kind of time warp.

A strong beam of sunlight poured through the stained-glass window and cast many-colored shadows on the landing; light fell there in exactly that way thirty years ago. Even the odors I smelled now were the same as those I had smelled then: linseed oil, verbena, beef roasting in the oven downstairs. Back in the long ago, Sunday dinner would be served in an hour or so, and for our supper, just before going to bed, Tim and I would be served a bowl of fresh fruit packed in ice with a plate of crisp graham crackers and butter—or perhaps a shrimp salad on a bed of crackling lettuce—washed down with ice-cold glasses of chocolate milk.

I knocked gently on Tim's door.

"Nick?"

"Right."

"Come in, please."

The words seemed to arrive from a long distance away. I went through the study—ceiling-high with bookshelves on three of the walls. The fourth wall was solid glass and looked out over a redwood deck. Books in bookcases, on top of bookcases, piled on tabletops, on the glass cabinet that held a collection of trophies: several statuettes of tennis players, skaters, a football player. There were also an autographed football and a number of photographs, some of them shots of Tim with me or other members of our family, a few of them group shots: a football team, an army platoon.

The room was, in a way, Tim's autobiography—at least up until the day of the accident.

A second door led from the living room into Tim's bedroom; that door was ajar.

"I was hoping you'd come out for a visit," Tim said.

I stepped into the bedroom, smiled, and waved at him. It would never do to let him know by the expression on my face how saddened I felt, how inconsolable, each time I saw him—although I'm sure he knew, somewhere in that part of his being where he alone confronted the inadmissable.

Let me say, complacent as it may sound, that I love my brother as he is, not just as he used to be. As he is now ... well, today he was lying in bed covered with a light cotton blanket. Under that blanket and under the robe he was wearing lay his legs, withered and useless, I knew. Outside the blanket his arms and hands appeared as normal as yours or mine—if anything somewhat more muscular, though quite pale, so white they seemed translucent. I could see the blood vessels pulsing in his wrists. His face was heavily lined, but as handsome as it has always been; his hair was thick, black, shot through with flashes of gray. His voice was light and musical, oddly elated. I was never quite sure when I came to visit him how he would sound. Depressed, bitter, determined,

24

resigned; I had heard him ring every possible change of feeling through the years.

"Almost three weeks since you were here last," he said, looking up at me with his dark, deep-set eyes.

My brother Tim has not walked or stood upright since that April day when he attempted to climb a hundred-foot tree in an open field near our property. Homemade ladder rungs had been nailed into the tree all the way up the trunk. One of the rungs was loose, and Tim's weight was enough to dislodge it. He fell over fifty feet. And—you know how it is—all the king's horses and all the king's men . . .

Why, just at the moment he chose to climb the tree half a dozen teenagers had just climbed, did the rung break? Having posed the question to psychiatrists, astrologers, ministers of the gospel, and at least one professional philosopher, I have yet to receive a single satisfactory answer. Such answers as *have* come my way lay the blame at various doors, from God's (watch out for those almighty dice) to Tim's (something in his nature impelled him to prove that he was as brave, or as reckless, as any teenager around). His reward was a broken spine.

I once put the question directly to Tim, who paid me the compliment of taking it seriously.

"I make it from one day to the next by recognizing that I was probably meant to die in that fall," he said. "Meant to die—yes, really—but somehow I beat it. I beat death, Nick, even though death took part of me with it. At first, of course, gratitude didn't come easy." I knew that he'd once tried to smash the trophy case in his study and had lacked the strength at the time to carry it through. "But knowing I'm alive when by rights I ought to be dead made it possible to keep going. Like Robinson Crusoe, I have to make my life day by day out of what I find at hand."

And so he did. Of course it helped that there was family money, enough to install an elevator, provide him with a motorized wheelchair, build a fully equipped exercise room and a heated indoor pool, and pay for a physiotherapist. But in the end the fact that Tim's spirit survived the destruction of so much of his body came down to Tim himself. There is a line in one of Sir Philip Sidney's essays that describes him: "He ranged far and wide within the zodiac of his wit." He missed nothing, remembered everything. He invented word games, devised puzzles in logic, solved cryptograms. The computer might have been invented so that Tim would be able to explore its wonders. He began his day by solving the *Times* crossword puzzle—the London, not the New York, *Times*—and ended it by reading Marcus Aurelius in Latin or Plato in Greek. An autodidact in every sense of the word, he had taught himself several other languages, including Russian. There was a certain desperation in all this, perhaps, as if he dreaded confronting a single idle or unproductive moment. He wrote well and was a superb editor. I used him constantly to supplement my staff, and he was the only person other than myself I trusted with our mysteries.

His first question today was "What are you reading?"

"The new Dick Francis."

"Like it?"

"Enormously," I said. "I wish it were one of our books." Every publisher lives to find a mystery writer who can break out of the field and find a broad popular following. We do not deprecate our best-sellers, however the reviewers might choose to trash them. And though we do our share of whoring, we still remain capable of falling in love. Which of us wouldn't want a P. D. James or a Ruth Rendell, a Patricia Highsmith or a Tony Hillerman on our list?

"I've brought some manuscripts out for you," I said, and dropped a bulging attaché case on Tim's bed.

"Maybe we'll catch a rabbit," he said, invoking our family joke about the recipe for rabbit stew: first you catch a rabbit. "Anything promising?" he said.

"A book on Polynesian mysticism that may appeal to the Shirley MacLaine market," I said. "Hypnotize yourself and reexperience your former lives."

"Better than MacLaine?"

"No worse. Tim, ..." I said, more loudly than I had intended, "what do you think?"

He motioned for me to raise the head of his bed. At the

same time I plumped up his pillows and held a water glass to his lips. He drank from it greedily. Some of the water leaked out of the side of his mouth and dripped down on his robe. When I started to look around for a towel or a napkin, he shook his head fiercely.

"Fu ... fu ... *forget* it," he said.

"So ... what do you think, Tim?"

I didn't need, I hardly ever needed, to tell him what I meant. Tim was always one step ahead of me mentally.

"Jordan Walker," he said, "was an asshole, I suppose."

"You might say that. Many have."

"But what kind of asshole, Nick? Careless?"

"Anything but."

"Extravagant?"

"No again. Oh, Jordan lived well, but with the calculated miserliness of a man who can still remember his boyhood poverty, complicated in his case by the Great Depression. He was scared to death that he might wake up someday and find himself without a cent to his name. So he—well, how shall I put it? He saved string."

"What?"

"He used to ask one of our New York salespeople to drive him to JFK so he might avoid the expense of a taxi or limousine—that sort of thing. There was a rumor he recycled his Christmas cards."

"And yet he lived on Madison Avenue?"

"Oh, he was capable of spending grandly, lavishly, on his own living quarters. But one of his former wives once told me he did his writing in a miserable little office somewhere downtown."

"Where do we begin to look for a motive?" Tim said. "What was he working on?"

I told him. "The police," I added, "seem to think it was a felony murder, plain and simple."

"You and I, on the other hand, have minds that run along more fictional lines. A belief in order, or a conviction that nothing happens by accident. Do you know Jung's theory of synchronicity?"

"I remember it. Vaguely."

"It explains away the idea of coincidence. Whenever two apparently isolated but somehow related events occur, they must in fact be connected. *Not* coincidental."

"So?"

"Murder is not likely to take place at random."

"A publishing pun if I ever heard one."

"I'm not joking," Tim said. Nor did I think he was; Tim's mind always ran along a different track from mine; his thinking was always clearer.

"I agree with you. But still, think of all the random violence in the city, the country, the world. Terrorism, vandalism, felonious assaults, murder almost by indifference. 'Casual slaughters,' as Shakespeare called them in *Hamlet*. Who's to say Jordan wasn't just another victim of the latter-day barbarism?"

"What about the attaché case, Nick? Where is Jordan's new manuscript? Do you know?"

I shook my head. "He hasn't—hadn't—delivered it yet."

"Have you read what he's done so far?"

"I never see any of his stuff until it's finished. He preferred it that way."

"So where is the manuscript now?"

"It usually comes to me from his agent, Jeffrey Burgal. When it's finished, of course."

"How was it sold to Talent Associates? An outline—or a synopsis?"

"Probably. That's his agent's job."

"Then, if I were you," Tim said, "I'd start with Burgal."

"What do you mean, start with him? Start what?"

"If you're obsessed about this business," he said, with insight amounting to smugness, "you'll just have to indulge the obsession until you've worked it off."

"Pfui."

Tim grinned. "Where is Nero Wolfe now that we need him?"

"I'd settle for Archie Goodwin, myself," I said.

That pretty well finished off the Walker Affair for the day. Or as Tim called it, "The Case of the Missing Attaché Case." We talked of other matters. Tim announced that he had just solved a chess problem that gave him mate in four moves, but when I pressed him for the solution, he refused to give it to me. "We'll be playing one of these days, and I'll spring it then," he said.

I would not want to create the impression that my brother is conceited about his intellectual achievements. He is rather proud of his IQ, which is well above the genius level, but he bears it lightly.

He proceeded to regale me with the latest news from his celebrated pen pals, a list that included John Kenneth Galbraith and Stephen Jay Gould, as well as a senator or two and one Supreme Court justice—the only liberal left on that particular bench. I countered by telling him some of the office news and industry gossip. I was in the middle of a story about the latest merger rumors (Simon & Schuster merging with Macmillan, and both being courted by Time Warner) when Mother joined us and announced dinner. We helped Tim into his wheelchair and into the elevator.

Downstairs we took dinner in our formal dining room. Mother's cook is not quite as versatile as my Pepita, but she does well by prime rib, and the Barlow wine cellar produced a passable burgundy to go with it. Tim, as usual, ate dutifully (the body must be served, after all) but hardly with what I would describe as gusto; Mother, also as usual, ate in a ladylike manner but left nothing on her plate. I must confess that I was the only one at the table who called for seconds. When I was a child, Mother used to press all the leftovers at dinner on me to finish off, claiming that if the bowls were empty, "we'd have a stormy day tomorrow." I almost believed her but cleaned up the leftovers anyway.

During dinner Mother informed me, in the excessively animated fashion with which people convey news *they* find exciting, that Graham Farrar had called.

"Well?" she said.

"Well what?"

"Aren't you going to call him back, Nicholas?"

"No, I am not."

She pursed her lips. Not call back the famous star of stage, screen, and television? How could I not? For all her savoir-faire, Mother was incurably star struck.

"Look, Mother," I said, "I have no desire to talk to Graham Farrar today, or his agent, or his secretary, or Steven Spielberg, or George Lucas, or *anybody* in Hollywood at all."

"Nicholas, will you be serious for a moment? You have a crisis to think about."

"No, Mother. I will not. Today I will be carefree. In the immortal words of Margaret Mitchell," I said, with my best attempt at fluttering eyelashes, " 'I'll think about it tomorrow.' "

There was still light enough after dinner to take a walk around our property. I needed to be alone, for starters. Much as I love them both, a little of Mother's furious curiosity and commanding manner goes a long way.

When this oppressive anxiety, this intense feeling of being a caged lion, comes over me, I need to walk around our land. I've stepped on every foot of our acreage so often that I could do it blindfolded, but whatever the season, the land never fails to work its restorative magic. I marveled now at how many shades of green there are in April, from the lemon green of the forsythia buds to the sea green of the spruce branches tossing in the gentle wind. The air was quick with promise.

About five acres of our land is forest: deep, massive woods, thick with pine, oak, and ash. On the way back from the woods, I crossed our meadow: six acres of wild grass, short now, but in August it would be knee-deep and golden. Harry Dennehy, mounted on a tractor mower, cuts it twice a year. *The birds, I see, are coming back,* I thought. *What birds? What are their names? And what difference does it make?* I did my best to push out of mind anything that might spoil the peace of my walk, most particularly the murder of Jordan Walker. Or the reasons why Graham Farrar had called. *You could have returned his call and found out, idiot. And where is the manuscript? I don't know, I don't want to know, not now!*

I'll think about Jordan Walker and Graham Farrar when I feel like it. Whenever.

4

Monday after Jordan Walker's murder. I am in my office by fifteen minutes past nine, early for me. There are already several people waiting. One—a sallow, bony gent dressed in black with a white shirt, old-fashioned string tie, and a porkpie hat—has a worn leather briefcase propped on his lap. Withered shanks protrude from his hitched-up trouser cuffs, barely covered by wrinkled white silk socks. I know what is in that briefcase without opening it: a manuscript, his life's work, his heart's blood, the child of his genius—at the very least, a masterpiece. I feel the onset of pity, an emotion hard to distinguish from contempt and perhaps at bottom the same thing. He is a fellow creature, and I respect his humanity. He is also an Author, God help me.

And his book? A gloss on *The Bhagavad-Gita*, perhaps? Forty years in the life of a country day school principal. Or, worst-case scenario, a multigenerational family saga set in the province of Manitoba. What it will *not* be, most assuredly, is a steamy romance full of heavy-breathing sex or an international thriller full of derring-do and state-of-the-art military hardware. Books such as these I might be able to publish and sell.

A second occupant of the couch rises as I pass the receptionist's desk on the way to my office. I have instructed the receptionists not to call me by name when I pass by; I want to remain incognito at least until I've had the chance to get my hat and topcoat off. Somehow this one seems to know who I am. She hurries toward me, trapping me before I can get by the reception desk.

"Mr. Barlow . . . please?"

"Yes?"

She smiles up at me. An attractive smile, open and guileless. Her face, too, is attractive—not beautiful, but ripe, unlined, olive tinted. Full lips and dark, slightly windblown hair. I can't tell what her figure is like under her loosely draped coat, but I can see she's wearing nail polish that matches her lip gloss. I like that. I suppose I look at every woman, especially one I'm meeting for the first time, somewhat lustfully. But then, lust is the verso of gallantry. A world without both lust and good manners—well, I simply can't envision it.

"I know you're in a hurry, Mr. Barlow," she says. Her voice is soft, with just a hint of throatiness. "I'm a friend of Margo Richmond."

"Oh?"

"I'm Jane Goodman."

"Oh?" A slightly less comprehending inflection on the query this time.

"She didn't mention me?"

"Not so far as I can remember, but then . . . Jane *Goodman*, you say?"

She nods.

"Job hunting?"

She smiles again, showing a fine set of teeth, even and bright. This time I sense a certain mockery in the smile, but directed as much against herself as me—with perhaps a dash of rue.

I bow slightly, to show her that I bear no inherent malice toward job hunters. I am about to say, as nicely as I can, "Shove off, no jobs today," when I see her lips tighten and her shoulders go back. Instead, I find myself saying, "If you don't mind waiting, Ms. Goodman, I'll see what I can do to fit you in. At least I'll get you to our personnel manager."

"I appreciate that."

"I don't suppose you made an appointment?"

"No, I didn't. I'm sorry, but my name wouldn't have meant anything to you—and you see, I know how hard it is to make an appointment with you."

"Oh?" A touch of irritation this time.

"I've tried so often."

"Well, we'll see."

"Thank you, Mr. Barlow."

"Don't mention it." But she doesn't hear me; she's already on her way back to join Gramps on the couch. And I'm on my way to one of the ghastliest Mondays in forty-odd years of Mondays.

5

When I had my office decorated, the architect asked me what atmosphere I preferred to work in. What I had in mind was something like the House of Burgesses in Colonial Williamsburg or the headmaster's office at Phillips Exeter. What I got was a comfortable and fairly dignified cave. Many books, not all of them published by my firm; dark wood paneling; a Persian rug I know to be at least three centuries old, which, in consequence, is displayed on the wall instead of the floor. Portraits in oil of my father and paternal grandfather. A thick burgundy carpet, an Eames chair and ottoman, overstuffed chairs for visitors, and some good reading lamps. Oh, yes, and windows that really open. Altogether, a place in which I'm happy to spend my days—alone, at work.

Solitude was not to be mine today, however. I had scarcely unfolded my *New York Times* when there came a soft knock on the door, followed almost immediately by my editor-in-chief, Sidney Leopold. Sidney, a slim, dapper man somewhere in his thirties with a tonsure ringed by a wild halo of frizzy brown curls, is the only person other than my secretary who has immediate access to my office.

"Yes, Sidney?" I lowered my paper and raised one eyebrow.

"I can't tell you," he said, speaking with the slight stammer that occasionally reduces him to an eye-popping silence,

"How shocked I was at the news. J-J-Jesus! To be butchered like that!"

"Not a pretty sight, Sidney, to be sure."

He gasped. "You *s-s-saw* him?"

"In the morgue."

Sidney is frightened by many things: air travel, packed elevators, thunderstorms, runaway horses, and unleashed dogs; but mostly he is frightened by blood and gore. That's why I keep him away from the harder-boiled mystery and suspense novels, reserving the right to acquire and edit them myself. When it comes to facing down an author, an agent, or a manuscript in need of severe cutting, however, Sidney is absolutely fearless. That is why I pay him a salary in the low six figures, plus generous bonuses when he brings in a big bestseller. But when faced with a threat to his person, Sidney is the most timid of men.

He has but one vice that I'm aware of: ice cream. He chose his East Side apartment for its proximity to several ice cream shops; of an evening he goes from Häagen Dazs to Baskin-Robbins to Sedutto's and back again. Occasionally Sidney will visit the same store twice in one evening, in which case he may change his jacket or don a hat so he won't be recognized.

"Sidney," I said, while he made faint percussive sounds with his lips, "I would like to call an editorial meeting. This morning, if possible."

"Sure, Nick. Only . . ." I waited while he struggled to speak. "So?"

"Prudence . . ." This was going to be a challenge. "Heh . . . heh . . . *heh*-enderson Harte is here!"

Prudence Henderson Harte. The American Agatha Christie, although I personally found her novels to be alarmingly overpopulated with cats. Sales in the millions of some fifty or sixty books, I forget exactly how many. Reprint sales, book club sales, movie sales, television miniseries sales. Creator of at least three different popular detectives. The joy of publishing her is that she does not need much editing and turns her books out like cupcakes, each of them dictated to a secretary in a matter of weeks. Her manuscripts need only routine copy-editing before immediate transmission to a computerized typesetter. Within a short time finished books flow out of the bindery and into the eager hands of booksellers, and thence to her avid fans.

"I should see her, but I'd rather not see her today—d'you mind, Sidney?"

"She'll be c-c-crushed. Utterly."

"Too bad. Do your best. Say that we're all in mourning for Jordan Walker. Tell her whatever, I don't care."

"Our . . . p-p-premiere mystery novelist, and you w-w-won't see her?"

"Even so."

"She's determined."

"All right then." I sighed deep and long. "We'll give her the coat trick."

To pull off this gambit, Sidney signals me when he is helping an unwelcome guest on with his or her coat. Just as the guest is being shown into the foyer, I pop out of my office, obviously on my way to someplace important, like the washroom. Time enough to shake hands and utter a few platitudes, and then I am off, with a minimum loss of time.

"If that's . . . the best you can do . . . OK."

Sidney departed and I opened my *Times* again. The buzzer on my phone sounded.

"Yes, Hannah?"

"A gentleman from the police department to see you." She spoke in low, guarded tones; whoever it was, he was probably hovering over her desk. Like most of us, my secretary finds the presence of policemen unnerving.

I swore under my breath, then again out loud.

"It wouldn't be a Sergeant Snyder from Homicide, would it?"

"No, it's a Lieutenant . . . excuse me, your name? . . . a Lieutenant Scanlon."

"All right. Send him in."

Scanlon was quite presentable: one of your college-educated cops with an obvious grasp of the right fork. A Literary Guild subscriber, probably. Bachelor apartment in the Heights or Park Slope, Dewars and water, or Jack Daniel's with a splash of soda. Just short of six feet tall, dark hair tightly coiled on his scalp, and smelling faintly of a lime-scented cologne. Not a jock, but that wasn't flab under his Harris tweed jacket.

He thrust out a hand; I shook it, expecting a firm grip. It was all that and more.

"Mr. Barlow. Good of you to see me."

"Glad to, Lieutenant, if it's about the Walker murder."

"Right."

"I'll do anything I can to help you catch the man who did it. Anything."

"Man—or woman," he said. "Anyway, I'm glad you feel that way. Some questions?"

"Ask away."

"Frankly, Sergeant Snyder's preliminary interview, while satisfactory for a start, was . . ." He searched as carefully as any of the authors I deal with for the exact word. ". . . tantalizing."

"Ah."

"Yes?"

"Just *ah*."

"The sergeant reported that you were somewhat evasive, Mr. Barlow. I hope you don't mind me being . . . well, blunt."

"Not at all. I shall be the same. But I assure you I wasn't so much evasive as disoriented."

Scanlon mulled this over briefly, then nodded.

"I trust I'll be of some help now."

"Good," he said. "for starters, is it true that Jordan Walker was working on Graham Farrar's biography?"

"Yes, that's right."

"So!" The word was followed by a low, soft sigh of appreciation. Graham Farrar was not only a star, he was also authentically macho, a onetime barroom brawler who had played a number of policemen in his career, always the tough, incorruptible types. He'd been made an honorary member of the Los Angeles Police Force—an honor he accepted in person.

"Have you read the manuscript?" asked Scanlon.

"Not yet."

"Has anyone?"

"I assume his agent, Jeffrey Burgal, has read it."

He took out his pocket diary. "How do I get in touch with this agent?"

I gave him Burgal's number, then asked, "Do you think the book might have something to do with it? Sergeant Snyder seemed to think it was a classic felony murder."

"We have to follow every lead we can," he said. "Was Walker a gambler?"

"Well, Lieutenant," I said, "I suspect Jordan laid a bet down now and then, and he did vacation occasionally in Las Vegas. But I would doubt he was a heavy plunger, he was too stingy for that. He had a bookie, though."

"Yes?" The pocket diary was out again.

"Whose code name was Victor."

"Real name?"

"I have no idea."

"Any idea where I might find him?"

"I believe he operated out of a Burger King in Jackson Heights."

"Thanks a lot."

"You're most welcome."

"You could be very helpful to us," said Scanlon.

"How?"

"I'd like to get a copy of the book Walker was working on when he was killed."

"Books, Lieutenant. There may have been others I know nothing about."

"Are you publishing any others?"

"No. Only the Graham Farrar. You'll have to ask his agent if there are any others in the offing."

"But you'll get me the Farrar?"

"If it's available, nothing simpler. Have you read any of Jordan's earlier books?"

"Not that I know of."

I reeled off several of the titles for him. He drew a blank on most of them.

The phone rang. It was Sidney, who said he'd set an editorial meeting in the conference room for four o'clock.

While I was on the phone, Lieutenant Scanlon wandered over to my bookcase and examined it, running his hand lightly over several of the volumes, taking one out and leafing through it. I couldn't help noticing that he had the look of a small child standing in front of a toy store.

I hung up the phone. "Sorry," I said. "Where were we?"

"These books," said Scanlon. "You published them all?" He gave the word "all" an almost reverent stress.

"Most of them."

He whistled softly. "Impressive."

Impressive? Well, so it was! But I hadn't thought it of it in that way for years. One of the hazards of being a publisher, I suppose, is that you lose some of your sense of wonder about books as literature. Too often we come to think of them as *products*, God help us, and they come to cloy on us, in much the same way as workers in a candy factory must ultimately lose their taste for chocolate.

Scanlon continued to ask me questions, some of them innocuous, a few of them leading. Did I owe Jordan any money? No, his last royalty statement had been sent to his agent, Jeffrey Burgal, who would have peeled off his cut and then forwarded the balance. Did Walker owe me any money? No, I lend money only to the poor, struggling authors, not to the fat cats like Jordan. In fact, I don't lend money at all, I *advance* it, assuming I believe in the author and the book.

Then I had a question or two for him.

"Tell me, Lieutenant, do you like to read?"

"Yeah, I do whenever I get the chance."

"I could tell by the way you looked at the books in my collection. Have you ever thought of writing a book?"

"Well, on occasion. . . ."

"Fiction or nonfiction?"

"Oh, I couldn't do fiction. I'm no Joseph Wambaugh."

"You can't know that until you try."

"Anyhow," he said, "I've been making notes. I think of it as a kind of diary, you know what I mean? A record of the life of a homicide detective over the period of a year, maybe. I've worked on a couple of big cases, Mr. Barlow, know one or two things nobody ever brought out in the open, certainly not the newspapers."

I began to detect the scent of rabbit, the promise of a book in the making—*my* kind of book.

"Well, I *would* be interested, Lieutenant." I was doing my best to walk the line between cautious enthusiasm and encouragement. "I'm always interested. We never know where our new books are going to come from. Of course it will have to wait until all this is over—this Walker business."

"I see." He shifted uncomfortably in his chair.

I could tell he did. And I now knew why Sergeant Snyder had been relieved from the case, or at least why he had been assigned to ride shotgun. This was Lieutenant Scanlon's baby now. And I was, too. His melancholy baby.

Do I need to explain that as a publisher I am the target of not a few authors in embryo? I have been confronted with a potential manuscript ("I have this terrific idea for a book, Mr. Barlow. . . .") while sitting in the barber's chair, while dealing with the local tradespeople, even while sitting stark naked in a sauna. ("It's my life story, Mr. Barlow. Don't you think there's a market for the memoirs of a free-lance gynecologist?") Then there was the gimlet-eyed bookkeeper who sat next to me on a transatlantic flight, subjecting me to an eye-glazing rundown on his hobby, which he thought would make a wonderful nature guide: *Extinct Birds*. And just the other day, a woman who arrived at the office claiming to be a friend of my father, which was the only reason I had been willing to see her at all, asked me "if I had heard of Amelia Earhart." I admitted I had, but why? "Because a message from her has come unto me," she said, "and I would be happy to write a book about it."

Scanlon took his leave, promising to get back to me again, leaving me to wonder why he had seemed so uncomfortable toward the end of our interview. Could he be suspecting that I was attempting to bribe him with my suggestion that I might be interested in his work in progress? Conceivably he was thinking: "This guy, this suspect, for that is what he is, wants to make sure *I'm on his side*." Careful, Barlow. Watch your step. You don't pal around with a detective investigating a murder.

6

By the time Lieutenant Scanlon made his exit it was nearly noon, and I'd hardly accomplished a thing—hadn't even finished reading my *Times*. Then Sidney got on the phone, and it was time to play the coat trick. When I emerged from my office, I found Sidney in the foyer, with his author in tow. Prudence Henderson Harte is a Barbara Cartland look-alike—intentionally, I believe. From her mound of frosted white hair through her heavily corseted, imperious bodice to her tiny black leather pumps, gold buckles aglitter, she is the perfect picture of a lady. Not many of them left, alas; they just aren't turning them out anymore.

I bowed instinctively, then raised her bony hand to my lips. "My dear Miss Harte."

"Oh, Mr. Barlow! At last we meet."

"Long overdue." A murmur.

"Mr. Leopold says you won't be able to join us for lunch." A coquettish pout. "I'd so hoped we could have a *good long talk*."

A Good Long Talk? GLTs were exactly what I didn't need at the moment. I apologized, citing the pressure of business affairs, then added, "I really must take this opportunity to tell you how pleased we are with the sales of your latest book."

"*Matters Mysterious*," Sidney said, knowing full well I probably wouldn't remember the title. He was wrong; the sales had been much too brisk for me to forget it. Murder in a fashionable country house in the Hamptons, a famous fashion designer the victim, poisoned at the height of a poolside cocktail party, surrounded by all his friends and enemies. Whodunit? Leave it to society detective Ben Halberston to find out.

Prudence Henderson Harte awarded me a beatific smile.

"Oh, Mr. Barlow," she said. "You really *do* like my books?"

"Very, very much," I said.

"Of course we do have to give at least a teensy bit of credit to Mr. Leopold. He really is the most *marvelous* editor."

"The best." And I meant it too.

I stood rocking back and forth on my heels. Why were they loitering so long? My stomach rumbled. Why weren't they getting hungry?

"I do have one tiny complaint, however."

"And what might that be, Miss Harte?"

"The car that met me in the airport."

"Oh? It wasn't satisfactory?"

"It was a late model Cadillac limousine."

I sighed with relief. Prematurely.

"Mr. Leopold knows that I expected a Rolls-Royce."

I turned to face him. "Is this true, Sidney? Was Miss Harte subjected to a ride in a *Cadillac*?"

"We did our level b-best to find a Rolls." Sidney bowed his head in a convincing show of contrition. "But the Carey people didn't have one available."

"Then you should have kept trying until you found one. Next time"—I turned to the American Agatha Christie—"you shall have your Rolls."

"Thank you, Mr. Barlow, I knew you'd understand."

"Thank *you*, Miss Harte, for the pleasure you've brought to mystery readers everywhere."

"And ... Mr. Barlow, *please* ... could the Rolls be a white one?"

Dear God, if this woman weren't making money for us the way a cow makes milk ... "Of course, Miss Harte."

It's important to remember that in publishing as in show business, there is clearly a star system. Star authors are not treated like other authors. They are given the red carpet treatment, and quite properly. We need them. Tiresome and demanding as these creatures can be, we smile and give them everything they want except a piece of the company. They represent the difference between happy stockholders and mutiny in the ranks. And so, when we do find our superstars, we lavish perks on them, we make allowances for them, we grant them one goddamn boon after another. You bet we do.

Exit Prudence Henderson Harte with Sidney trailing along behind her. Just before their elevator door closed, he gave me a wan smile. I didn't envy him lunch at La Caravelle with a lady who does not swear, drinks only Perrier, eats nothing but fruit and vegetables, and has an attention span—unless the attention is directed on her—of about ten seconds.

As I returned to my office, I saw the young woman who had asked for an interview earlier—Jane Somebody—still sitting in the lobby. When I passed by, she looked up from the book in her lap. I nodded, smiled, but didn't speak. Somehow I'd have to fit her into a schedule that was already overflowing.

· · ·

Once back in my cave and comfortable, surrounded by leather, well-polished wood, and fine bindings, I pressed the intercom.

"Hannah," I said, "I need Jeffrey Burgal. Tell him it's urgent. Spell the word if necessary."

"Gotcha."

Jeffrey Burgal is a literary agent, which means, in the words of one of the more honest of the species, that he sells unlaid eggs on consignment, then charges the hens for laying them. In an ideal world, his profession, like so many in American business life, would not exist, because it is inherently parasitical. But this is not an ideal world, and one needs the Jeffrey Burgals.

Hannah had the agent on the phone in a matter of moments.

"Nick, I can't tell you how I feel about this. It's . . . well, it's devastating. Just devastating! And insupportable—that some-one, goddamn it, could do this to Jordy.... My God, nobody is safe in this town these days. *Christ.*"

"You'll be at the memorial services tomorrow?"

"Well, as a matter of fact, Nick—"

"It's at Frank Campbell's. Surely you're planning to be there. What the hell, the man was one of the best producers in your stable, don't you think you owe him that much?"

"It's just that I planned to fly to the coast tomorrow," Bur-gal said. "And anyway, you must know how *depressing* I find these things. I'm sorry about what happened to Jordan. Still ..."

Surely Jordan deserved a better excuse. The coast—Jeffrey was forever flying to the coast, or somebody on the coast was flying to him. For me there is only one coast, and I was on it now.

"Jeffrey, please tell me—where is Jordan's manuscript?"

"Ah ... which one?"

"Which one? Graham's biography. It's the only one of Jor-dan's books I have under contract."

"Oh, Graham Farrar. Yes, of course."

"Who the hell did you think I meant? Are you all right, Jeffrey?"

"Of course I'm all right. What do you mean?"

"Is there anybody with you? Can you speak freely?"

"Certainly I can."

"Well, then, where's the goddamn manuscript?"

"You don't have it?"

"No, we do not have it. We'd love to publish it eventually, you know. And there's a little matter of the police wanting to see it. Along with any other books Jordan might have been working on before his death."

"Oh."

"So how soon can we have it?"

"Right away, Nick, of course. It's a bit messy. Perhaps I could have it put through the word processor one more time?"

"Is that really necessary?"

"The last few chapters, anyway."

"So when might we expect it?"

"I'll have Miss Regan get to work on it tomorrow. You ought to have it by Thursday."

"Miss Regan?"

"A free-lance. She did all of Jordan's typing."

"That'll be fine. One copy for us and one for the *police*."

"The police, yes. But I don't think—"

"What?"

"I doubt there's anything there that will help them one way or another. Unless it's the chapter about his last wife."

"Angela?"

"You know, the unindicted felon."

I surely did know. Angela Farrar had been the actor's greatest and most mysterious mistake. Born into a socially prominent family from upstate New York, she had originally attracted Graham because he thought she was a lady, and he hadn't had much experience with that particular breed of woman. Well, she may have known which wine to serve with the turbot or the beef Wellington, but I suspect her real expertise was in poisons.

At any rate, when Jordan's biography of Graham was announced in *Publishers Weekly*, her lawyer got in touch with us and suggested that we either not include any material about Angela in the book—under threat of a libel suit—or that we permit her to review whatever Graham said about her and delete or change anything she found offensive. When I asked him if he had read the First Amendment recently, he snorted and bade me good day. I wondered if I should have mentioned this exchange to Lieutenant Scanlon. So far we had been thinking only of *Jordan's* exes, not Graham's.

"Tell me, Jeff. Was there more than one copy of the Farrar manuscript?"

"I suppose so. Why do you ask?"

"Because it seems odd that Jordan's attaché case was taken from his apartment."

"It was a Mark Cross alligator case, I happen to know. Quite valuable."

"Bullshit. Pardon my French, Jeffrey, but nothing of that kind would bring as much as it's worth in a pawnshop or anywhere else. Money is what thieves want, good old money. Untraceable, immediately usable. My point is, there might have been a manuscript in that case."

"I don't know. I . . . I just don't know," Burgal said. "If there was another copy of the manuscript, that is. And why would anyone want it? By the way, who found the body?"

"According to the lieutenant I talked to, a cop found it, a uniformed patrolman. The building superintendent called the police when a neighbor reported hearing a violent argument, complete with furniture being tossed around."

"Anything else, Nick? I mean, any theories about Jordan's death?"

"Not on my part. My brother, Tim, has an interesting theory about it."

"He does?"

"Yes. Has to do with the book, as a matter of fact—Jeff, listen, Hannah's buzzing me, I'm expecting an important call—from California."

"I understand. We'll talk again, OK?"

"By the way, I do hope we'll see you at Campbell's tomorrow."

"What? Yeah, I guess. Good-bye, Nick."

He was silent. Then, as I offered a polite good-bye, I wondered about Jeffrey's strange reluctance to attend Jordan Walker's funeral services. Squeamishness? Quite possibly. For an agent, he was peculiarly shy and reticent, almost withdrawn. Still . . . it was odd that he felt *that* reluctant.

7

On with the day. I tried calling Graham Farrar in California—no luck, and nobody I talked to seemed to know where he was, either. I read my mail, took out my father's old Dictaphone, one of the few truly user-friendly machines in my office, and dictated until after twelve, then buzzed Hannah.

"Yes, Nick?"

No formality around this office, thank the Lord. Another lapse in tradition—my father must get more exercise spinning around in his grave than he ever got in life. In his day they used to have afternoon tea, for God's sake. I like to think I'm carrying on in his footsteps when, at five-thirty or six, I sometimes wheel out the portable bar and fix cocktails for the late workers.

"Would you try Graham Farrar again?"

She did, again without success. Leaning back in my chair, I ruminated for a while about Jordan's murder, Jeffrey's disinclination to attend the service for his most productive client. Then there was Lieutenant Scanlon, enterprising detective and putative author. A man worth cultivating—

The phone again. A paperback house wanting to know when I was going to auction Jordan's new book. Actually, I was mildly surprised I hadn't heard from them even before rigor mortis set in. Here was poor Jordan stone cold dead and hotter than ever. He would have appreciated that.

Then came an unexpected visitor, Warren Dallas. The late Ian Fleming in cowboy boots. Another star of the "cloak, dagger, and paranoia circuit." All of Warren's novels are thick, that is to say, larded with plot and special effects just begging to be filmed. And all of them have three words in their titles, "The" followed by some exotic combination of adjective and noun, such as *The Levantine Persimmon*, or something of the sort. Where John le Carré's novels rest on an intimate knowledge of the twisted and vagrant world of international espionage, Warren's books exploit only violence, coincidence, and cinematic revelations and reversals. In his own way, and on his own hill, Warren Dallas is king. Some hill!

I won't say I deplore mediocre popular fiction, I just don't want my publishing house widely known for it. No danger there; I publish too many books that receive estimable reviews while racking up lousy profit and loss statements. In any event, nobody in the general public remembers a particular publishing house anyway, for anything. Not anymore.

Warren breezed in shortly after my call to Jeffrey Burgal. Making himself right at home, he hung his wide-brimmed Stetson on the Jo Davidson bust of my late father, which rests on a bookcase in the corner of my office.

"Ah, Warren," I greeted him, "you're just in time for lunch."

He consulted his watch, a Rolex which does everything but play "Dixie"—a gift from Barlow & Company on the occasion of his first half-million-copy best-seller.

"No can do," he sang out. "I'll have to get back to my hotel pronto."

Can't have lunch? *Warren Dallas* turning down a free lunch? Will miracles never cease! Warren Dallas, one of America's favorite authors, is one of the cheapest men God ever made. He lives in San Francisco, in a beautiful house on Nob Hill—where else?—and he'll never again want for money, not as long as he lives, given his handsome royalty checks and his continuing sales, but I can remember him treating me only

49

once in our long association. Just once! He bought me a cup of coffee at a Dunkin' Donuts.

"Rain check on the lunch?" he said.

"Sure enough. Anytime."

With Warren, I'm lucky if I can get away with some relatively inexpensive place like the Four Seasons or "21." On his last trip it was Windows on the World for lunch and the Rainbow Room for dinner. The tips alone on one of my lunches with Warren would keep your average American worker in food for a full week, and a Chinese peasant for a month.

I claim no credit for Warren's success. He did it all himself, God bless him. In fact, I admire him for it. A one-time English teacher, he turned himself into a best-selling writer by sheer determination and by putting himself to school with the works of the best-selling authors he most admired—or envied. But he *is* hard to put up with. And I cannot understand why he worries so much about money. As though he would need to be concerned about it more than a few minutes or so every year, when his accountant hands him his income tax form to sign. Then I remembered something my father once said that struck me as quite wise: "If you're worried about money, you usually don't have anything to worry about."

Anyway, Warren's greediness is by no means the worst of faults. As Samuel Johnson put it, "There are few ways in which a man may be more innocently employed than in getting money."

"Good to see you, Warren," I said. Another little white lie added to my balance in heaven. "What brings you here?"

"A new contract," he said.

Fair enough. When Warren isn't writing books, he's working on contracts, which sometimes take longer to complete than his novels. Warren is on a multibook agreement with us, which pays him an extremely large sum of money each year, though far from as much as he earns. The income is spread in this fashion to keep him from personally supporting his entire local IRS office. But what he objects to in this arrangement—

"What I object to in this arrangement," he said, "is the income spread."

"Oh? It was worked out to keep you from paying more taxes than David Rockefeller," I said. "You might end up doing just that, you know."

"I understand that David Rockefeller, like so many of the rich, doesn't pay any income taxes."

"I wouldn't know about that, Warren. I do know what would happen to you if you took all your royalties at once. You'd probably end up paying for a nuclear submarine all by yourself. In a good year, certainly."

"Not necessarily. Moreover, I resent the fact that *you*, Barlow and Company, are earning interest on the money you do not pay me in this arrangement. *You* have the use of *my* money, and *I* do not."

"All right, what do you have in mind?"

"I've found a new agent."

Now we were getting to the point. Whenever an author is unhappy about his income, his reputation, his reviews, or whatever, he first blames his publisher and then his agent, never the fickle public or the reviewers, who might just have gotten tired of him. Obviously Warren had just dumped his agent. And was there a new publisher in the wings as well?

"Anyone I know?" said I, with as much bonhomie as I could muster.

He named a quite highly touted attorney, a man who had practiced both civil and criminal law: spectacularly in both areas, so spectacularly that he was frequently in the news and gossip columns. He'd been *People*'d, or whatever you call inclusion in that magazine that seems to feature only rock stars and orthodontists living in Terre Haute or Buffalo. Warren's new agent had also been the subject of a book himself; there were rumors it might be turned into a movie. Well now, think of that!

"I've heard of him," was all I said.

"And I expect you'll hear *from* him," said Dallas, with a slightly vulpine smile.

"Does he have much understanding of the publishing business, Warren?" I asked.

"His understanding of tax law," said Warren Dallas loudly, stressing every word, "is encyclopedic."

"How handy for the feds," I said, "to have him around to explain things for them."

"He's got a plan in mind," Warren said, ignoring my remark, "that will require a new contract."

"But the old one hasn't expired yet." I could feel my adrenaline flowing faster, my heart pumping a call to battle stations. *We'll see about that, Dallas. Click, click—cock your piece, Barlow. Ready, aim—*

"That's a matter of opinion," he said. "As long as we both agree to renegotiate—"

"I'm not in principle opposed to negotiation. Still—why?"

"I was hoping you'd be reasonable, Nick." Warren was pouting now, and given the thickness of his lips, it was no ordinary pout; you could use it to lick postage stamps and seal envelopes.

"Have I ever not been reasonable?"

He did not answer. I had the feeling he had come to my office just to provoke an argument, the better and quicker for his new attorney to get in touch with my old one. But I wondered: couldn't we speak directly to each other any longer? We had always been able to before, even when he'd had one of the worst agents in the business. Especially at the beginning, when he'd had no agent at all. We had helped to make each other prosperous, with the edge somewhat in his favor, since I had many authors to worry about, and he had only one. Had it come to this—that we couldn't even sit down and work out a new agreement together? It was sad. But was it also inevitable?

"Warren," I said, "we've always been able to talk things out, reach a meeting of the minds, you know what I mean. Well, can't we still do that?"

"It's out of my hands, now, Nick."

Well, fuck him, if it's a fight he wants . . .

"I don't feel you've really been giving me much attention lately, Nick," he said.

"Oh, Warren, how can you say that? You're never far from my thoughts."

He ignored the irony in my remark. "Your mind, it seems to me, has been on other authors ... other things."

"For instance?"

"That dippy dame Prudence Whatchamacaller Harte for one. The old bag who writes those dainty murder mysteries ... the ones all set in the vicarage garden."

I raised my eyes and hands heavenward. "So help me, Warren, there's nothing between Prudence Henderson Harte and me, nothing at all. She belongs to Sidney Leopold."

"Even today you seem ... well, preoccupied."

"Surely you've heard the news about Jordan Walker."

"Oh, that—" said Warren, naming an only too common and explicit sexual deviant. One of those words that still hasn't appeared in a Barlow & Company book, I hope, considering Mother's sensibilities.

"*De mortuis nil nisi bonum*, Warren," I said. "I'm sure your Latin is up to speed on that well-known piece of counsel. Always speak well of the dead, right?"

"Horseapples. Anyway," he said, "I'm talking about a general *trend* in your attitude toward me ... long before Walker packed it in. Moreover, there are less violent ways to lose an author, may I remind you."

"Is that a threat, Warren?"

"Take it however you wish." He rose. I remained seated, but said: "Sure you won't reconsider lunch?"

"No, thanks. But you'll be hearing from us." He started toward the door, then turned back. "Incidentally ..."

"Yes?"

"If we can't come to terms ..."

"Go on. Go on."

"There *is* an offer on the table from another publisher. I won't say who, I'm not at liberty to give out the name."

"You *prick*."

"What?" His voice rose to Mickey Mouse pitch. *"What did you say?"*

"Why, you dumb bastard, you've always had offers on the table from other publishers, don't you suppose I know that?"

"Now ... now calm down, Nick."

"I will *not* calm down, and don't tell me what to do." By now I too had risen and was leaning over my desk. "And don't try that cheap bidding-threat trick on me, Warren, for God's sake. That's all right for some tight-assed editor just out of Yale, but not me, not your publisher who's known you for twenty years or more."

"Fifteen."

"Fifteen then, what the hell difference does it make?"

And what a fifteen—I still think it was more like twenty—years it had been. Warren's first novel—a turkey! His second novel—a best-seller! His third, fourth, fifth, and sixth novels, each one a better seller than the best-seller before it. His seventh novel, actually a rerelease of his first turkey, also a best-seller. Over those years, I'd considered us friends as well as colleagues. Well ... anyhow ... *the next best thing* to friends. Together we'd gone with our wives to Disneyland and to the Metropolitan Opera production of *Tannhauser*, suffering acutely and in silence at both. I had come to feel for Warren Dallas, if not exactly *love* in the Christian sense, then surely what St. Paul identified as *caritas*. Charity. The last thing a rich bastard like Warren needed. We'd wined together, dined together, gotten loaded together—granted, always at my expense, but who knows whether it is better to be the one who always picks up the tab, or the freeloader? Who controls the situation, the host or the guest, and whose character is enriched the more by the exchange? You tell me.

"Nick," Warren said, "this *is* a business, you know. My business is writing novels, yours is publishing books. Friendship is all very fine, but it stops at the royalty statement. The well-known bottom line."

"Is that also one of your problems?"

"Well, now that you mention it—"

"Dallas, you *amaze* me."

"We would like to do an audit on my earnings for the past two years. That is, if you don't mind."

"If I don't *mind*, you say. Audit your pants off, anytime you feel like it. Anytime you feel like paying through the nose for some CPA to rummage around in our account books. But may I remind you that no author has ever even *accused* me of cheating. My books are always wide open."

"Unlike your office door."

More than ever before, I felt like giving Warren Dallas the finger. I restrained myself.

"Oh, and one other thing, Barlow," he said, putting some rather nasty English on my surname.

I could hardly wait. What now?

"My attorney ... agent ... whatever you want to call him—"

"How about 'shyster'?"

"Insults won't get you anywhere. He doesn't want just a commission."

"So?"

"He'll also expect to get a fee."

I shrugged. "So what?"

"Naturally, I'll expect *you* to pay it."

"You'll *what*?"

"You heard me."

"You're hiring a man to represent *your* interests, a man whose primary aim will be to screw *me*, and you expect me to pay his fee?"

"I do." Warren—or that damned Dallas, as I had now decided to think of him—edged closer to the door, as though he feared I might attack him. By God, he was *afraid* of me, he really was. I began to feel much better about the whole thing. I'm sure I still looked outraged, but inside, I was beginning to smile. This last assumption of his was just too much. The excessive demand that would restore the balance of power.

"You do?" I said.

"Sure." He grasped the handle of my office door and opened it tentatively, still looking at me. Then, bravely: "You *bet* I do."

Drawing myself up to my full height and placing my hands on top of my desk, only the fingertips touching the wood, I called upon one of the legendary heroes of my young manhood, and said, John Wayne to the life in perhaps his finest role:

"That'll be the day."

An angry snort, a loud slam of the door, and Warren Dallas was gone.

For a moment or two after his exit, I sat and considered the implications of his untimely visit. At worst, I was going to lose one of my most profitable and productive authors, at a time when I was already in jeopardy because of the still absent Jordan Walker opus. I could ill afford to lose Warren Dallas. At best, we would work out an uneasy compromise, with neither of us completely happy about it—both of us sullen, peevish, distrustful. In other words, back to normal. Once upon a time, when I was a calf in this business, agreements were negotiated with a simple handshake to seal them. Publishers and authors trusted one another—most of the time. Once upon a time ... but no matter. These days even the milk of human kindness is 99 percent fat free.

As I was thus meditating, I spotted Warren's ridiculous Western hat, still perched irreverently upon my father's tonsured bronze head. I wondered: what would Father—in his youth a companion of Henry James and Edith Wharton, a fellow clubman with John Steinbeck and Ernest Hemingway—what would he have made of Warren Dallas? What would he have said or done?

I looked at Warren's hat again, picked it up, and examined it closely. The crown was slightly crumpled and turning gray. The sweatband was stained dark brown. The initials "W.D." at one end of the band and the number "8¼" on the other. Of course! I always *knew* he was a fathead. I turned the hat around and around in my hands. And then—

And then the demon that has always lurked within me since I was a small boy—whether heeded or sternly suppressed and denied voice—that demon whispered a mischievous suggestion.

No-no, I thought. *That would be a mean thing to do. Malicious.*

Quite so, replied my demon. *The very thing!*

I pulled and tugged at Warren's hat, grasping it in both hands and exerting all my strength, waiting for the gratifying sound of felt ripping. Nothing happened. The hat, like its owner, was obviously made of sterner stuff.

If I may make another suggestion ... My demon again. I listened. I smiled. Who was I to resist such a delicious temptation?

I opened the window. I'm one of the few New York publishers fortunate enough *not* to have one of those glossy midtown offices in a high-rise built by Harry Helmsley or Donald Trump. Barlow & Company occupies a building raised almost a century ago on Irving Place, quite near Gramercy Park. Inside, all is conveniently modernized: air-conditioning, computer terminals, up-to-date wiring, you name it. But outside, ah, outside—nineteenth-century charm. And the windows really open.

I opened mine and leaned out.

There, three stories down, a bareheaded Warren Dallas emerged from the front door of our building, bent forward like a clenched fist. At the corner, not too far from my window, he stopped for a traffic light. At that point I called out his name.

His head came up. He looked from side to side. Then, failing to see me, he shrugged and prepared to cross the street with the green light. I called out again, louder. This time he turned and looked up, mouth agape, eyes squinting against the glare of the afternoon sun.

"You forgot your hat!" I yelled, and scaled it out of the window, into a gentle westerly that caught it and lifted it up and tossed it wantonly about. Down it floated, spinning from side to side, finally landing with what I hoped was an audible *plop* in a gutter visited only too frequently by the neighborhood schnausers and Pekingese.

Warren rushed toward the landing site to retrieve his hat. Too late! At that same moment a sanitation truck rumbled down Irving Place, sweeping all before it into its cast-iron maw. *Grang grang grang*—its great broom relentlessly picking up cigarette wrappers, beer cans, newspapers, dog-do— and Warren's hat.

Needless to say, I hadn't meant *that* to happen. How could I know the sanitation truck would come along at just that moment?

I thought I heard an anguished scream, and the roar of the truck as it swept on by, so rapidly I could just barely catch the lettering on the truck's flank—ALLERGRO SANITATION—and then it turned left on Eighteenth Street. Miraculously the hat had not been scooped up and digested. Instead, it had been spun back out on the street again, and from my distant vantage, it looked flattened, crushed.

Warren reached down for the poor thing, picked it up, brushed it off, whacking it clean, doing his best to restore it to its former state of hatness. No use. It began to come apart in his hands. Shoulders bowed, he walked to a nearby trash container and dropped it in. Warren Dallas For A Cleaner New York.

Then he screwed up his shoulders, threw out his chest, and looked up toward my window. His lips parted and moved, but I could only catch a fragment of his speech.

"... of a *bitch!*" he cried out between bared teeth.

I smiled and closed my window. I knew I should feel guilty, but I didn't. Let my demon feel guilty.

Top that one, Dallas, I said to myself. *If you can.*

For several long moments, I savored the sweet taste of revenge; afterward, I must admit, the rosemary was mixed with rue.

"Hannah?"

"Yes, Nick?"

"Would you call the Banana Republic, please, Hannah, and order a safari hat for Warren Dallas? Size eight and a quarter. Send it to his room at the Algonquin."

"A hat?"

"You heard right."

She sighed. "Mine not to reason why." And rang off.

More telephoning for quite some time, I lost track of exactly how long. No matter; while it might have been the worst day I'd had in weeks, it wasn't all that different from the best day. When people tell me they envy me my apparently glamorous occupation, I wonder if this is what they mean. Too busy to go out to lunch, let alone a lavish expense-account lunch. One phone call after another. Consultations with bankers and potential investors. For a smallish, independent publishing house like mine, there is always a struggle for capital. I spend hours every day and days every week beseeching the local money bags to open the strings for me. Sometimes it works and we prosper, sometimes we're fortunate just to survive.

Then Margo called, and at once I felt better. Shoes off, toes comfortably planted in the carpet, I made a date with her for that evening, and then we chatted on idly.

"Margo, I wonder if you'd do me a special favor."

"If I can, Nick. What is it?"

"Go to a funeral with me."

"Sounds like a fun date."

"Please?"

"Jordan's funeral?"

"Tomorrow. I'd feel much better if I had company. You know how I dislike funerals. I always feel so alone at them, so isolated, even if I know everybody there—Well, I'll spare you the psychological interpretations."

"Of course I'll come with you, darling."

"I'll appreciate it. One other thing."

"I'm listening."

"A woman named Jane Goodman has come to see me about a job, says she's a friend of yours."

Silence, and then: "Sorry, Nick, I can't place her. Jane Goodman?"

"Can't be much of a friend."

"Oh, I may know her, but offhand . . ."

"Okay, I guess that's that. So long, my dear."

Around three forty-five Hannah came in with a Post-it note in hand and stuck it on my phone. When I finally finished the call of the moment, I picked it up.

Ms. Jane Goodman is still waiting to meet with you, though God knows where she gets the patience. Don't you think you ought to fit her in somehow?

Oh, *God*. How could I keep anybody waiting that long? I'd have to see her, I'd even have to apologize. As I reached for the phone to tell Hannah to bring her in, Sidney popped through the door.

"Editorial meeting, yes?"

"Yes." I'd almost forgotten. Ms. Goodperson would have to wait.

The editorial meeting is only one of many meetings held weekly at Barlow & Company, as it is in virtually every other publishing house. It is quite the most important meeting we have, for it is there we determine which of the books that have passed muster with our editors will actually be published. I must admit that I conduct my editorial meetings in the same way that President Lincoln conducted his cabinet meetings. Lincoln was in the habit of sounding out all his cabinet members on any given subject, eliciting their opinions, and then calling for a show of hands on whatever issue was at stake, emancipating the slaves, perhaps, or firing one of his generals. Up went the hands. The cabinet was unanimous in voting "aye" on the issue. "I vote nay," Lincoln would say. "The nays have it." Although I encourage all the members of my staff to think of themselves as "publishers," there can be only one Publisher in the end.

That's not to say that I don't listen attentively to my staff, for I do. I listen particularly to my sales manager, Mary Sunday, and to my comptroller and chief financial officer, Mortimer C. Mandelbaum. While Morty is not exactly in Ebenezer Scrooge's league, he does wield a fearsome calculator. Profit and Loss and Return on Investment are his daily bread. As for Mary Sunday, she and her sales force have to take our show, whatever it may be, on the road, and they are prompt to bring us to book when we have failed to deliver the product. There's that word again. Oh, well. Let it stand.

I won't go into detail about the books we turned down at the meeting: two first novels and a book of heavy-breathing poetry. Of one of the novels, Morty Mandelbaum offered the most telling critique: "a negative ROI." Sidney Leopold described the other novel as "promising but too 'midlist.' " "Midlist" these days is the kiss of death: a book of some merit that falls between the rock of commercial fiction and the hard place of literary distinction. As for the poetry, we do publish one or two books of poems a year, and we had already filled our quota.

We accepted a new private-eye mystery called *Say It with Bullets*, set in Buffalo and featuring a tec named Homer Blank. When asked about the author's track record, Mary Sunday produced a satisfying string of five-figure sales for his previous books.

Next came a science fiction anthology, always dependable merchandise at Christmastime, and a library staple: the memoir of a prize-winning angora cat as told to the owner of a grooming center called The Cat House, and a New Age manuscript entitled, predictably, *The Channeling Response*. One of our junior editors, much into crystals and the Tarot, sponsored that book; I could only take her word for it, since I am deeply unmoved by parapsychology.

Back in my office again, I was beginning to droop, like my philodendron when it needs water. Time to recharge the old batteries. I shut the door, told Hannah to take all calls, and stretched out flat on my back on the rug. Normally, I close my eyes and within five minutes or so, off I go for the pause that refreshes. No such luck today.

"Mister Barlow."

"Unghh?"

Lying there on the floor, I probably resembled a beached whale. An embarrassed beached whale. I grunted a few times and finally hauled myself upright.

Erect, I faced the Job Hunter, standing in my doorway, a

look of patent disapproval on her face. Actually, it was a quite attractive face: clear skin with a slight olive tint, eyes of that intense blue usually found only in Siamese cats, nicely shaped ears.

"Look, Ms. . . ."

"Goodman." Her voice made me think of gin on the rocks.

"I know. Ms. Goodman, I wish you'd wipe that frown off your face."

"Oh?"

"After all," I said, "I'm not the one who walked into somebody's office without knocking."

"I did knock first."

"Oh. Sorry."

"You were probably sound asleep."

"Yes, I expect so. Well then, I won't charge you with breaking and entering."

"Mr. Barlow," she said, "I have been waiting *all day* to see you—"

"Surely you haven't spent *all day* in our reception room?"

"I took a coffee break, a short lunch hour, and a midafternoon walk. I also finished reading one of your new novels on display out there."

"Persistent, aren't you?" Not just a polite comment; I was in fact quite impressed.

"And you're—well, if you ask me, you're pretty damned rude."

Her lips began to tremble. Tears, I feared, were about to flow. She struggled to suppress them. I struggled to suppress my feelings of guilt.

"You did promise to see me, you know. And here it is practically five o'clock."

"Lord, Ms. Goodman, I'm sorry about that, really. It's just been . . . that kind of *day*. Please accept my sincere apologies. Please."

"Well . . ."

"Since you've waited so long," I said, all bonhomie now that the crisis had passed, "and it's come that time of day, why don't we have a drink together?"

"Mr. Barlow, I appreciate your offer, but I'm not here for a friendly drink, I'm here for a job."

"Certainly," I said. "First things first. May I see your résumé?"

She handed it over as I waved her into a visitor's chair.

I scanned the résumé quickly, pausing here and there to absorb the details. Vassar . . . several years with Doubleday, starting as a trainee and ending up an assistant editor (half the people I knew worked for Doubleday at one point or another; what a turnover they must have) . . . three years or so with Little, Brown in Boston. . . .

"Why Boston?"

"I was married at the time and my husband worked at MIT."

"I see." I read on. I was not surprised to see Jordan Walker's name on the list of authors she had worked with, since I knew he'd published several books with Doubleday.

"There's a missing year here," I said.

"I beg your pardon?"

"1983 to 1984."

"I was . . . free-lancing."

"Oh?"

I've read enough résumés to know that "free-lancing" usually means the same thing as "consultant," which means "unemployed." I let it pass.

"Well, Ms. Goodman . . ." I leaned back in my chair and made a steeple out of my fingertips. "Your credentials look fine. Now tell me why you think you'd like to work for Barlow and Company?"

"To tell you the truth—" She had barely opened her mouth when the phone rang. I excused myself and answered it. Where the hell was Hannah? After five, I supposed, and she'd gone home.

It was Margo. "Nick," she said, "I remember your Jane Goodman after all. Only . . . I knew her as Jane Ryan. She was married to a professor somewhere."

"MIT," I murmured. Jane Goodman sat up straight in her chair and stared at me.

"That's right," Margo continued. "Anyway, Nick, I thought

she was a super person. We weren't intimate friends, but pretty close. I forgot that her maiden name was Goodman. And I did suggest that she call you if she was ever looking for a job in New York."

"Ummm."

"You sound funny. You can't talk freely."

"Mm-hmm."

"Is she there with you?"

"Mm-hmm."

"Bye! See you tomorrow, Nick."

"That was Margo Richmond," I told Jane Goodman. "Just in time to save me from making a stupid mistake. I should be so lucky all the time."

The Goodman person raised her brilliant eyes. "Mistake?"

"Forget it. Go ahead—why do you want to work for us?"

"You have a reputation for intelligent, fair-minded, conscientious publishing."

Dear me. We sounded like the Boy Scouts of America.

I got up, with résumé in hand.

"This is what I'd like to do. I'm going to take you in to talk to Sidney Leopold, our editor-in-chief. You may very well be just what he's looking for."

"I hope so." She gave me a 250-watt smile.

In a way I hoped so too. She looked good on paper and in person.

Apparently Sidney agreed, for he spent almost an hour with her. When he did appear, it was to recommend that we hire her as associate editor, starting immediately.

I already knew what manuscript I wanted her to work on. If we ever got it, that is.

8

Tuesday was officially the first day of spring, and for once the calendar and the vernal equinox were in accord. I woke to dazzling sunlight streaming thorough the bedroom curtains, which rose and fell gently in a soft southerly breeze. The air was so sweet and fresh that I bundled myself up in my favorite terrycloth robe and climbed a flight of stairs from my bedroom to the roof garden. From there I could look out over Gramercy Park, past the FDR Drive to the East River, glittering fitfully as the sun rose over the Brooklyn waterfront.

Immediately below were tiny clusters of green buds shivering on the branches of the park's noble trees. My own little forest of trees and shrubs, constrained in their clay and wicker pots, also showed new green life. With every breath I inhaled the odors of spring in the city: smog and automobile exhaust fumes mixed with the fragrance of flowering mulberry and hawthorn. That latter scent has always evoked Gramercy Park to me, just as the boxwood trees in St-Germain-de-Prés fill the air with the essence of the Sixth Arrondissement.

Gramercy Park, you see, is my village, the neighborhood I know and love best in the city. It is my Kensington Gardens, my Vieux Carré, my Camelot.

It is also the only private park left in the city of New York.

In fine weather the park follows a predictable daily cycle:

first several elderly folk with the morning papers and food for the resident squirrels. Later come the mothers and nursemaids with their strollers and carriages. During the latter part of the day and the early evening, lovers perch on the benches, holding hands and murmuring, I suppose, "heavenly sibilants," to borrow Wallace Stevens's phrase. Runners circle the park outside the fence; workmen perch on the ledge near the railings and brown-bag it: models pose in next season's fashions for photographers from *Vogue* and *Glamour*. Dogs lead their owners on leashes.

In the center of the park, the great nineteenth-century actor Edwin Booth, elder brother of the infamous John Wilkes Booth and patron saint of the Player's Club, stands, head slightly bowed, dressed as the Melancholy Dane, his flowing bronze hair and dark robes set off against the green of the hedge encircling his statue.

It has been proposed at times that Gramercy Park be made open to the public. A ridiculous suggestion! Gramercy Park is one of the most thoroughly civilized squares left in Manhattan, restricted as it is to members of the Park Association, who all hold keys. If it ceased to be private, it would surely become, like so many other metropolitan parks, a haven for dope smokers, pushers, hookers, pimps, and panhandlers.

What a shame it was that on a spring morning as beautiful as this one I had to attend a funeral.

Two hours later, freshly groomed, dressed in a sober, navy-blue pinstripe suit, and fortified by one of Pepita's bravura breakfasts, I sat with Margo Richmond in Frank E. Campbell's on the Upper East Side, waiting for Jordan's services to begin. Up front, banked with rings and tiers of spring flowers, stood a coffin of dark, gleaming mahogany—shut tight, thank heaven. Horrible, depressing place, the more so because its atmosphere aspires in such a vulgar way toward the ecclesiastic: thick carpets, gloomy wooden furnishings, nondenominational religious paintings, and stained-glass windows.

"Well, it might be worse," I whispered to Margo.

"How?"

"Could be a wedding."

"Cynic."

I looked around, the way one does at funerals, to see who has shown up and who hasn't. In the first two rows, where the family of the departed usually congregates, were two of Jordan's ex-wives and three of his children—two daughters and a son, ranging in age from twelve to perhaps twenty. They all looked healthy, attractive, solemn. Jordan, always the doting father, had attended lavishly to their needs. As for his misfortunes in marriage—who am I to pass judgment? One of his wives wore black, your basic black with a matching cap and veil, and a rope of seed pearls; wife number two wore green, probably Givenchy or St. Laurent—Margo would know. I was about to ask her when she touched my arm.

"Who is *that* with Jeffrey Burgal?"

I followed her gaze to the back of the chapel, where Jeffrey and an overdressed, heavily made-up bleached blonde had just taken seats. Jeffrey, as always, looked like a slightly spoiled college student gone to fat, or maybe like a failed actor, which in fact he was. He had yet entirely to lose his good looks, but they were beginning to go, gradually sliding out of focus as he neared fifty.

Whatever Jeffrey had lost, he'd obviously gained an admirer. The blonde on his arm fairly radiated attentiveness. I studied her for a moment. Amply endowed by nature, she had enhanced her assets by wearing a pink silk dress at least one size too small. As she twitched about in the pew, nodding and smiling to all her neighbors, she brought to mind an early arrival waiting for the opening curtain of a Broadway show.

"Who *is* she?" Margo said.

"I don't know," I said. "Let's find out." I passed the question along to Sidney Leopold, who sat on my left.

"I'm not s-s-sure," he said, "but I think it's J-J-Jordan's typist."

Typist?

"She didn't wait long to find a new position," Margo said.

"Now who's being cynical?"

Despite his companion's devotions, Jeffrey appeared to be desperately uncomfortable. Miserable, in fact.

As I sat there in the chapel watching other slightly familiar faces pass by, I wondered if it was at all possible that Jordan's murderer might be among them. Doubtful . . . but there *is* that familiar plot twist about the murderer's retaining an obsession with the victim. I saw no one in the room, however, who looked even faintly murderous, other than a Hollywood producer I know and a book reviewer for *Time* magazine.

Just then I spotted Lieutenant Scanlon standing near the doorway. He was looking around the room, shifting from one foot to the other. With him were several burly fellows, obviously not friends or relatives of the deceased. They were hatless to a man. I wondered who or what Scanlon was looking for.

The services began, finally, with an organist playing "A Mighty Fortress Is Our God" much too loudly, followed by a prayer delivered by a funeral director, one of those generic prayers that would be suitable for any faith or even for a nonbeliever—which, it occurred to me, Jordan probably was. He had certainly traveled far from the faith of his ancestors. Starting life as young Jordan Goldberg, *ben brith*, he had now become—in fact, if not in spirit—a High Episcopalian.

The eulogies, mercifully brief, would have pleased Jordan. He was praised for his achievements as a writer and father; his shortcomings in both areas were passed over. His charities were mentioned. He had given much—both at home and at the office.

My facetiousness in these matters is, of course, an act of self-defense. More than once during the service, when I felt a congestion in my throat not to be confused with phlegm— pity for Jordan and his children, relief, self-pity perhaps, anger, especially anger—I pressed Margo's hand fiercely and felt the answering pressure of her fingers on mine. I don't cry easily and I didn't cry then, but the tears were there all the same.

One disturbance alone marred the tranquillity of the service. At the first mention of his paternity, wife number one, the mother of his two daughters, let out a plaintive shriek, not quite a full-fledged scream. Then, sobbing, she was led from the room by an attendant.

The service went on. And on. And still on. Various celebrities, whose lives Jordan had done his best to lend an air of significance to, spoke well of him, as well as they might. There was a note of insincerity, even hypocrisy, in all of this, which I resented. No matter what was said of him, it wasn't him; no one even came close to the truth. The fact is, Jordan was star struck. He really took these foolish people—overnight sensations most of them—seriously. He saw them as they wanted him to see them, and he gave their own images to the world more faithfully than any press agent ever could. No wonder they loved him.

I couldn't say that I loved Jordan, or even particularly liked him. My sharpest emotion was anger. Jordan did not deserve to die the way he had. His death was an outrage, an offense against every person in that room. It cried out for retribution. For vengeance, if you will.

Jeffrey's companion, I noted, was dabbing at her eyes with a lace handkerchief during the eulogies, sniffing audibly, and now and then heaving a deep sigh, the kind Prudence Henderson Harte would describe as "heartfelt." Those sighs, I could see, were putting the upper half of her pink silk dress in mortal peril. Jeffrey looked, if possible, more wretched than ever.

When the last notes of the organ postlude had died away, we all rose and moved noisily toward the foyer, where people were lining up to sign the guest register. On the way out I caught up with Jeffrey Burgal.

"Thank God that's over," he muttered.

"I agree."

"Let's hope you're satisfied," he said.

"Me? Why should I feel any satisfaction?"

He frowned. "If you hadn't pressed me, I wouldn't have come."

"Really?" I couldn't help smiling. "I didn't know I had any moral influence over you, Jeffrey."

"Business first. You're a good client. And so, as you pointed out so persuasively, was Jordan."

"Well, that's it for the poor bastard. Next stop, the crematorium."

"Can't we change the subject?"

We were being herded toward the door by now, pressed on all sides by people who were chattering away or uttering little squeaks of recognition. There was a forced gaiety in the crowd, as though everyone wanted to show how vitally alive they still were.

"I want to get together with you, Nick," Burgal said. "This week. About the manuscript. *Oh, Christ.*"

"What's the matter?"

"Somebody, goddamn it, stepped on my goddamn foot."

I looked down to make certain the offending foot wasn't mine.

"Sure," I said. "Tomorrow?"

"Can't."

"How's Thursday?" We both groped for our pocket appointment diaries.

"Fine as far as I know," he said. "The Players at twelve-thirty?"

My turn to scowl. "Lunch is out, but let's make it drinks and dinner."

He nodded.

"See you Thursday," Burgal said, and then, almost as an afterthought: "Oh, Nick, I'd like you to meet Miss Regan. Dori—meet Nicholas Barlow."

"Nicholas Barlow, the publisher?" Jeffrey's blonde warbled. I hadn't been trilled at like that since my encounter with Prudence Henderson Harte.

"How do you do?" I extended my hand. "And this is Margo Richmond. Margo—are you still with me?"

"Right here, Nick," she said from behind somebody's flowered hat. "Hi. You worked for Jordan, Miss Regan?"

"I did his typing," she said. "And made him happy when he wasn't writing and I wasn't typing. And it's Dori, Miss Richmond."

"Call me Margo," my quondam wife said, smiling. "I hope you made Jordan very happy."

Dori Regan hoisted a lightweight shawl up to her shoulders and drew it over her cleavage. Even though she was standing quite still I could see she was in almost constant motion, her hips swaying ever so gently, her eyes flickering from Margo to me to Jeffrey. When she smiled, a trace of lipstick showed at the tips of her dead-white teeth.

She looked Margo straight in the eye. "You bet your booties I did."

And you'll make Jeffrey Burgal just as happy, I thought, *although not at the moment.*

"Do you suppose we could get the hell out of here?" he asked.

Just then a light bulb went on in my head. Jordan's computer files, of course. Dori Regan was Jordan's typist. Surely she would know where his office was. Not only that, but she probably had a key. If Scanlon and I could persuade her to take us to that office . . . I opened my mouth to speak to her. Too late! Dori and Jeffrey were swept away from us in the crowd. Margo was close enough now to breathe in my ear.

"Darling," she said, "did I make you happy in those halcyon days when we were forever fighting and making up?"

"Can you ever doubt it?"

"*Very* happy?"

"You bet your booties you did. And will once again, my love?"

"Not likely," she said. "I'm having too much fun comparing notes with you to think of you as a love object."

"I disagree," I said. "But I'll take what I can get."

"Precisely."

We were still breasting our way through the crowd of mourners, not half fast enough to suit me. Comments of various sorts were falling all around me; I could not help but eavesdrop.

"Did you know what Jordan's favorite charity was?" someone asked.

"Himself?"

"Sarcasm, darling? It's unworthy of you. No, it's my understanding he gave simply *thousands* to Trinity Parish, my dear, but nothing, *nada*, to B'nai Brith."

"Still less to Israel, I expect."

"Yes, but now and then to Planned Parenthood."

"What about his wives, what did he leave them?" The inquirer this time was male.

"Not a penny. Disinherited them all. His children will get money in trust, of course."

By now we were at the exit, ready to make the last plunge through the crowded foyer to the street.

The way was blocked—politely, not menacingly—by Lieutenant Scanlon and his plainclothesmen.

9

M r. Barlow," said Scanlon. "Could I talk with you for a few minutes?"

So *I* was the reason he had trekked all the way up to Eighty-first and Madison.

"Of course," I said. "Glad to."

"I hate to intrude on your ... grief."

"Grief is probably too strong a word, Lieutenant." I ignored Margo's elbow prodding my ribcage. "Let's talk, by all means, but outside."

Once outside, Scanlon motioned his men out of the way. They got into an unmarked car parked at the curb—in a No Parking or Standing zone, of course. It's only us civilians who get ticketed.

There were almost as many people standing around on the sidewalk, chatting away, as there had been inside. Nothing like a funeral to bring old friends and acquaintances together.

"Gets so I find somebody I know on the obit page at least once a week," I heard someone say.

"And if you ask me, the best writing in the *Times* is on that page" was the response.

This fell Sergeant death, so strict in his arrest ...

Lieutenant Scanlon cleared his throat and claimed my attention.

"Mr. Barlow," he said, "we've taken the seals off Jordan Walker's apartment. I'd like you to come along with me and check it out." He shoved his hands deep into his trench coat pocket. "If you can spare the time, that is."

Not wanting to appear *too* eager, I shrugged. "I suppose so, Lieutenant. I'm afraid I may not be of much use, though. I've never been in Jordan's apartment, I wouldn't know what to look for."

"You're a publisher, after all. You know how writers work. When it comes to authors, I don't have a clue, frankly. Maybe you might spot something we've missed." The accent on the word "something" was a touch wistful, hence appealing. I was beginning to take quite a liking to Lieutenant Scanlon.

I turned to Margo.

"Don't worry about me," she said. "I'll make my own way downtown."

After giving her a friendly kiss—on the cheek, unfortunately—I got into the squad car with Scanlon and three of his cohorts. Scanlon introduced them as Officers Berk, Murphy, and Cohen.

"We've identified the murder weapon," Scanlon said on the way to Jordan's apartment building. "One of our crime-scene people spotted the metal shining in a pile of garbage bags in the basement. He thought it was funny anyone would throw away a Sabatier carving knife."

"Curious," I said. "Pretty fancy blade for a burglar."

"Curiouser and curiouser," Scanlon said. Hadn't I sensed from the start that he was literate? "The knife came from a set in Walker's kitchen."

"So you think—"

"He might have gotten into the apartment—the killer, I mean—before Jordan Walker got home."

"Or else Jordan let him in."

"In which case the list of suspects becomes considerably smaller, doesn't it?" Scanlon said.

"Do you have any?"

"Any what?"

"Suspects."

"We've rounded up the usual ones."

Very good, I thought. "What about the doorman?" I said. "Can he recall Jordan's visitors?"

Officer Berk spoke up from the backseat. "We checked him out first. His name is Benjamin Harrison Cody. He said that Jordan had three visitors that day, all three between five and six-thirty in the evening. That squares with the neighbors who heard the commotion in his apartment, but we dug a little deeper, of course. Apparently Cody takes an occasional break, heads downstairs to his locker and knocks back a few from a bottle he has stashed there. Meantime the door is left unattended."

"Locked, I assume."

"Sure," Berk said, "but it's easy for a stranger to get in. You just have to wait for one of the tenants to show up, look respectable, smile, apologize, and there you are."

"Three visitors, at least, then. Who were they?"

"One of them was Graham Farrar," said Scanlon.

I pursed my lips but did not whistle. I can't whistle, a deficiency I've regretted ever since I was a small boy.

"And?"

"The second—actually she was the first to arrive—was Angela Farrar. At least, that was the name the doorman re-membered, as close as I could make it out. He didn't need to remember Graham's name, the face was unforgettable."

"And the third visitor?"

"A man. Gave the name of Spelvin, George Spelvin."

"Mean anything to you?"

"No," said Scanlon. "But we'll check it out."

"So that's your murderer," I said. Case closed.

"Not necessarily. The doorman claims he saw him leave before Farrar."

"Before?" This time I managed a modest whistle, but I doubt that Scanlon even heard it.

"This Spelvin," he said, "the one we'll call—"

"The second man," I said. "Or third person, if your prefer."

"Spelvin was spotted by one of the building's porters," he said. "A man named Angel Cordoba. And there's something else."

"Yes?" I was, as they say, all ears.

"Our man Spelvin was carrying a briefcase when he left the building." Scanlon frowned. "I only wish Cordoba was a more reliable witness. He's got a record—rape, aggravated assault, breaking and entering. He's changed his name, but his prints are on file. Murphy"—after a particularly jolting stop—"for God's sake, take it easy. We're not in *that* much of a hurry."

Scanlon turned to me again, with an apologetic half-smile. "Where was I? Oh, yes, we've got Cordoba downtown now."

"How does he look?"

"Guilty as hell." This time it was Officer Cohen who rang in on the conversation. "Though exactly what about, who knows? We do have his prints in Walker's apartment, but . . ."

"What?" I was barely able to conceal the tingle of excitement I was feeling, the kind of kick that comes from being on the inside looking in.

Scanlon spread his hands. "He says he's often done work for Walker—repairs in his apartment, that sort of thing. Besides, we don't have a motive."

"Where does that leave us? I mean you?"

"We're working on him."

He did not elaborate on what that particular phrase meant, but I assumed it was whatever the police do now that they're denied the third degree. The fourth degree?

"What about Spelvin?"

"We're looking."

. . .

We pulled up in front of Jordan's high-rise on East Sixty-fifth Street. The doorman stepped forward and opened the right front door of the car. His welcoming smile vanished when Scanlon stepped out and flashed his gold shield.

"Police," he said.

"Oh. Sure."

"Murphy, you stay here," Scanlon said. "Cohen and Berk, you come along." He turned to me. "We haven't checked out all his neighbors yet."

Once we reached Jordan's floor, Scanlon sent his men about their missions—Cohen to interview the neighbors on the floor, if any were to be found, Berk to grill the staff again, with special attention to the doorman. "Cody is sure that Spelvin left before Farrar—too sure, if you ask me. Check it out, Berk."

"Sure, Lieutenant."

As though he had forgotten I was present, Scanlon said, almost to himself: "Nobody remembers much of anything. See no evil, hear no evil, speak nothing at all."

As a fan of police procedurals, I have developed the notion that criminal investigation may well be the dullest work on earth. Dig, dig, dig—plod, plod, plod. Even though they're not walking beats, most detectives are still plodding along, looking for a crack in the case, waiting for a break, and still drawing a blank most of the time. As I watched the men troop off to their divers duties, I could see I was probably right.

Scanlon opened the door with a passkey.

I don't know what I expected to find inside—some hint of Jordan's recent presence there, I suppose. An aura, a tangible odor, an unmistakable, lingering impression of Jordan himself. I remember as a child prowling around my grandfather's attic and finding old clothes hanging in closets, ancient suits and overcoats that seemed still to exude the essence of the people who had worn them: perspiration, tobacco, the animal pungency of the body itself still clinging to the fabric.

Jordan's apartment was immaculate, precise in every detail—so pristine it might have been one of those model apartments furnished by designers to show prospective buyers what life will be like in Ivory Towers or Wistful Vista. Even the plants, of which there were many—dumb cane, philodendron, Swedish ivy, ferns, and amaryllis—looked plastic. Only a hanging wandering Jew in the living room showed the brown edges of neglect on its leaves.

The furniture was all expensive stuff, of course—a curiously bland, high-tech mixture: white and black leather, extravagantly thick rugs, leather cushions the color of light liver. The art hanging on the walls was minimal, mostly color-field and hard-edged oils. I recognized a Frank Stella and a Jasper Johns in the dining room and, in Jordan's bedroom, a Morris Louis Veil. Obviously he'd been well advised in his collecting; I knew full well that Jordan, left to his own devices, would have bought color-coordinated velvet paintings by the yard. An erotic sculpture—erotic if you don't insist on a representational human figure—stood in the foyer. There was also an oil painting of Jordan in his prime, along with several studio photographs of him near the portrait.

"Looks unlived in, sort of, doesn't it?" I asked.

"Yeah."

"I would guess that he used this place for sleeping, for entertaining, and for screwing. Certainly he didn't work here. No desk, no typewriter, no word processor. Hardly any books to speak of, except a few thrillers and his sex manuals."

"Well, all that's obvious. But do you know where, exactly, he *did* work?"

"He kept an office somewhere downtown."

"There's something else," said Scanlon.

"What?"

"The mirrors."

I knew what he meant. I felt disquieted by them, too. They were everywhere, Jordan's mirrors. Not only in the bedroom and living room but in the foyer as well. There was even one in the kitchen and, predictably, a large ceiling mirror over the sunken tub in his bathroom.

"The Narcissus of Madison Avenue," I said.

For a man who was so unassuming, so self-effacing professionally, a man whose identity as a writer was overshadowed by so many well-known names, Jordan was certainly obsessed with his own image. Overcompensation? Egomania? Vanity? Any one of these or all of them, we'd never know.

"I'd hate to have to look at myself wherever I moved," I said.

"Me too," Scanlon said, with rather less reason to feel modest than I have.

In the kitchen we checked through Jordan's cutlery. Sure enough, a Sabatier knife was missing—the fish knife. I shuddered, remembering the condition of Jordan's body in the morgue.

His refrigerator was filled with champagne, imported beer, caviar, paté, some sour cream, and a few raw vegetables.

"The diet of your typical everyday sybarite," I said.

"We found a pistol in the drawer of his bedside table," Scanlon said. "A thirty-eight automatic, loaded, unused, and registered in his name. There was also a pocket diary and engagement book."

"Anything unusual in the diary?"

"Nothing that meant anything to us downtown. Maybe you'd take a look at it? Something might occur to you."

He handed over the diary. A Tiffany pocket diary, naturally, bound in full leather with marbled endpapers, Jordan's name stamped in gold on the cover. I stuck it in my jacket pocket.

"Whatever you do, don't lose it," said Scanlon. "It's an important piece of evidence."

I felt vaguely queasy, almost depressed. I realized I had not really known the man who lived in this apartment; from what he had left behind, I would find it hard to guess who in fact he was, or what. Even the clothes in his closets, rack upon rack of them, had reminded me only of the excellent men's stores they'd come from, not of the man who had worn them.

One thing was sure—they'd never hang a commemorative plaque on Jordan's door.

"Where was it found? The body, that is?"

"Over there." He pointed to a spot behind the sofa. "There was a fair amount of disorder—drawers open, his pockets turned inside out. After the crime lab boys finished with their work, we cleaned the place up."

"They find anything?"

"Some latent prints, nothing we can identify yet. There

must have been blood on his attacker's clothing, a lot of it, but . . ." He shrugged. "We'll see."

"Is there anything else, Lieutenant?" I asked.

"The manuscript he was working on," he said. "The Graham Farrar book—anything on that yet? We'd like to see it. Badly."

"Nothing so far. But I'm working on it."

"There's something else that might be helpful."

"Shoot."

"You said something about his having an office somewhere downtown."

"I suspect he did."

"Do you know where it is?"

"Offhand, no, but I may have met someone who does."

"Who?"

"Jordan's typist, a woman named Regan."

"We'll want to talk to her. Do you know where to find her?"

"I suggest you try Jeffrey Burgal," I said.

"Good. I'll get on it. And if you get anything from the pocket diary, you'll let me know."

"Of course."

"And be damn careful with it, won't you?"

"Of course."

"Oh." He gave me a wide smile. "There's something else, Mr. Barlow. I hate to impose on you, but . . . ah . . ."

"Yes?" Just the right inflection, casual but interested.

"I told you I had been thinking of doing a book?"

"I remember."

"Well, I thought you might be willing to read a piece I wrote last year. For the *Police and Fireman's Journal?*"

"I see."

"You probably haven't heard of the magazine, but it's well-known in my bailiwick. And anyway, it might give you some idea of whether I can write or not. I'd be grateful if you'd take a look at it."

"Of course, Lieutenant." I put on my happiest face. This was beginning to look more and more promising. A possible book—that was one thing, and not to be taken lightly. But a contact this close with the NYPD, Homicide Division—even better!

"I'm sure you have my address, but here's my card," I said. "Do send it to me."

Scanlon blushed, I swear.

"Actually," he said, "I have it with me. In the car."

10

On my way to meet Jeffrey Burgal for dinner at The Players, I saw a man walking a duck.

I swear to God that's a true statement; there *is* a man in my neighborhood who keeps a pet duck and walks it as regularly and proudly as any dog owner. The duck follows him at a respectful distance of a yard or so, waddling along contentedly in its master's shadow. I am reliably informed that the duck attached itself to this fellow one evening and has yet shown no inclination to wander off.

Passing the two of them at the southwest corner of Gramercy Park, I was tempted to ask the duck walker if he was observing the pooper-scooper law.

Our date was for 6:30. I got to The Players early, and since I have been a member of this illustrious club for some fifteen years and a regular, I made myself at home in the grill. Jeffrey is a relatively new Player, having joined the club only this past year.

The Players' home is a fine old brownstone on Gramercy Park South, built in the Italian Renaissance style, remodeled by the architect Stanford White in 1888 for Edwin Booth, who bought the building from Clarkson Potter's widow the previous year. Booth set out to found a private club for actors—rather, a club where actors could meet gentlemen of other professions, since in the Manhattan of Booth's day, those who wore the buskin were not always welcome in established clubs. Joining Booth as founders were such worthies as Samuel L. Clemens, Augustus Belmont (beloved by racing fans everywhere), and curiously, General William Tecumseh Sherman.

Now, a century later, the club accepts women members as well as men. *O Tempore! O Mores!* Still, The Players remains primarily a theatrically minded hangout in tradition, and stocked higgledy-piggledy with marvelous works of art and memorabilia. Publishers too are welcome, and the library is first-rate. Quite a few of the books I bring out wind up there, EX DONO NICHOLAS BARLOW. I myself wind up there frequently, because my home and office are both so near. Doesn't everybody need a home away from home—a favorite pub or other pit to stop?

For a half-hour or so, I stood at the massive oak bar in the Grill Room, under a mural bearing this legend from Shakespeare: YOU SHALL NOT BUDGE: YOU GO NOT TILL I SET YOU UP A GLASS. An appropriate sentiment, if incorrectly applied. Hamlet's glass was of course a mirror, not the perfect dry martini I held in my hand. I sipped happily, waiting for Jeffrey and eavesdropping on the conversations around me, since I knew no one there except by sight.

There were no famous actors that evening, just a few stalwarts standing at the brass rail nearby, and four elderly gentlemen, regulars all, playing bridge. Three of the foursome, I guessed, were in the theater, probably unemployed. The fourth I recognized: a short, elfin man, a retired journalist of ninety or more. Andrew Holt, his name was, quite well-known in his day. "Once," he told me, "back in 1925, when I was on the staff of *Judge* magazine—the name won't mean anything to anyone under the age of seventy—I sat at a lunch table between Scott Fitzgerald and John Held, Jr., the two men who between them created the Jazz Age."

"And what was the subject of their conversation?" I asked.

"I can't remember," said he.

Lest I leave the impression that The Players is frequented

only by old fogies and tosspots, let me hasten to add that I have spent some of my happiest hours there, in charming company. True, there have been mildly scandalous incidents. A young actor, son of a famous movie character player, showed up in a goatherd's costume one night, barefoot and leading a gigantic Dalmatian, which proceeded to evacuate its bowels on the floor of the Grill Room.

My favorite story—it's also attributed to the Lambs—is about the matinee idol who got drunk at the bar one evening, picked up his cane, and carelessly knocked over an entire shelf full of glasses with one broad, sweeping gesture. He was suspended for a year. Back at the bar on the day his suspension was lifted, he was asked by one of his companions what he'd done to be so punished. "This!" he said, picked up his cane, knocked the glasses down again, and was instantly suspended for a second year.

This evening, however, nothing more passionate or violent occurred than a double and redouble at the bridge table, followed by a small slam. I had started on my second and last martini when Jeffrey showed up, slightly out of breath and making apologetic noises. He'd been caught in traffic; also, it had started to rain. At his suggestion we moved our drinks to a table in the corner and called for menus.

Club food, unfortunately, is not the kind Pepita serves me, or the kind Pierre Franey and Marian Burros give houseroom to in the *Times*. No, club food is food for clubmen, men eating in order to fill their stomachs as a cushion for all the alcohol they've been drinking, or plan to go on drinking.

I studied the menu, decided to take the path of least resistance, and ordered a small sirloin rare, so I'd be sure to get it medium rare.

"Salad?" said Jeffrey, who had decided to treat, although we are both members. His pencil was pointed above the order card.

"No, thanks, Jeffrey. I subscribe to Dr. Sam Johnson's recipe for salad."

"And what might that be?"

"Take a lettuce," I said. "Wash it. Dry it. Season with salt, pepper, oil, and vinegar. Then throw it away."

Burgal shook his head.

"Salad is just about all I can eat these days," he said.

"Dieting?"

"Doctor's orders. *Crise de foie*, as the French call it. No spicy foods, no fats, no alcohol."

"Pity." I sipped my cocktail; Jeffrey sipped his Perrier.

"It's not so bad," he said. "I'm beginning to feel the way I used to."

"When you were a quarter-miler?"

"Not *that* far back. More like I felt when my tennis game was still strong."

Once again I looked at Jeffrey, more closely than I had at Frank Campbell's. His face was not that of an aging matinee idol; it was that of a failed human being. Disappointment was etched in every feature, along with the deep lines characteristic of a heavy smoker. Nevertheless, when he was relaxed and comfortable, Jeffrey Burgal's smile could be positively incandescent. He must indeed have been a handsome young man, hoping to crack Broadway, making the rounds from one producer's office or casting call to another. Somewhere along the way he'd accepted the fact that he would never make it as an actor, and became that strange amalgam of lawyer, financial adviser, friend, psychologist, and critic that most literary agents have to be if they are to succeed.

And Jeffrey was nothing if not successful, at least financially. He was even a past president of the Society of Author's Representatives, a luncheon club where prosperous agents sit around boasting about their fees—or so I surmise; I've never been invited to one of their gatherings. Publishers and agents are enemies by nature, always on a collision course. Jeffrey and I would be sitting at a table calling each other thieves and crooks one moment and trading jokes the next, the best of buddies. So to speak. Because when you get right down to it, we can't function without each other, any more than either of us can survive without authors.

Right now, fortunately, Jeffrey wasn't feeling combative. He stubbed out his cigarette, leaned back, and sighed.

"I love this place," he said after a moment. "You know, Nick, the thirties are alive here." He was looking at the drawings and engravings on the Grill Room wall.

"So are the twenties," I said. "And even the nineties, in a way."

"I miss it," he said.

"Well, surely you can come here more often."

"It's not easy." He sighed again, a deep one this time. "Christ, I don't know how to keep up, there's so much going on."

Now, I knew, he was ready to talk business.

"I've brought Jordan's manuscript—the Graham Farrar book," he said. "It's upstairs, in the cloakroom."

"Good."

"It is, I suppose, vintage Walker."

"Which means that it's corny and rather trite, but salable. Well researched, polished, and salable. Upbeat—and extremely salable."

"Salable, certainly," Jeffrey said. "But, you know, I think this is a better book than Jordan ever wrote before."

"Maybe that's because his subject is Graham, not your usual Hollywood twit."

"It's Graham to the life, you're right, and no one could do a really sappy book about him. All you have to do is quote him and report on his romances, his wives, his brawls, and you've got enough gutsy stuff to draw a crowd. But"—he ran the fingers of his right hand through his thinning blond hair— "it's also, oddly enough, Jordan Walker to the life. There's a lot of *him* in it, too."

"Not too much, I hope," I said. "I'm buying Graham's biography, not Jordan's. By the way, Jeffrey, why are you selling me on this book? We've already bought it—for a price I consider ruinous, by the way—and I'm eager to publish it. A good deal of my firm's money is at stake here." I did not want Jeffrey to know how much of our money was at risk, or why I so badly needed the Farrar book on my next list. Never give an agent any idea of the depth of your wallet, that's my motto. "Why the violin music, old buddy?"

"Shit, Nick, I don't know. I almost feel that the book is too personal to be published. Too intimate. I kind of hate to let it go."

"Consider it gone. It's already in the catalog for my fall list."

"Of course," he said. "Graham insisted on your firm, you know."

"Yes. Graham has always said that if he ever wrote his memoirs, he wanted me to publish them."

"You've known him for a long time?"

"We were in college together, and ... there were other times." I decided to cut the reminiscing short, I didn't want to get into auld lang syne just then. Graham may have been an old friend, but his book was just another book. A lead book on the list, a crucial book perhaps for our finances, but only a book. And this was just another dinner, which, about then, arrived on the table.

For the next half-hour or so, we were busy dining and murmuring platitudes. And exchanging jokes. Good old Jeffrey and good old Nicholas. Citizens and statesmen in the country of Literature. Gossiping, swapping inside stories, speculating.

After dinner and cigars and brandy (a snifter for me and none for Jeffrey), we headed out, feeling cosseted and well stuffed. At the table near the cloakroom, I picked up the manuscript neatly packaged in Jeffrey's distinctive Nile green paper, so the world of book publishing would know it came from his agency. I hefted it, as I usually do; it weighed in at about 550 pages or so.

"Anything new about the murder?" Jeffrey said as we got into our topcoats.

"Not much."

I told him what Scanlon had told me, that the murder weapon had been found and had turned out to be Jordan's own knife. I also told him that Scanlon had given me Jordan's appointment book, to see if I could make anything out of it. I omitted only what Scanlon had told me about Jordan's visitors. I hesitated only because I considered it somehow privileged information.

"And have you looked at it?"

"Um?"

"The appointment book."

"I haven't had time to study it carefully," I said. "I have it with me now. And I'll show it to my brother, Tim. He may have some thoughts about it. I also have an article Scanlon wrote for some police magazine. He's asked me for an opinion."

"Well, well. A detective who writes," Jeffrey said. "And a publisher who detects, no doubt. Whoever did it, they'll catch him for sure."

"You think nobody gets away with murder?" I squared my hat, tucked my stick under one arm and the manuscript under the other.

"Only literary agents and publishers."

We headed out in the velvet spring night. The rain had stopped, and above us the stars were thick and bright in the sky; the streets around the park were almost deserted. Past ten-thirty, and I could not suppress a yawn. Oh, well . . . and so to bed.

But not quite yet. As we rounded the corner of the park, heading toward my house (Jeffrey had agreed to stop by for a cuppa, although I was eager to slip between the sheets and tackle the Farrar manuscript), two men came our way, taking up most of the sidewalk between them.

I'd like to say I got some atavistic warning of danger ahead, a rising of the hairs on my neck or a shiver along my spine, but no such thing occurred. I was simply annoyed that the sidewalk was blocked, and uncertain whether we should push on or step aside. Stepping aside seemed more appropriate, or more prudent, so we did. Almost automatically, Jeffrey moved to the right, near the fence around the park, and I stepped into the gutter.

I didn't see their faces at first; they were only dark figures in leather jackets and jeans. Big, both of them. A stink of marijuana and sweat struck my nostrils like a blow.

What happened after that gets rather confused. Out of the corner of my eye, I saw one of the two men wheel suddenly and swing at Jeffrey, who doubled over, expelling his breath with a *whoosh*. Then he collapsed backward and sat down—fell down, I suppose—against the fence.

By that time my own hands were full. The other thug moved toward me on the balls of his feet, dancing in for the kill. Not a word from either of them, but I saw a flash of metal in the light that reached us from the streetlamp on the corner.

I didn't need to be told what this was. A massive surge of anger and wild energy filled me. *Jesus Christ—the son of a bitch!* I shifted the cane until the shaft was in my right hand, just above the ferrule. Then I brought it down hard, hard, hard—three times. Once on the shoulder of my attacker, once on his upraised arm, and then on the blade of the knife, which spun away, clattering into the street.

Now! Once again I brought the cane down on his shoulder. I could feel the impact of the ash striking the bone and smashing it; could feel the force of the blow in the palm of my hand and in my forearm—as though they'd been stung. He screamed and clutched his shoulder. I felt a sudden burst of primal exultation, a satisfaction deeper than any civilized pleasure. *You bastard.*

Now the man who had gone for me was turning and running, and the second one was coming toward me. The manuscript had fallen from my arm and was lying on the sidewalk. Jeffrey was still slumped against the cast-iron railings of the fence. I raised my stick again, grateful I hadn't broken it. Just raising it was enough; mugger number two also turned and ran.

Damn it, I wanted to stop them both, or if I couldn't do that, at least one of them! Remembering what Wallace Beery, playing Long John Silver in the 1934 movie *Treasure Island*, had done with his crutch, I hoisted my cane by the tip, drew back my arm, and hurled it. Threw it end over end, aiming at the black jacket of Number Two.

And missed! The cane struck the fence and, bouncing off, rattled harmlessly into the street. I briefly considered running after them, but they were already disappearing around the corner, one of them clutching his shoulder in what I hoped was excruciating pain, the other just hightailing it.

I bent over to attend to Jeffrey. As far as I could tell, he was unharmed, just out of breath.

When he could finally talk—or wheeze, which would be more accurate—he said: "Jesus, Nick . . . Jesus."

"Are you all right, Jeffrey?"

He nodded, but he looked ghastly: pale and wretched and above all humiliated, a grown man disabled by a punch in the belly.

He said something I couldn't make out, so I learned over and got my ear next to his mouth.

"Did they get anything, Nick?"

"Not a thing. Can you make it up?"

He was struggling to get to his feet, so I put my hands under his arms and pulled him to a standing position. Then I set about to pick up the manuscript.

It was nowhere in sight.

Gone, by God! One of them must have taken it. I was able to retrieve my poor battered cane, and while I was about it, I fished the mugger's switchblade out of a puddle in the gutter.

Rather more slowly than we'd started out, rather the worse for the booze, the adrenaline, and the roughing up, we made our way to number 2 Gramercy Park.

Oscar was understandably shocked at the sight of the two of us, disheveled and tottering and, for all he knew, dead drunk. Still, his face showed no sign of censure. He helped me get Jeffrey into the hallway and onto a chair, then turned to me for further instructions.

"Call the police," I said. "Nine-one-one. Tell them it's an emergency. Then fix us both a drink."

Jeffrey was not too far gone to raise a protesting hand.

"Make that just one drink," I said.

Still sitting in the hallway, Jeffrey began to make soft moaning sounds.

"It's all right, Jeffrey," I said. "We're safe now. Here, let me give you a hand."

I helped him to his feet and guided him into the living room. There I deposited him on the couch, unlaced his shoes and took them off. Tears dribbled down his face. He covered his eyes with his hand.

"Nothing to worry about now," I said.

He shook his head slowly back and forth.

Oscar reappeared with my drink and assured me that help was on the way. Only then did I allow myself the luxury of a long swallow of Napoleon brandy, followed by a deep, deep sigh of relief.

11

"You ought to've known better," said the young cop from the Thirteenth Precinct. "Beating up on muggers is a damn good way of getting killed."

It was nearly midnight, and Jeffrey and I were seated in my parlor, with two patrolmen on the couch facing us. *One* patrolman, I should say, a good-looking black who insisted we call him Artie; and a patrolwoman, also good-looking, who was taking notes. Artie was calling her Buster, with obvious affection. The two of them might have posed for a recruiting poster for the NYPD.

"What would you have expected me to do?" I was still somewhat swollen with pride at having fought off our attackers.

Artie considered my question for a moment.

"Give them what they want," he said. "It's the only intelligent thing to do. Then hope for the best. I know, afterward you'll wish you had a machine gun so you could mow them down. Still—"

"But I don't know what they wanted, they didn't ask for anything, they just jumped us. What if they wanted to kill me?"

"All the same—"

"Officer," I said, "I am, as you must have guessed, an intelligent, reasonably well-educated person. The product of one of our finest universities—and, I might add, a good example of the contemporary liberal mind, neither tightly closed nor open at both ends. At any rate, that's what I think I am when I'm about my father's business. But," I said, "clearly, somewhere inside that envelope of urbanity and cultivation is a ferocious savage—a truly uncouth ruffian with a lead pipe in his paw and a temper with a boiling point of about forty degrees. That troglodyte, that throwback to the Neanderthal Man, it was he who struck out at those sons of bitches in the park, not the calm, rational man you see here in my living room."

"All right, all right," he said, smiling. "Just remember that caveman can get the man of distinction killed. So be careful."

"Fine," I said. "Now can we get on with it?"

He leaned back on the sofa, looking from me to Jeffrey, who sat slumped in the other armchair—sullen and, for him, silent.

"Let's start at the beginning again," Buster said. "When you walked out of The Players . . ."

.   .   .

"And what did they take?"

"A manuscript."

"What?"

"A book, in manuscript form." By the expression on his face, he clearly didn't regard the loss as worth recording.

"Is that all?"

"I think so."

Artie frowned. "You're sure?"

"*Look*, officers." My turn to frown; the policewoman called Buster nibbled at the eraser end of her pencil.

"Can't you please give it another shot?" she said. "Your best one?"

"Jesus, I don't know what more I can give you." I sighed deeply. I felt tired and bored and very sorry for myself. I'd been closeted with Jeffrey Burgal and the two cops for almost an hour now. I'd told them everything I could remember. I'd turned the switchblade over to them, not that it was likely to be of much help unless they could find prints on it, and that wasn't likely, since I'd picked it out of a puddle. Now they were doing their best, and also their worst, to pry descriptions of our assailants out of Jeffrey and me for their Identikits.

Jeffrey hadn't been much use at all, beyond contributing the information that the men were both white and that one of them was swarthy. I had their heights down fairly closely; one of them could look me in the eyes and the other one would have had a good view of my shoulder blades. Identifying scars or marks?

"The younger one," I said, "had a terribly pockmarked face."

"How old would you say he was?"

"Which one?"

"The younger one. Pockmarks."

"About twenty-five, I would guess. Midtwenties, anyway."

"And the older one?"

"I don't know. Somewhere between thirty-five and forty, I'm only guessing."

"Anything else about the older one?"

"Especially dark and thick eyebrows, much in need of a trim. All in all, a pretty ugly pair."

Artie nodded while Buster scribbled a few notes.

And so it went, for almost another half-hour, until the two of them were apparently satisfied with our descriptions.

"Okay," Artie said. "Now we can start looking for these two. Oh, there's one more thing we might try that could help."

"And what's that?"

"Would you mind submitting to hypnosis? The department has an expert. From time to time hypnosis helps witnesses remember things that have been lost to the conscious mind. Purely voluntary, of course."

"Why not?" I said.

"No," said Jeffrey.

The vehemence of the reply startled me, the police officers, and I think, him as well.

"We're extremely careful about it," Buster said. "You're allowed to have an attorney present—and your doctor, if you wish. We don't want to embarrass anybody. And there's a taped as well as written record of it for the subject."

"Oh, I don't know," Jeffrey said. "I remember so little anyway. Besides," he winked broadly, "everyone knows an agent is incapable of the truth, even under hypnosis."

"Well, it was just a suggestion," Artie said. "It may not be necessary, after all."

"Can we call it a day now?" I said.

Both cops got to their feet and started for the front door where Oscar waited to show them out, his face drawn tight in disapproval. Just before he reached the doorway, Artie turned suddenly.

"One other thing, if you don't mind. I'd like you to look through our album of muggers."

Jeffrey, looking altogether desperate, waved an SOS signal at me. I raised both hands.

"Another time, Officer," I said. "Mr. Burgal and I have had a hard night and day with this. We could use some rest."

"While those faces are still fresh in your mind? Please?"

"You ask too much of us," I said.

"I see." Artie shrugged and murmured something inaudible. His partner tucked away her notebook, and they went out into the night.

As for Jeffrey—my ashen-faced Sancho Panza, as I was beginning to think of him—when we were finally alone, I asked if there was anything I could get him before he left. Coffee, maybe, or hot milk? He shook his head. He hadn't been much help to me or the police so far. Just walking through his part. His primary emotion seemed to be embarrassment—that he hadn't acquitted himself better during the attack. He said as much while we were waiting for a hired car service to come and drive him home.

"At least you did *something*, Nick. Probably saved our lives, at that."

"Oh, hardly."

"If it had happened ten years ago," he said, "even five . . . well, they wouldn't have put me down so easily. You should have seen me then, Nick."

"I know, Jeff, don't worry about it."

"I've let myself get out of shape, you see."

"Haven't we all? Don't punish yourself about it."

"I'll try not to."

"Meanwhile," I said, "doesn't it strike you as odd that we should be mugged so soon after Jordan's death?"

"Odd?"

"Attacked with a knife," I said, "which the police now have as evidence. While we were carrying Jordan Walker's manuscript."

"That *manuscript*," said Jeffrey. "I wish I'd never had anything to do with it."

"And I," said the head of Barlow & Company, "can't wait to get hold of it."

"I'll do my best."

"Your best? What do you mean, your *best*? Surely there's another copy of it."

"Of course I have another copy, Nick. You know as well as I do that an agent always keeps copies on hand of all his clients' manuscripts.

"So whip it over to me, won't you, Jeffrey?"

"Of course. First thing tomorrow."

12

When I arrived at the office the following Monday morning, there was an urgent message to call Jeffrey Burgal. I did so, with an inexplicable feeling of apprehension. The manuscript I wanted so badly had still not arrived. I was about to deliver a reproof to Burgal when he forestalled me.

"Nick—something terrible—"

"What?"

"It's godawful, Nick, and I'm really pretty damned upset about it, but my office was broken into over the weekend. Broken into ... trashed ... things tossed around.... God knows what was stolen. I haven't been able to take an inventory yet, but—"

"Don't tell me—"

"Yes, there are manuscripts missing. One of them is Jordan Walker's biography of Graham Farrar."

"Oh, *shit*."

"My sentiments exactly."

"You've notified the police?"

"Most certainly. Though I hardly expect it to be a high-priority crime."

"It is for me, by God. Anyway, how are you holding up, Jeff?"

"First the mugging, and now this. I'm beginning to wonder if I'm cut out for life in these United States."

"So what now?"

"Well, first I have to get my office straightened out. You have no idea what a mess."

"I mean—what do we do about Jordan's manuscript?"

"Nick, there must be another copy—yes, there must be," Jeffrey said. "Jordan worked on a computer. A word processor."

"So?"

"The question is," said the agent, "where's the disk he wrote it on?"

Where indeed? I thought.

I had no sooner hung up the phone than Hannah buzzed me to say that Ms. Jane Goodman was on board. "Send her in, Hannah."

Notebook in hand, our new associate editor entered my office. "You're here bright and early," I said.

"Eager to get started, even. Is that unusual?"

Publishing does tend to attract more than its share of night people, I've found. Sidney is a good example—seldom in before ten or ten-thirty in the morning, or out before seven or seven-thirty at night.

"I like to be in early," I said, "but I don't make a fetish of it. I don't want clock watchers working for me. Give me geniuses instead."

Jane Goodman smiled her endearing smile and bowed her head slightly.

"I hope I can live up to that, Mr. Barlow."

"I'll give you every opportunity. For now, welcome to Barlow and Company. I hope you'll like it here."

"I feel good about it already. Your reputation precedes you."

"Reputation? For what?"

"Caring about good books. Putting your authors first. Most of all, not selling out to a conglomerate."

I preened, I couldn't help it. Everything she said was true, with reservations—I thought of Prudence Henderson Harte.

But she was right about the authors; by and large, we let them rule the roost. As for conglomerates, anyone who thinks you can sell your company to one of those monster corporations and still be your own boss is brain damaged, that's all there is to it.

"Enough of ceremony," I said. "I might as well warn you that I occasionally lose my temper."

"So I've heard."

"And sometimes use words that can't be printed in a family newspaper," I said.

"So do I, I'm afraid."

"Don't be."

"What?"

"Afraid. This is not a family newspaper. You'll forgive me, I trust, if I sometimes sound abusive. It's not really personal. Actually my character was formed by the works of Laura Lee Hope."

"Who?"

"Creator of the Bobbsey Twins. But enough about me. You, I hear, have edited at least one of Jordan Walker's books."

"Yes," she said. *"Mister TV, The Ron Reilly Story."*

"Good. I'd like you to check in with Sidney Leopold to see what manuscript he wants to turn over to you."

"Mr. Barlow—"

"Nick."

"Nick. I was hoping I might be assigned the Graham Farrar biography."

"I don't blame you," I said. "I just wish we had the damn thing."

"I know that one copy was stolen, but—"

"We still don't have another copy. I just learned that Jeffrey Burgal's office was broken into and his other copy was stolen."

"You mean—someone bothered to steal a *manuscript?* But why? Why would anyone bother?"

"I know," I said. "It's just so much used paper to anyone but a publisher. Still . . ." I shrugged. I had no explanation.

She brightened. "Well, maybe it will turn up."

"Let us pray. But don't worry. I'll be the first to look at the manuscript when it comes in, Sidney will be the second, and you'll be next in line."

And she went on her way to Sidney's office, a self-starter if I ever saw one.

Hannah buzzed me just as Jane Goodman left my office. "Angela Farrar, no appointment. Says she has to see you."

Why, for God's sake? She had, of course, threatened to sue for libel if we published Graham's biography and she found anything offensive in its pages. And if Graham told only half the story of their somewhat scandalous union, I had no doubt she would be offended. But that didn't explain why she, rather than her lawyer, wanted to see me.

"Send her in," I said to Hannah.

Angela Farrar is a tall, slender woman with the face of an Egyptian princess and, according to Graham, the carnal appetite of a praying mantis. Swathed in mink, she swept into my office with all the self-possession of a process server, imperious features set in paint, eyes like a pair of bullets aimed straight at my forehead.

"Mrs. Farrar," I said. "What brings you here today?"

"You've already heard from my attorney. Do I have to repeat what he told you?"

"I wasn't, ah, cooperative, as he undoubtedly informed you. I don't like threats of any kind, and I especially don't like threats of lawsuits. In my opinion there's already too much trivial, unsubstantiated, downright foolish litigation in this country as it is. I merely hoped to discourage your attorney from initiating any more."

"Foolish? *Trivial?*" Her voice rose an octave, and a flush darkened her ivory cheeks. To the manner born, all right. She who must be obeyed. "How can you possibly call my complaints *un*substantiated?"

"Madam," I said in my quietest voice, "Graham Farrar's biography has not been published yet. It therefore being unlikely in the extreme that you have read a word of it, how can you know what he may or may not have said about you? What grounds can you have for a complaint?"

"Why . . . why . . . I can *imagine* what that bastard might say about me. Anything to get ev—to make me uncomfortable."

"Yes, I am told a vivid imagination is a continuous feast, Mrs. Farrar. Sit down, though. Please."

She settled into a chair and draped her fur over the back of it.

"Let's be reasonable about this," I said.

"What do you mean?"

"I certainly don't want a lawsuit, and I'm sure you don't want any . . ." I was going to say "dirty laundry" but edited myself. ". . . any embarrassing details of your marriage to Graham made public."

"I beg your—"

"Which, if you'll be good enough to let me finish, would surely happen if a libel suit came to trial."

She mulled this over briefly. And then that impassive, not to say icy, face of hers broke up in a smile. Her voice lowered by half an octave, and her glare softened to a gaze.

"Mr. Barlow," she said, "you're a gentleman."

I inclined my head slightly to acknowledge the compliment, if that's in fact what she meant it to be.

"And I'm sure you're not without gallantry."

This time I smiled.

"I'm going to throw myself on your mercy," she said. "I don't know if you're aware of it, but I'm engaged to be married."

"I'm afraid I don't really follow the society columns," I said. An absolute lie, I read them religiously. And I knew damn well that Angela Farrar was planning to marry Mr. C. Austin Blackwell III, heir to a South African fertilizer fortune.

"Anyway," she said, "you can see how the—how shall I put it?—the silly mistakes of past years . . . might seem more serious if they were cast in the wrong light."

Silly mistakes? Heavy drug use? A long series of lovers, including a Cuban laundryman, a Jamaican car wash attendant, an Iranian arms merchant, a chapfallen British nobleman, and an abalone fisherman from Baja, California, among others?

"At least," Graham had once said, "she showed no prejudices, either of race, creed, or color." Nor, I believe, even of gender.

Graham obviously did not care particularly about these transgressions—all this having transpired B.A. (Before AIDS) —but he drew the line at her forging checks on his personal bank account to finance her drug habit. He threw her out but failed to change the locks. The result? While he was out on location for a picture, she got back into his Hollywood Hills home and trashed it. Something like twelve thousand dollars in damages, not counting the artwork she slashed. He had her arrested and charged. It took a good deal of her own and her family's money to get *that* "silly mistake" off the books.

Oh, well, none of us is perfect.

"When is the marriage?" I asked.

"Sometime in June."

"Well, then," I said, "I promise not to publish the book before September. That should get you off the hook."

Angela Farrar studied me for a moment, the ice flowing back into her cheeks, the fur coming back up around her bony shoulders. No more Mrs. Nice Gal.

"I take that back," she said.

"What?"

"That crap about your being a gentleman. You're not a gentleman, you're a goddamn son of a bitch. Fit company for Graham!"

"I've been called worse."

I rose to show her to the door, but she snatched it open without my assistance, then slammed it behind her.

• • •

Later that morning Scanlon called on me to ask about Jordan's manuscript—and had I made any progress in finding Jordan Walker's hideaway?

"Negative on both counts," I said.

"About that mugging," said Scanlon, "and that burglary of your agent's office."

"You know about them both?"

"Look, Mr. Barlow." The exasperation in his voice was unmistakable. "You and Mr. Burgal are involved in a murder investigation, like it or not. Obviously the two episodes are connected. And while we're on the subject of the mugging—"

"Yes?"

"Whatever possessed you to put up a fight?"

"You sound like the cop who interviewed Jeffrey and me."

"Don't pull a Bernie Goetz with muggers," he said. "Give them what they want."

"Suppose they intend to kill you anyway?"

He let that one slide. Then he said: "It doesn't make sense."

"What doesn't?"

"Why would anybody steal a manuscript? What value would it have on the street?"

Half a million dollars, I thought, *to me.*

"If it sheds any light on Jordan's death—"

Scanlon finished for me. "Then someone out there doesn't want it to get into our hands. Yes, that's possible. Look, Mr. Barlow. I think you and Mr. Burgal ought to get down to the station and check out those mug shots."

I groaned.

"Can I tell you something, Mr. Barlow?" Scanlon said softly. "One of the things I've learned in ten years on this job?"

"Please, Lieutenant, spare me your philosophy of criminology. Save it for that book you're going to write."

"No philosophy," he said, "and I'll put it in very few words. How do you suppose we're going to do anything about crime, especially street crime, if people like yourselves—good, conscientious citizens—won't give us all the help they can? You were attacked when you were going peacefully about your business. You have every right to feel outraged. And I would think you'd want to *do* something about that outrage to get even. But the only way to do that is to help us catch those two. End of sermon. I won't pass the hat."

I have always found guilt to be a wonderful persuader.

"All right," I said. "I can't speak for Jeffrey, but I'll be glad to look at the picture collection. As for that book of yours ..."

103

"Yes?"

"I haven't had the chance to read your magazine article with everything else that's come up, but I will. Soon."

"I appreciate that. All I ask is your frank opinion."

"And you will have it."

My frank opinion? *Nobody*, but *nobody* wants that. What every writer wants is praise, encouragement, raves—or help, in the form of intelligent, enthusiastic, useful editorial suggestions. But a frank opinion? Never.

"I've checked out Jordan's ex-wives," Scanlon said. "Jesus, what a bunch. I'd hate to put them in the same room together."

"Did they give you any trouble?"

"That first one . . . what's her name?"

"Viola?"

"Viola, yeah. Well, she said it served the bastard right, and if she'd had any sense when they were married and he was fooling around, she'd have done it to him herself. But now she has better things to do."

Viola I remembered as a termagant, beautiful in a spidery way but essentially shrewish and vindictive. It was she who would threaten to attack Jordan's royalties if he fell but a week or two behind in his alimony payments. I had heard rumors that she now planned to sue his estate, so that the alimony payments might go on and on. Poor Jordan, to be harassed thus even in his grave.

"And the other two," Scanlon said with a low whistle. "One's a drunk, the other looks like a two-hundred-dollar call girl."

"With reason," I said. "Didn't she press her phone number on you, Lieutenant?"

From the silence that followed, I knew she had. It was then that I told him about my visit from Angela Farrar.

"Why didn't you mention this lawsuit threat before?"

"I didn't know if it was important."

"*Everything* connected with Jordan Walker or Graham Farrar is important," he said.

"Yessir," I said. "I'm sorry."

He cleared his throat. "Come on, Mr. Barlow, I'm not trying to give you a hard time, really. I just want to know whatever you know that might be helpful."

"Done and done."

On that note we headed off to look at mug shots.

As it turned out, when it came to making an ID, I couldn't. A grim-looking bunch of faces altogether, most of them unsavory, some of them absolutely depraved, but none of them rang the bells of memory. I did my best as a good citizen, but it wasn't good enough.

Jeffrey, as I expected, was a no-show.

13

When I left for Connecticut that weekend, I took Margo with me. We both felt she needed and deserved a restful stay in the country. As for me, I'd had my fill, temporarily at least, of crime and punishment, and that included television reruns of the cops-and-robbers shows. I wanted to walk through the sun-dappled woods of Weston with our two golden retrievers, Zachary and Bonnie.

I hoped Tim would be able to shed some light on the Jordan Walker mystery. Why would anyone be willing to kill for a manuscript? What was in it that made it worth a mugging as well?

At some point during the trip out, I fell asleep, out of sheer exhaustion, I suppose, or brain fatigue. Another wild and woolly dream ensued, complete with missed connections, mislaid clothing, and a dark, saturnine figure—a man who somehow embodied consummate evil. Then I was running down a long crepuscular tunnel, fleeing from I knew not what. Above my head a whirring sound, the beating of bats' wings overhead. And then the tunnel ended abruptly, and I was falling, falling. . . .

Margo woke me by rubbing her fingertips gently across my forehead.

"Whfunk?"

"Nicholas," she said, "I'm worried. You're starting to hyper-ventilate."

"Oh, God," I said, "nightmares in the middle of Saturday morning."

"Poor baby," she said, with a goodly helping of irony in her voice. I grunted and cleared my throat. Somehow I expected more sympathy from a contented ex-wife.

I was looking forward not only to a walk in the woods but also to a romp on the feathers with Margo. It wasn't going to be easy, as she'd given me no encouragement whatsoever. She seemed, in truth, to have taken the vows, and celibacy, an increasingly popular choice in this day and age, clearly suited her. Well, what could I do about it except wait? And hope.

Harry Dennehy met us at the Westport station and drove us to Weston along the usual route: from the Saugatuck Station to Route 33 and Lyons Plain Road. The Saugatuck River was running high, almost overflowing its banks, bringing the last of the melted snow from the Berkshires to Long Island Sound. It was a beautiful pea green, foaming white around the rocks and sunken trees. Lyons Plain Road was heavy and golden with forsythia; I saw, darting among the branches, cardinals and blue jays.

"Looks like spring for sure, Harry," I said.

"Yessir."

"How's my mother?"

"Fine."

"And my brother?"

He did not reply at once. Then he said: "Ah, that's hard. *Hard.* But nobody could do any better with it than him, y'know?"

When we turned into the driveway, Margo remarked again on the tiny Colonial graveyard on the hill near the road. She found it enchanting that we might have our own historic cemetery: five ancient headstones, the oldest of them dating back to 1790. Some of the names and dates had worn away in the snow and rain, but one inscription could still be read if you bent down and cleared away the earth and grass:

Stranger, reflect, as you pass by
As you are now, so once was I
As I am now, so shall you be
Prepare for death and follow me.

That's about the gist of it all, isn't it? Actually, I found the presence of these old bones oddly comforting. There was in all this a continuity that made death itself seem more manageable, almost domesticated.

Mother stood near the front door to welcome us, dressed in her gardening costume: a floppy felt hat, ancient gray sweater covered with a flowered smock, heavy canvas gloves, a trowel in one hand and a fork in the other. Harry did the heavy work around the grounds, or Mother would call in the nursery people. But the fine-tuning around the place, the care of the shrubs and flowers, she reserved for herself. Even at seventy-plus, she was not about to turn her roses, petunias, and azaleas (which even now were beginning to display their glorious colors) over to strangers.

She waved and smiled as we got out of the Cadillac.

"Hello, children." She patted me on the shoulder and embraced Margo when we got close enough. Mother liked Margo and had at times hinted that I ought to show the good sense to remarry her. Even though I have at times been inclined to agree with her, I mostly feel singularly unattracted by marriage. As an institution it has much to recommend it: solidity, stability, children, affection, conjugal pleasures, property rights, and all that. Still, like Mae West, I just don't feel like moving into an institution again. Not yet, at any rate.

"Are you all right, Nick?"

"Yes, Mother."

"You're quite sure?"

"As sure as I can be, Mother."

She made a face. "Those horrible street crimes! No one, no one at all, is safe. Perhaps you should move back out here and commute to the city, as your father did. Five days a week on the New Haven, in on the eight thirty-five and out on the six-oh-five."

Since I can't be convinced that twentieth-century Manhattan is any more dangerous than fourteenth-century Paris or nineteenth-century London, I ignored this suggestion, as I always do. Besides, if I lived in Connecticut full-time, I'd have no such beautiful place to visit on weekends.

"No use, Gertrude, dear," Margo said. "Nick is uncomfortable when he gets too far away from Manhattan. He travels only when he has to—on business, for the most part."

"Connecticut is all I really need," I added.

"A pity. What are you up to this weekend?"

"Primarily I want to see Tim," I said. "I'd also like to unwind, if I can."

"Before you go upstairs, Nicholas, I've had some thoughts myself about this Walker murder."

"Oh? Like what, Mother?"

"Well . . ." She raised a bony index finger. "Why couldn't the murder have been committed by one of your competitors?"

"I beg your pardon?"

"I mean a competing publisher, of course. Someone jealous of your success, or disappointed because your Mr. Walker left his firm for yours. Isn't jealousy a perfectly good motive? Or envy?"

"Mother, to be truthful, that theory doesn't make much sense."

"And why not, may I ask?"

"Because a publisher might be likely to murder another publisher—always provided he could get away with it—but not an author. They are our source of income, and we wouldn't do away with our geese if there were golden eggs to be laid, now would we?"

"But, Nicholas," she said, "you yourself have told me more than once that *you* would like to kill one of your more difficult authors, haven't you?"

I sighed and retreated from the field.

As soon as Margo and I had gone to our rooms and unpacked, she to the second-floor front and me to the apartment in the attic I occupied when in the country, I headed for Tim's room. He was in his wheelchair, bent over a book. The sunlight streaming through the window that lit up the fine lines and planes of his face made him look like a piece of Greek sculpture. His skin was so pale it seemed almost translucent— usually he avoided direct sunlight, but today he seemed to be drinking it in.

"Did you bring the Farrar manuscript, Nick?" he asked, without looking up from his book. I glanced at the title. Baudelaire's *Petits Poemes en Prose*.

"Still waiting for it." I explained the situation to him.

"Damn and *damn!*" Tim said. "I've been looking forward to it." He closed the book and put it aside.

"I hate to disappoint you, Tim."

He shrugged. "You certainly didn't plan on being mugged."

"That's true. Can I do anything for you?"

"Just let me know when lunch is ready."

Half an hour later we were all seated around the dining room table. Mother's Honduran cook served us up an oxtail soup that must have taken her all morning to prepare. It was accompanied by crisp oven-dried bread rounds rubbed with sweet butter and garlic, all washed down with a slightly chilled vintage burgundy. Even Tim, who usually picked at his food, cleaned his plate. As for me, after coffee and one sip of brandy, I couldn't repress a yawn.

"I may fall asleep any minute now," I whispered to Margo.

"Nonsense, Nicky," she said. "Time for a brisk walk."

So we headed out into the woods to inspect the signs of new life: vernal energy everywhere. The earth was spongy and soft, though its crust of matted leaves had begun to dry out and in places snapped crisply beneath our feet. The gray of winter was fast disappearing, to be replaced by flashes of pale green and yellow.

Cheeks bright red from a biting wind, we returned to a silent house.

"I think it's time for a nap," I suggested to Margo. "You in your bed—"

"All right."

"And me in your bed too."

"Well ..." she said.

"Yes?"

"No."

And so to bed, alone and not too distressed. After all, well fed—and an hour later, well rested.

Later that evening I paid another call on Tim, vodka martini in hand.

"You're really worried about this one, aren't you?"

I took a deep swallow of my drink. "Yes."

"What is it?"

"Well ..." And I laid it out for him. We weren't exactly skirting bankruptcy, not by a long shot, but I had gone out on a very long limb with a couple of large advances for books that hadn't worked out too well. So the numbers weren't so good right now. A Jordan Walker best-seller would come in timely.

"The bank is unhappy," I said. "My controller Mr. Mandelbaum isn't so happy, either. And any minute I expect Mother to get on my case."

"While you're waiting for another copy of the manuscript," Tim said, "It might be helpful if you could find Jordan Walker's office."

"What the hell—I could kick myself, Tim. I ought to have gotten around to that before now!"

"Then why haven't you?"

"Too many damn meetings. It'll soon be sales conference time, you know. But I will get cracking on Jordan's office as soon as I'm back in the city."

"Like how?"

When I told Tim about Dori Regan, Jordan's typist, and how I'd met her at the funeral service, he brightened.

"Why not talk to her, Nick? You have to follow every lead you have."

"I told Scanlon about her, and I have no doubt he's already spoken to her." Then I began to laugh.

"What?" Tim said.

"Listen to us. 'Follow every lead,' indeed. We're beginning to sound like a bad detective novel. 'Come, Scanlon, the game's afoot!' "

111

"Well, what's wrong with that? Enjoy it while you can."

Actually I was. I felt a surge of excitement such as I hadn't felt since . . . well, since the last time I fell in love. When I had started out with this murder business, my main interest had been to get a book out, Jordan's book, one that would go two-stepping out of the bookstores. A book club selection, even a best-seller. Just a *book*.

Now I knew I was at least knee-deep in a murder investigation, and as happy about it as a schoolboy in June. Moreover, the detective in charge was becoming a bosom buddy, all because he hoped I might publish his book, or so it seemed. And yet . . . and yet, I felt I *could* be helpful to him. *Oh, my God, what did I do with Scanlon's article?* I had to find it and read it!

"You think I ought to go ahead with this, Tim? What about the police?"

He stared at me for a moment, then shook his head.

"Don't be an ass," he said. "You're already involved in this case, up to your chops. So you might as well put some legwork into it. Anyhow . . ." He turned away and looked out at the fields, lit now only by a rising full moon. "Anyhow, the murder case *is* the book."

14

Another Monday morning.

I sat in my office brooding. As usual, the correspondence piled up in my In box had proliferated over the weekend, like a malignant growth. As usual, I ignored it. I felt no desire to pick up the phone and begin the day's flurry of business and personal calls. Tim's words were still reverberating in my mind: "The murder case is the book." *And you*, I said to myself, *are a detective as well as a publisher.*

Nonsense.

Yet there was a seductive logic to it. Was there an affinity between my peculiar trade and Lieutenant Scanlon's? Consider it this way. A murder is a problem to be solved. So is a book: the problem of how to get the author's vision from the bare outline of a manuscript to a finished book, then to market it. Or, if this doesn't sound too frivolous, let us posit that a book is a crime committed by its author. It is then my duty as a publisher to unravel the mysterious threads of this crime, to expose the author's "guilt" to a public (for which, read "jury") ready to exonerate or condemn. No less than Scanlon, I have my unsolved crimes (unsold books, failed visions of literary glory), a professional life charged with frustrations and baffling clues. (What do they *want* out there, those book-buying multitudes?) And the moment I think I have figured out the secret of this publishing business, I am confronted with yet another mystery. The money men, the M.B.A.'s from Harvard, the bottom-liners, the corporate pinstripers, all think *they* can figure it all out. Little do *they* know! Below the bottom line there is always another bottom line; behind every solution to a problem, there is still another problem, and behind that problem, as if it were a curtain, there is another curtain, and behind that an endless corridor of beguiling veils—and behind those veils . . .

No doubt all this is the purest sophistry, and I questioned its validity even as it passed through my mind. Still . . . I no longer felt so eager to dismiss Jordan Walker's murder as none of my business. My business as a publisher, I mean.

And now I was ready to get down to work.

Just then, riffling through the papers on my desk, I came upon the copy of *Police and Fireman's Journal* that Scanlon had given me. I pushed the rest of the reports and manuscripts on my desk aside, picked up the magazine, found Scanlon's article, and began to read.

The title of the piece was "A Policeman's Lot."

When constabulary duty's to be done/Does a policeman's lot have to be an unhappy one, as W. S. Gilbert contended in *The Pirates of Penzance?* I think not. I personally like being a cop. I deliberately chose law enforcement as a career from a number of other callings, including the law, politics, and government service. So when I hear people talking about how much they hate the fuzz, or the blues, or the flatfeet, or whatever they decide to call us, it rankles. I want to say: look, I didn't go into police work because I was too dumb to find employment. I went into it because I believed—and I still believe—that it was work as useful as any a man or a woman can do.

I suppose the desire to become a police officer was born in me when I was a small boy in grade school. I grew up in a tough Brooklyn neighborhood, quite near Coney Island. I hated fighting, hated violence; I still do. But you had to fight to survive in my part of Brooklyn. Even more than fighting, I hated the bullies who forced me into using my fists, and I promised myself that if I ever had the chance to do something about those who prey on other people, particularly people weaker than themselves, I would smite them hip and thigh.

Even though there are rogues in our ranks, crooked cops, greedy cops, stupid cops, the policeman's calling is still as fine and noble a calling as there is anywhere. We may not be priests in uniform, but we are certainly defenders of the faith. . . .

I read on. There were indeed surprising depths in Police Lieutenant Joseph Scanlon. When I had finished the piece, I put a buck slip on it, directing it to Sidney Leopold's attention.

"There may be a book in this man," I wrote. "Shall I see if we can't get it out of him?"

A rhetorical question. Already I was on the phone.

"Lieutenant Scanlon?"

"Yes, Mr. Barlow?"

"Any developments?" I adopted what I hoped was the right note of curiosity mixed with genuine concern—a good citizen's concern.

"We're still plugging away, Mr. Barlow. We'll have something soon, I promise you."

"How about Jordan's typist? Have you spoken to her?"

"Of course we called her!" The asperity in his tone brought me up short. "She wasn't much help. Apparently she never set foot in Walker's office, he brought his stuff to her and she reworked it at home. Or so she claims."

"You don't believe her, then."

"She *might* be telling the truth."

"How about that porter? What was his name—Cordoba?"

"We still don't have enough to hold him. He's a druggie, by the way, which gives him his motive. Robbery. We still don't know what all was missing from Jordan Walker's apartment."

"I see. I was just wondering if, perhaps, there is some help I can offer you?"

"It would help if I could talk to Graham Farrar," he said. "In fact, it's essential we see him. He was one of the last people to see Jordan Walker before his death. Do you think there's any chance he'll come back East?"

"It's certainly possible. You want me to take a shot at it?"

He hesitated a moment, then said: "It might be easier for you to persuade him than us."

"I'll do what I can, Lieutenant."

"Thanks," he said. "Let me know if you can arrange something."

"Before you hang up . . ." I said.

"Yes?"

"I've read your story."

He said nothing, but his silence was almost palpable. How many times have I spoken those words—"I've read your story," or "your book"—knowing that what I said next would inspire either joy or despair, and seldom any emotion in between.

"This is a strange business," I said, "risky in the extreme, and there are no sure things, at least not where a new writer is concerned. Entrances are sometimes exits, it's often a matter of 'Hail and farewell.' We who have the gall to call ourselves publishers have to go by our instincts, our hunches, guesswork seasoned by experience, if you will."

"Yes."

"I have a gut feeling that you can write a good book. One I'd be proud to publish."

"You think so?"

"It's at least a strong possibility. One editorial suggestion. Excuse the pun, but I think you ought to get down to cases."

"Oh? Oh, sure, I see what you mean. Details about the crimes I've investigated."

"Precisely."

"Chapter and verse, so to speak."

"Right, the first-person narrative, blow-by-blow approach.

We can discuss that further next time we have a chance. Right now ..."

"I know," he said. "Right now our hands are full of a murder."

"And a mugging."

We rang off, and I buzzed Hannah.

"As soon as it's a decent hour in California, would you see if you can get me Graham Farrar on the phone?"

"Will do."

To work. Work? I did my best, but it was hard to settle down to the mundane details facing me. Not that Mary Sunday, my sales manager, is in the least ordinary. Female editors, publishers, and subsidiary rights directors are not uncommon in book publishing today; there are distaff opportunities galore. Consequently, women swell the ranks not only of publishing houses but of the publishing courses and classes that supply so many of our recruits. There are, however, relatively few female sales managers. Perhaps that is because so few women start their careers in sales, or because sales managers have to deal with occasional hard-bitten types: sales reps, for example, or retail book buyers, and it takes a certain toughness to survive. Mary Sunday is small, ash blond, rather birdlike, I think, but tough, all right, though she can also charm the birds out of the trees. And she certainly knows how to charm me—usually.

"Boss," she said, settling down in a visitor's chair, "what do we do about the Walker bio?"

"Eh?"

"You know, the Graham Farrar?"

I groaned. "I have heard of it," I admitted. "What about it?"

"Well," she said, "we were planning to have Jordan Walker talk to the sales force at conference, which, as we all know only too well, is just two weeks away."

"Unless you have connections in that great remainder house in the sky, Jordan is certainly out as our guest speaker."

"In that case, what do you think our chances are of getting the great actor himself?"

117

"Negligible to zero," I said. "I have a favor I must ask him, but it definitely is *not* that one."

"Just a thought. There's also the matter of the advance bound galleys we want to send out."

I thought it wise to let Mary in on the extent of our predicament.

"You mean—*no* reading copies for the reps, even as they start out on their appointed rounds?"

"Indeed."

"But a copy of the manuscript has to turn up soon, doesn't it?"

"Let us fervently hope so. You might also try prayer."

There were other matters Mary wanted to bring up. Was the Sign of the Dove all right for the end-of-conference bash? Too pricey, in my view. I suggested "21." We were planning to use a smallish midtown hotel for the conference itself; not for me the Bahamas or sunny Florida. I leave that to the Simon & Schusters and Random Houses. Besides, the pinch was on—not just the economic climate outside, but the recession in our cash flow had to be taken into account. Anyway, I hate playing golf.

Exit Mary Sunday, and I buzzed Hannah.

"Any luck on getting Graham Farrar?"

"Not yet, Nick. I believe he may be shooting. At least, that's what I read in the entertainment section the other day. I'll keep trying."

"Do, please."

It seemed, and undoubtedly was, hours later when I got through to California.

"Graham," I said. "I was thinking today of that evening back at Princeton—you remember, our last poker game?"

"What? Oh, yeah. You son of a bitch—that straight flush."

"That's the one. Graham?"

"I hear you."

"I figure I beat you out of a ticket home. I'd like to send you a first-class ticket from L.A. to New York to make up for it."

"Come on, Barlow, you wily bastard, what's on your mind?"

"Truth and consequences. Jordan is dead, and we're all doing what we can to find out who killed him. We need you to help us, that's all."

" 'We?' Who the hell's 'we'?"

"Well," I said, somewhat lamely, "I happen to be assisting the New York homicide squad with their inquiries. Ah . . . in my capacity as the deceased's publisher, you understand."

Silence. Still more silence. I could imagine what he was thinking—*Who the hell does he think he is, bothering me with this shit?* Then, in a snarling tone familiar to moviegoers the world over, "Nick, I happen to have a few things to do with my time. You don't know how busy I am or you wouldn't—"

"If I have any due bills at all with you, Graham, I'm calling them in now. Please."

"I don't owe Jordan Walker anything now. I didn't even *like* him, the little jerk."

"He wasn't exactly my favorite companion, either, but I think he's entitled to rest easily in his grave. Come back and help us."

"I doubt that I can."

"You never know."

Silence—to the point that I thought maybe he'd hung up on me.

"Graham . . . are you still there?"

"OK," he said. "I'll give you two days. But two days is absolutely all, Nick, and even that will cost me more than you can possibly know. But, Nick—"

"I appreciate it."

"We'll be quits, Nick, just remember that. No more due bills. I won't owe you, you won't owe me."

"If that's the way you want it, Graham."

"That's the way I want it."

After talking to Graham, I put the phone down and leaned back in my chair. Graham Farrar. One of the finest actors of the century, he'd been called more often than I could remember.

In our college days, of course, he was just another student actor, so unsure of his calling that he was in his midtwenties

119

before he finally gave up his alternative choice of careers: medicine, the surest road to riches for a boy from the hinterlands of the Midwest. Thus did the world lose yet another sawbones and gain a superb actor.

A born actor, in fact. When he showed up at the Triangle Club at Princeton, he hadn't had any formal training at all. I first saw him on stage playing Danny in *Night Must Fall*, a part that calls for an uncanny blend of naive boyish charm and sinister malevolence. Both qualities were there, in abundance—you could *believe* he was carrying a severed human head in that hatbox. The applause at his curtain calls was exuberant and prolonged; to Graham, I'm sure, addictive. I know . . . once I was stagestruck, too. Nothing quite replaces it.

Granting that, how is it that Graham Farrar has not been on a legitimate stage for years and now only makes movies? I suppose, as Willy Sutton remarked when asked why he robbed banks, "Because that's where the money is."

One episode especially stands out in my memory: Graham, two other friends, and I playing poker at my eating club—Tiger Inn—on a June evening just before classes ended. We were all going on our separate ways the next day. Graham, I knew, had just enough money to get back to his hometown in Nebraska and not much more. We were playing a game of seven-card stud, probably the last hand of the evening. Any player with a pair showing could raise the bet from fifty cents to a dollar, with unlimited raises. Graham had a pair of aces, a ten, and a nine. Last draw and a final round of betting—a long round. Graham and I kept raising each other until there was actually about two hundred dollars in the pot.

"Jesus, Graham," I said, after about the sixth raise. "This could go on all night."

"Getting nervous, Nick?"

"Aren't you?"

"Your bet, Nick. Speak up—or fold."

"Hell, there's no way I can fold."

"So . . .?"

I put in one more raise. Graham called and raised me again.

"Oh, shit," I said. "Show your cards, Graham. I call."

He spread his hand. A full house, aces over tens. Just what I expected him to have.

"I'm counting on you," he said, "for a flush."

"So it is, pal." I put my cards down one by one. They were all hearts, all right—a two, three, four, five, and six.

"*Straight* flush, Graham."

Why did I have to draw it out so? I suppose I was savoring the moment of triumph, poker being a game rich in sadomasochism.

"Well, that's show business," Graham said, then put his hands behind his head and smiled. To this day I swear he smiled as though he had won, not lost. And all the time I knew he was out his plane fare home.

"Why didn't you give him his money back?" a woman friend once asked me when I told her the story. "You knew he'd probably have to hitchhike home."

"Probably."

"And you certainly didn't need his money."

"Certainly not."

"Then why?"

"My darling," I had said, "I wonder if you really understand poker. Or Graham Farrar." *Or*—I thought, but did not say —me.

15

I knew Graham would be as good as his word, and he was. On Wednesday morning the phone rang, and when I picked it up, I recognized the snarl.

"So I'm here."

"Where?"

"New York, goddamn it, where d'you think?"

"I mean where in New York?"

"The Carlyle. Long as I'm here, I might as well enjoy Bobby Short."

"I agree. But I think we should meet at a less public place. The Players?"

"No, my treat. Make it the Athletic Club. Noon?"

"The NYAC it is. And, Graham . . ."

"Yes?"

"Thanks for coming."

"The hell with it," Farrar said, and hung up.

The NYAC is Graham's club, not mine. Like most actors, he works out whenever he can. When your body is such an important part of your professional equipment, I suppose you have to stay in shape somehow. I might as well admit that I don't care much more for the Athletic Club than I care for working out. The club strikes me as a rather dull place: the decor is basically heavy leather and sporting prints, and the people there are either affluent businessmen running to flab or slim, well-built yuppies. All in all, about as appetizing as a high-school gymnasium.

I got there first and was nursing a cocktail when Graham joined me, trim, tanned, and elegantly clad in a light brown shantung suit. As always, all eyes were upon him. I suppose all eyes are always on him wherever he goes. Even the waiters, often so indifferent to their duties, snapped to attention when he passed their stations.

He nodded, smiled, and sat down. "Now that I've had my daily dozen," he said, "I'm ready for a Bloody Mary."

"How's the Carlyle?" I asked.

"Dependably understated. But it's quieter here, refreshingly boring."

Just then the headwaiter brought Lieutenant Scanlon over to our table: my little surprise. Graham looked annoyed when I introduced him, but he quickly got over his pique and began playing it polite if not gracious. After all, Graham was a famous police buff, always an infallible sleuth on-screen.

I had suggested to Scanlon ahead of time to be as unassertive—and as unthreatening—as possible. Not that it was all that hard—he looked as though all he wanted to ask of Graham was his autograph.

"You keep your membership here," I said for openers, "but you probably don't get here more than once or twice a year. Why bother?"

"I don't know," he said. "It's not a bad place for a workout, a massage, a swim, you know? And nobody really bothers me here. No requests for autographs, no drunks who think they're tougher than my on-screen persona, no promoter who wants me to endorse a Graham Farrar line of luggage, or what have you. I can relax and feel like an ordinary human being for a change. I can get away from those people who think that paying seven or eight dollars for a movie ticket gives them the right to rip the pocket off my sports coat."

I thought fleetingly of the young and struggling actors who

would send their aging mothers out to scrub floors rather than take a steady job—anything to land that perfect part, to achieve the fame Graham found so burdensome.

"Besides," he added, "the drinks are bigger and stronger here than anywhere else in town."

After one more each of the biggest drinks in town, we settled down to our feeding. Graham ordered a Golden Buck. I picked the trout amandine, it being hard to go wrong with the catch of the day. Scanlon seemed shy, hesitant to order anything lest he seem presumptuous, but he mustered up his courage and asked for a club sandwich.

While we were ordering, I studied Graham more closely. The lean, craggy good looks were even more pronounced now that he had reached his early forties. He could no longer play young leading men, of course; but then, those roles seldom appealed to him. You couldn't imagine Graham Farrar walking into a drawing room, swinging a tennis racket, not even at the beginning of his career. He had played villains and, with makeup, old men; bizarre juvenile roles, psychopaths, men with strange and passionate causes. In Westerns, he was the outcast or the gambler, shunned by all decent folk in town. Yet his was still an emblematically American face, complete with long Scotch-Irish jaw, high cheekbones, and piercing, ice-blue eyes. He needed a hairpiece for some roles but still had most of his own.

"Another drink, Graham?" I asked him.

He nodded, then said: "Did I ever tell you I was in AA for a while?"

I shook my head.

"I didn't quite make the ninety days they say to get your head minimally clear."

"Why'd you drop out?"

"Hell, I don't know. I enjoyed the stories those drunks told in the open meetings—some of the wildest stuff you can imagine. Like the guy who said he'd decided to commit suicide but didn't have the guts to pull a trigger or drown himself. So late one night he starts walking though the deepest, darkest part of Central Park, waiting for the ultimate mugger.

He goes in one side and by the time he comes out the other, he doesn't have a stitch of clothes on his body."

We laughed, none more appreciatively than I, who had flirted with AA myself at one point. Like Graham, I had found the confessions of alcoholics fascinating—and sometimes hilarious in a macabre way—but I had been put off by the quasireligious, at times sanctimonious, proceedings, and all the prosletyzing that went on. AA is after all a circle, and one closed as tightly as any other.

"Why did I drop out?" said Graham. "I suppose because it is clearly an impossibility now for me to remain anonymous. Anywhere."

"Now," he said, "I'm what I would describe as a functional alcoholic. I need booze every day. Some days I drink moderately, some days heavily. My moderate drinking would probably look heavy to a teetotaler, but when I'm working, I don't drink at all. Between times I do what I feel like doing. I don't have hangovers and I never miss shootings. I know my lines, I don't bump into the scenery. That, as you must know, is the Spencer Tracy School of acting, to which I certainly belong. I would add one more rule to Tracy's two for the benefit especially of young actors—be sure that your every word can be heard clearly in the last row of the theater."

Graham was now off and running, cocking his head first in my direction, then in Scanlon's, playing himself to an audience of two, and a bravura performance it was. I had long ago immunized myself against the actor's professional seductiveness, which, I felt, properly belonged only in the theater or on screen. I wondered, however, whether Scanlon, who had never before been exposed to the full force of Graham Farrar's personality, might succumb to the actor's savage charms and forget why he was here. It wouldn't be all that surprising if he did. However, I am no slouch myself at upstaging and can also steal a scene when the occasion calls for it. This occasion obviously did. I did not intend that Scanlon and I continue to be the Wedding Guests to Graham's Ancient Mariner.

"We appreciate your coming here to meet with us, Graham," I said. "You could be quite helpful." The actor waved his hand in deprecation. Scanlon did not pick up the cue. Was it perhaps premature to bring up the Jordan Walker case? Or was he intimidated by Graham? I somehow felt he was tough enough, experienced enough, to hold his own. I decided to change the subject.

"What are you working on now, Graham?" Damnation! A tactical error. My question was enough to open the floodgates even wider.

"I am going to film," he said with quiet solemnity, "the most marvelous adventure story ever written. One of the first novels in all of literature, and still one of the most intricate and ingeniously plotted stories in print. Can you guess what I'm talking about?"

I shook my head.

"Ulysses," he said.

"Not James Joyce?" I couldn't visualize Graham either as Stephen Daedalus or as Leopold Bloom.

"I'm going to play Ulysses in Homer's *Odyssey*," he said. And with that he began to describe his dream. It was to be "a Graham Farrar production, of course." Producer: Graham Farrar. Director: Graham Farrar. Starring Graham Farrar. Screenplay by somebody whose name I didn't recognize, with Graham Farrar, based on the epic by Homer.

"We'll film it in the Mediterranean," he said. "Shooting starts in a few weeks. It's all there, the script, the financing—well, *most* of the financing. I have"—and he named one of the newest Hollywood nymphets-starlets—"as my Nausicaa. An all-star cast, Nick, you can take my word for it. There has never been a historical like it, nor will there ever be another one to match it. Oh, I know you're thinking of *Gone with the Wind* or *Greed* or *Intolerance*, perhaps, or *Ben-Hur*. Well, if you took all the money spent on those movies and multiplied it by three or four, you still wouldn't be close to the budget I've drawn up for my *Odyssey*. I tell you, Nick, it's going to be one of the most beautiful and elaborate movies ever filmed—we'll spare no expense, cut no corners, make no compromises."

For the first time I doubted Graham's chances of success. Wasn't all art in some way a matter of compromise? The compromise at least between an artist's ambitions, which can be infinite, and his abilities, which are not. Could anyone possibly put the *Odyssey* on the screen? If he did, would anyone want to see it?

It occurred to me that so much had happened to Graham and me since we last met—fame and adulation and money for him, fun and games and a life among books and bookfolk for me—that I no longer knew where he was, in any moral or philosophical sense. He lived *out there*, after all. Certainly his public statements reflected a fierce integrity, a compassion for the less fortunate, a determination to acquit himself honorably as an actor and as a man. This was the actor, after all, who had turned down several enormously attractive film offers to appear with the Royal Shakespeare Company in *Othello;* the man who had quietly supported several down-at-the-heel movie actors who could no longer pay their bills, whose generosity to friends and relatives was legendary. I knew too that he had given substantial sums of money to AIDS research.

"Now, when we film the part where Odysseus is cast ashore on the coast of Phaecia and meets Nausicaa of the white arms ... Well, of course he's nude—his clothes have been ripped from his body in the heavy seas—and Nausicaa and her maidens are bathing. We see them emerge from the sea, their skin glowing in the sunlight, and this strange bearded creature appears in their midst. Is he, perhaps, a god? He has the body of one. You understand, Nick"—he slapped himself vigorously on the stomach—"I'll have to go into training for this part. I'll need to wrestle and race and fight like hell, and I'll have to look like a forty-year-old wonder. Odysseus *was* middle-aged, you know, but he still cut a hell of a figure, especially with a laurel wreath to cover his bald spot."

At this point Graham took a well-worn copy of E. V. Rieu's translation from his pocket and began to riffle through its pages. I hoped he wasn't planning to read aloud. I hate being read to. The ear is so much slower, so much more imprecise than the eye. I admit Graham's voice is a superb instrument, but still . . .

Fortunately, he was simply searching for a chapter. "My God, this scene with the Cyclops will be brutal, gory—absolutely terrifying. A giant, by God! The special effects in this film alone will cost ten or fifteen mill, maybe more."

And so he went on, and on, and on, his voice rising, his hands waving to drive home his points, until all the diners around us were staring in our direction. Some turned their heads, shamelessly eavesdropping. I couldn't help reflecting on Graham's ego. An actor is not necessarily more childish or self-centered than a corporate CEO or senator, or even a garbage collector, but he more than they may have earned the right to be. Consider for a moment how insecure is the occupation, and how fragile the equipment: only one's body, a large supply of vanity, and a few secondary skills such as voice control and projection.

Graham had the good fortune to be able to play character parts, primarily; that was why he had survived. But at what cost to his humanity, I couldn't begin to guess. I doubt that he even knew, or would know, until it was all over. I hoped to God he would know when to quit.

In all this time he had not asked me a single question, personal or professional. I was reminded of Ambrose Bierce's definition of a bore: a person who talks when you wish him to listen.

Finally Lieutenant Scanlon bulled his way into the conversation.

"Have you any idea why somebody would have wanted to kill Jordan Walker, Mr. Farrar?"

Graham shook his head. "Not a thought, not a theory."

"Did you get to know him at all well?"

"He was practically in my pocket for a month." And with a wry smile: "It seemed like a year."

"He had his faults," I said, "but I can't imagine anyone hating him enough to want to kill him."

Farrar shrugged. "Somebody gets killed in this city on the average of once every few hours. Walker just ran out of luck, that's all. His number was up, law of averages, put it any way you want."

"He didn't ever say anything about his personal life that might have indicated he was in trouble," Scanlon said.

"Nope," Farrar said. And then awarded us his famous grin—crooked, sheepish, disingenuous. "I didn't give him much chance to. After all, he was out there to learn all he could about me. And that's what we talked about, for four solid weeks. Me."

Scanlon turned to me. "How about you, Mr. Barlow? Have you thought of anything special that might have been troubling Jordan Walker?"

I reflected for a moment, then said, "I can think of only one thing he ever discussed with me that would be relevant. He felt somehow that he had been pigeonholed as a writer of authorized biographies of celebrities—'celebios,' we call them—many of them about rather superficial people, shall I say? Oh, not you, Graham, by any means." Farrar laughed, but his laughter was sardonic, self-mocking maybe. "He thought he'd like to do a biography of a statesman or an important businessman."

"Mr. Farrar," Scanlon said, "you were in Jordan Walker's apartment the evening he was murdered."

"That's right."

"Do you mind telling me what you talked about?"

"What else? The goddamn book. My *biography*. More fiction than fact."

"Did you ... well, have words with Jordan Walker?"

"If you mean did we have an argument," said Graham, "no, we didn't. He took my complaints quietly. None of it was worth a fight."

"And when you left the apartment ..."

"The son of a bitch was alive and kicking."

"Were you aware," Scanlon said, "that your former wife Angela also visited Walker the evening he was killed?"

"No, I didn't know that."

"So you didn't know whether her visit came before yours or afterward?"

"Negative."

Scanlon had obviously struck a dry hole, so I changed the subject. "Graham, did you ever get a copy of Jordan Walker's final draft?"

"Not yet," Graham said, "but I'd certainly like to see what he made out of all those fucking hours of tape recordings he squeezed out of me."

So would I, thought I.

"Business all done?" said Graham. "Okay, let's get the hell out of here."

As the three of us left the dining room and headed for the front door, a beefy gent in rumpled gray flannel stepped in front of us.

"Hey!" he said, "Hey, Graham ... remember me?" He had obviously spent a lot of time at the bar.

Graham stared at him.

"No," he said. "Should I?"

"Upstairs," the big man said. "In the sauna. We talked about that TV series you did."

Graham sighed.

The man put his hand on Graham's shoulder. "Think you're all that important, do you? Just because ... you actors ... all alike. *Shit*."

"Take your hand off me," Graham said softly.

I looked around to see if anyone in uniform was in sight. Any kind of uniform at all, even a doorman's, would have been welcome. I saw Scanlon tighten up, like a cat ready to pounce.

What happened next went so fast I couldn't actually say I saw it. The big guy, I think, gave Graham a push, a contemptuous shove, and then started to turn around. He never quite made it. The next thing I saw, he was spinning around, ricocheting off a nearby chair, and landing on the floor. When he sat up, he was looking at his hands in a dazed way. There was a bright red spot on his left cheek and blood on his lips. He shook his head back and forth slowly.

"Are you all right?" Scanlon asked Graham.

"Piece of cake," Graham said.

We left the man who had accosted Graham to his own devices; someone on the club staff came over to help him to his feet. My only thought was to get Graham out of the place as quickly as possible.

As the three of us left the club and stepped out on Central Park South, a long black limousine pulled up in front of number 180. In the front seat were a driver and an ape in men's clothing.

Graham saw me staring at this no-neck caveman.

"My bodyguard," he said. "Goes with me everywhere, except in the AC, where they wouldn't allow him. And where I wish he'd been just now."

"It's that bad, Graham?" It saddened me to think of Graham, a rugged six-footer himself, dogged about by a hulk like that.

"That bad, pallie." I was of two minds about the "pallie" but decided to accept it in the affable way Graham had bestowed it. "You saw what happened in there."

"It didn't look as though you needed any help," I said.

Graham shrugged. "Another place I'll have to scratch off my visiting list."

At that moment a woman in a bright red cloth coat and a flowered hat walked by. She stopped dead in her tracks at the sight of Graham.

"Aren't you . . . ?"

"I am," said Graham pleasantly.

"I know you, I've seen you somewhere."

"Probably."

"I'm sure I've seen you, in the movies. You're—"

"You bet I am." With that Graham walked off toward his car. I had a feeling he might be just a tad disappointed that the woman hadn't been able to recall his name.

Mr. Muscle got out of the limo and opened the back door. As he did, he looked me over. I felt as though I'd been frisked. The eyes of Graham's bodyguard, sunk deep under bristling black eyebrows, were the meanest, most baleful I had ever seen.

"Wouldn't want to meet him in a dark alley," Scanlon said.
"If *you* wouldn't, imagine how I'd feel," I said. "Who do you think he is?"

"He's trouble," Scanlon said. "Your friend Mr. Farrar is not only protected, he looks overprotected."

"*Quis custodiet ipsos custodes?*" I said. "Who's watching over the watchmen?"

"My thoughts exactly," Scanlon said. "only in English."

"About what happened in there . . ." I said, pointing back to the club.

"He's good, isn't he?" said Scanlon. "Fast as a lightweight. That was some karate chop."

"Fast all right, and every bit as short-tempered. By the way, Lieutenant, was this interview any help to you?"

Scanlon mulled my question over for a moment before answering. "If Farrar left Walker's apartment before his ex-wife dropped in, it clears him. If it's the other way around, it clears her."

"What did the doorman say about the order of departure?"

"He described it three different ways and was absolutely certain of all of them. Not a good sign."

"No. And there's still the third visitor," I said.

Scanlon sighed. "No shortage of suspects," he said. "Let's try this scenario. Angela leaves first, followed by Graham. Walker is alive when Graham leaves, which means the third visitor must be hiding somewhere in the building. After Graham leaves, number three calls on Walker and does him in. There's some justification for this. One of the tenants on Walker's floor has reported that he saw the mystery visitor leave—after Graham Farrar."

"It makes sense," I said.

"Yeah, but any number of things can make sense without being true. Oh, could I trouble you for one more favor?"

"What is it?"

"I've decided to bring Angela Farrar in for questioning. Not an arrest, mind you, just a friendly grilling. Would you like to be there?"

Would I? Wouldn't I just!

132

"I assure you, Lieutenant, I wouldn't miss that particular scene for anything in the world."

.   .   .

That night I was scheduled to attend the New York City Opera with Margo: Puccini's *Il trittico: Gianni Schicchi, Il tabarro,* and *Sour Angelica.* At least that's what I found written in my engagement calendar. But I was much more interested in finding out what might be written in Jordan's, so I called Margo and asked her if she wouldn't mind giving me a rain check.

She did mind, but she gave it to me anyway.

So instead of joining Margo, I put away a splendid solitary dinner: grilled salmon stuffed with julienned carrots and celery hearts cooked in butter, to which truffles, mushrooms, and sherry had been added, all bound with a béchamel sauce, served with fresh lemon slices and a chilled white Graves.

"Pepita," I said, "that meal was one of your triumphs."

She blushed becomingly. Pepita is no Latin beauty, but she does have a sturdy, wholesome, peasant-girl quality about her. Like Oscar, her consort, she speaks a somewhat fractured English. "Oh, I like cook for you," she said now.

"I'm glad."

"You gentleman, I know, not work with hands, but—" She paused, searching for the apt phrase, I supposed. "You eat like *caballo.*" A horse, eh? Well, so be it.

After dinner I took my espresso and Jordan's diary into the study. Mendelssohn's ethereal Violin Concerto in E Minor was on the stereo, and with those singing, soaring opening chords in the background, I began to go through Jordan's appointments, from the first of January to the day of his death.

I noticed early on that while Jordan had been quite explicit in listing his out-of-pocket expenses ("cab fares, $7.50"; "gratuities, $5.00"; "train to Greenwich, CT., $6.75"; "magazine, $2.50"; "newspaper, 40 cents"; et cetera, ad nauseam), he got terribly imprecise when it came to his appointments. Most of them were just entered as initials ("MJC, 2 p.m."; "DR, 6:30"). By looking in the back of the diary, where names, addresses, and phone numbers had been listed, I was able to identify MJC as Mary Jane Carruthers, whoever she might be. DR I thought first might be a physician's appointment, but then I decided it must be Dori Regan. There were of blocks of time spent in "Calif." or "LA with GF," and occasional heartfelt comments, like "GF no-show, GF rude" and "Ugh, bad interview GF." There were also references I took to be sexual rendezvous, accompanied as they were by tiny stars and exclamation points. One such entry read: "MJC 5 p.m." and was followed by "**!!." *Multiple orgasms, perhaps?* I thought. I had to admit a certain admiration for a man who could be prolific both in his writing and in his sex life. Lieutenant Scanlon would undoubtedly want to talk to Mary Jane Carruthers, as well as to Jordan's other paramours.

Had Jordan Walker known I was doing my best to track his murderer through the pages of his diary, I'm sure he would have made more detailed entries.

On a separate piece of paper, I wrote down the names of all those people whose initials turned up more than once— those I could identify, at any rate. It was almost two hours later, midway through Poulenc's Concerto for Two Pianos and Orchestra, when I reached Friday, April 14th.

There was only one entry on the page: "FMS, 2 p.m."

FMS. I went through all the S's in his diary without success. Then I realized what I ought to have known instantly, unless I'm in the wrong business after all: "MS" was the abbreviation for manuscript, and "F" must stand for Farrar. The Farrar manuscript. But what about it? Did that mean a meeting with a person, and if so, who? Dori Regan, perhaps? Jeffrey Burgal? Graham himself? Or somebody altogether different?

I sighed. Why couldn't he have been more specific? I might as well have gone to the opera after all.

On the off chance he might be pulling the lobster shift, I dialed Lieutenant Scanlon's number. When I told him what I'd found—and also what I hadn't found—he was clearly just as disappointed as I was, but not discouraged. "Do me a favor," he said. "Write down everything you've deciphered from Walker's shorthand, and let me have it, along with the diary, as soon as possible. At least we know it's somebody or something connected with that manuscript. It all comes back to that. If only we could find Walker's office. There might be another copy of it there."

"No luck so far?"

"I've put a couple of men on it, but they've come up empty. You're sure there's nothing else in the diary of any importance? Something you might have overlooked when you went through it?"

"Negative, Lieutenant."

"Too bad."

"How about that interview with Angela Farrar?"

"She's been off on a Caribbean cruise with her husband-to-be," he said, "but the boat is bound to dock someday, and when it does, we'll bring her in."

Half in hope, half in desperation, I scribbled a hasty note to my brother, Tim, explaining my impasse and begging for his help. I stuffed the note and Jordan's diary into an envelope and addressed it.

It was still too early to go to bed, so I picked up my dog-eared copy of Scott Berg's biography of Max Perkins: a book of wonders that makes the life of a book publisher appear as romantic as that of a knight-errant. I always found Perkins' remark to Scott Fitzgerald especially thrilling: "Nothing in the world is as important as a book can be." Of course that was all long ago and now seems as distant and faint as the horn of Roland.

Good as the Berg book is, I just couldn't concentrate on it. Here I am, a man of the twentieth century, less than a decade away from the twenty-first, and yet I sometimes feel that I'm engaged in a nineteenth-century business. Oh, we have computers, electronic typewriters, copying machines, fax machines, calculators—all the sophisticated hardware of this high-tech age—but what we produce is not different in essence, and probably not much better in quality, than a Gutenberg Bible or Shakespeare's First Folio. Well, yes, I guess I may have published a book or two that's not *quite* as good as Shakespeare. On that note I laid aside *Max Perkins: Editor of*

Genius. I dialed Margo's number, listened to the melancholy ringing half a dozen times, then hung up. Oh, well. And why should I expect her home so early? Though it was now going on midnight.

I dabbled with the notion of calling Jane Goodman, whose résumé had helpfully supplied her home phone number, but decided against it, on the grounds that there was no way I could make the call sound like business.

16

"Sidney ... Sidney, I ..."

"Yes, Nick?"

"I'm going to need a favor, Sidney. Something above and beyond the call of duty, so to speak."

"Uh-oh."

"You know I'd never ask you to do anything *I* wouldn't do myself. If I could."

We were facing each other over a table at 65 Irving Place, a splendid restaurant arrogant enough to take its address as its name. In view of what I was going to ask Sidney to do, I thought I'd better face him over a good lunch. I urged a Beluga omelette on him while I nibbled on a seafood quiche, indecently creamy within and crisp without, ignoring the salad that came with it, suspecting that it might contain arugula, or another of those peculiar greens appearing on our plates these days.

"Okay," Sidney said, after pistachio ice cream and just before cappuccino. Nothing but the best. "Wh ... wh ... what is it you want me to d-do, Nick?"

I explained as succinctly as I could.

"Oh, God!" he said. "Not *that*."

"You won't actually have to *do* anything you don't want to," I said. "Just talk to her."

"Bu ... but I'm allergic to baby-faced blondes, you know that," he said.

"I have a feeling she'll be delighted to hear from you, Sidney. She took a shine to you at the funeral services, I could tell."

"Bull ... *bleep.*"

"Please, Sidney. Please?"

"All *right*. But, d-damn it, I'm going to keep it strictly business."

"Of course."

"Why me, Nick? You're the d-demon lover of the firm, not me. I'm an amateur."

"Precisely. I'd scare her off. With you she's more likely to open up." As was well-known around the office, Sidney was rather shy with women. Shy but not averse to them. It may just be that he never found time for romance. Given his work load, I wouldn't be surprised.

"So what is it you w-want?" I hated to see that look on Sidney's face, as though I'd short-sheeted him or something.

"Information," I said. "Miss Regan told the cops she doesn't knows where Jordan Walker's secret hideout—his office, I mean—is located. Scanlon suspects she *does* know, and I feel sure she does—she'd *have* to. See if you can find out. Or if she has anything to say about the Graham Farrar manuscript."

"You don't want much, d-do you?"

"And if, by any stretch of the imagination, she knows anything that relates to the murder of Jordan Walker, I want that too."

Sidney slumped back in his chair and belched softly. I knew then it was time to consolidate my gains, and beckoned for the waiter to bring the check.

· · ·

Bright and early the following morning, Sidney poked his head in through the doorway of my office.

"Nick?"

"Come in, Sidney. Sit down, for pity's sake, you don't look

at all well." In point of fact, he looked ghastly: pale, shaken, thoroughly miserable.

"I feel worse," he said, without a trace of a stammer.

"So tell me what happened."

"I told Ms. Dori Regan that my reason for meeting with her was to discuss employing her to retype certain manuscripts for Barlow and Company. I qu-questioned her especially on the original manuscript of Farrar's biography."

"And?"

"I must admit my m-mission was a c-c-complete and utter failure, Nick."

"Oh, *hell*."

"But let me tell you the whole story—just as it h-h-happened."

Which he did, with so much stuttering I won't attempt to reproduce it here.

"Ms. Regan—she insisted at once I call her Dori—greeted me in a maribou-trimmed white robe and a pair of baby-blue mules. She offered me a drink, either scotch or the Russian vodka that she herself was drinking—neat, from a large tumbler. I asked for Perrier. Since none was available, I settled for white wine—a cheap jug wine, I suspect. At any rate, I was able to get it down and keep it there.

"I explained that we were going to want Jordan Walker's autobiography of Farrar retyped, once we located it, and wondered if she might be interested in working on it.

" 'Oh, no,' she said, tossing her head."

"Sidney! She *tossed* her *head*? You'd never let an author get away with that."

"I know, Nick. Whenever I see the phrase, I write 'How far?' in the margin. But Dori is the heroine of her own romantic novel—something by Barbara Cartland or Janet Dailey, most likely—and true to form, she tossed her head. 'I'm not doing typing anymore,' she said. 'I'm in a completely different field now, Sid.' "

"Sid?"

"Sid. I asked her just what that might be.

" 'I'm a literary agent now, Sid,' she said, with considerable satisfaction.

" 'Oh, my . . . *good!'* I said. 'That's a very good career move.'

" 'I'm going to be a partner of Mr. Jeffrey Burgal,' she said. 'I look forward to my new career with great expectations. Who knows—we may even do business together, Sidney. You and me.'

"I couldn't help myself, Nick—I gulped my wine down in one swallow. I had hardly put the glass down on the coffee table when it was full again. What was worse, Dori had begun to toy with the, ah, zipper on her dressing gown. Playing with it almost absentmindedly, I assumed. At any rate, the damned thing was coming down, inch by inch.

"I confess I hadn't a single notion how to proceed. Still, I felt I had to do something.

" 'Dori,' I said, 'I'm sure Mr. Barlow will be happy to do business with you.' We've done worse, Nick. 'And maybe,' I told her, 'one of these days, you'll be opening your very own agency.'

"I could see I'd hit the right button there. I was pretty pleased with myself, only I kept watching the dangerously widening gap in her robe—that zipper seemed to have a will of its own.

" 'Oh, that'll be a while,' she told me, 'but once I have mastered the in*tri*cacies'—she actually accented the second syllable, Nick—'of the business . . .'

"At this point I brought up the subject of the murder.

" 'Mr. Barlow is terribly upset over it,' I said.

" 'Oh, yeah. *That.*' She shuddered—the zipper moved again—and she said: 'Awful. Just awful.'

"I pressed on. I told her you were so concerned about it that you've taken a personal interest in the investigation. Her response to that was to offer me more wine and to pat the cushion next to her on the love seat. I declined the wine, but I did move to the love seat—it seemed easier than arguing.

" 'Mr. Barlow is eager for any information that might lead to the solution of the murder,' I told her. 'Anything at all.'

That damned perfume of hers was beginning to get to me. I was afraid I might throw up.

" 'I don't know if I can help you there,' she said.

" 'We think you can, Dori.'

"At that moment, while she was holding the bottle of wine over my half-empty glass, she tripped over her own slipper. The wine spilled over my trousers. I could feel it seeping through my fly and down my pantlegs. She kept saying she was sorry, produced a napkin, and started dabbing away at the wine-soaked parts of my clothing. Especially the crotch, to which she gave rather prolonged attention, with a quite gentle touch. By now, the zipper on her robe had quite given up the struggle, and so, I'll admit, had I. There's a limit as to how far a man can go in resisting temptation, especially under the influence of cheap wine.

"Still, I also felt that I was doing my duty, and sometime later, after waiting for a decent interval to pass before making intelligible sounds, I said: 'Dori, you haven't answered my question.'

" 'What question?'

" 'Will you cooperate with Nick and me? About the Walker investigation?'

" 'How can I'—she made the 'I' sound like 'little me'—'help you?'

" 'For starters you might tell us where Jordan Walker's office is. I'm sure you *know* where it is.'

"She was silent. Gravely silent. Thinking, I believe.

"Finally she said, 'Well, love, I don't think I can do anything like that just as a favor to you and Mr. Barlow.'

" 'Oh?'

" 'You *know* what I mean,' she said.

"I didn't, Nick. Really, I didn't.

" 'After all,' she said, 'it's my neck on the line, not yours.'

"Then I got it. 'You'll expect to be paid, of course,' I said.

" 'Of course. I can't do anything, you know, just for kicks.'

" 'Anything?' I looked down at the two of us, naked as a pair of boiled shrimp, and at my pants, draped on a hanger over the bedroom door to dry out.

" 'Oh *that*,' she said, tossing her goddamn head again. 'I guess I just succumbed to your manly charms, Sidney. After all, this is only our first encounter.'

" 'Well, now ...'

" 'I hope I'll be seeing you again. You wouldn't want our relationship to be ... just a one-night stand, would you?'

"I didn't contradict her openly, and I couldn't complain, Nick—how could I? She had been the perfect hostess, in a manner of speaking. If not a friendly witness.

"Well, almost perfect. The ice cream in her freezer was a scandal—some kind of mushy custard.

"And that, dear boss, is that. I'm sorry to have gone on at such length, but you wanted a full report—and there it is."

Sidney leaned back in his chair, hands locked behind his head. He looked ever so much calmer and more composed than he had at the onset of his recital.

"Thank you, Sidney. I appreciate all you've done. All."

"So now it's your move, Nick," he said. "The lady is likely to prove costly. Is the information you want worth the price she might charge for it? In any event, leave my feelings about La Regan out of it. I'm actually of two minds about her, though I'm sure the more rational one will prevail."

After Sidney left, I sat for some time in my office mulling over the whole affair. If only a scale existed on which one could weigh alternatives. But I am aware of none, unless it is the human conscience, which, as we well know, makes cowards of us all. To pay off Dori Regan or not to pay her off? That was certainly the question.

I thought that to be on the safe side, I'd better consult my attorney, reliable old Alex Margolies. For once I got through to him on the first phone call.

I explained the situation quickly. What did he suggest?

"Well ..." I could almost hear the legal mind start clicking. Along with his billing clock. "I have to say, Nick, if you do this thing with—what's her name, Miss Regan?—you could be accused of subornation, withholding evidence. If the woman has anything to say that might be useful, she ought to say it to the cops. The best thing would be to sic Lieutenant Scanlon on her."

"You know about Scanlon?" I knew I hadn't mentioned the lieutenant to Alex.

"He's been to see me, Nick. I was also Jordan's attorney."

God! And I hadn't known! It took me a moment to recover.

"So you think I ought not to cooperate with Ms. Regan, Alex?"

"Did I say that? I didn't say that."

"Then what did you say?"

"I gave you one side of the matter. The other side is, if you pay her for it, chances are you'll get whatever information she has, whereas the police might not. She could decide to keep whatever she knows to herself—and then what's been gained?"

"So?"

"So there you are."

"With a typically straightforward, clear-cut, unequivocal piece of—"

"Knock it off with your sarcasm, Nick."

"Piece of legal advice, I was going to say."

"Well, I've told you the possible consequences of doing it. I've also told you the probable consequences of not doing it. In any event, I know you well enough by this time to realize you've already made the decision."

"I have?"

"You're going to do it."

"You're right, Alex. I am."

"Good luck," he said and, just before ringing off, added, "Call when they read you your rights."

I made a note to check on the penalty for subornation, then decided the hell with it. Full speed ahead!

I buzzed for Sidney.

•   •   •

That same afternoon Scanlon showed up. This time he had Sergeant Snyder with him. I wasn't crazy about seeing *him* again, but he was on his company manners—hat in hand, no cigar in his mouth, quiet as a great big clam. They both sat down on the couch facing my desk. I spent a moment or two shuffling papers before I greeted them; I wasn't about to take any unscheduled intrusion lightly, even if I was having a hard time concealing my curiosity.

"Well, Lieutenant?" I nodded to Snyder. "Sergeant."

"I thought you'd like to know," Scanlon said in his quiet way, "that we think we have found your mugger."

"You have? Now that," I said, "is good news indeed."

"And maybe," added Scanlon, "just maybe—Jordan Walker's murderer as well."

"Wonderful," I said, but I felt a sharp stab of disappointment. Could the chase be over already? Just a classic felony murder, after all?

"We're happy about it," said Scanlon. "I should tell you that Sergeant Snyder here turned up the suspect."

Snyder shifted awkwardly on the couch. His hand wandered into his inside coat pocket and then wandered out again, empty.

"Congratulations, Sergeant," I said. "That calls for a cigar, if not something stronger." I held my humidor out to him; he took out an Uppmann, fondled it briefly, then put it to work.

"Thanks," he said, exhaling happily. "Thanks a lot."

"You're welcome—you've earned it."

"If you don't mind, Mr. Barlow," Scanlon said, "we'd like you and Mr. Burgal to come to headquarters for a show-up."

"A show-up?"

"The lineup," Scanlon said. "We feel pretty sure that the man we have in custody was one of the two who mugged you and Mr. Burgal in Gramercy Park. But we'll need a positive ID."

"Doesn't the man have a name, Lieutenant?" I said.

"Marco. Salvatore Marco," Sergeant Snyder said. "A goddamn—" The big man sighed. "I just hope he doesn't get off this time."

"If he did it."

"He did it," said Snyder. "at least, we're sure he did the

144

mugging. Goddamn hood." He made that word ring with a profound contempt. I thought once again that I wouldn't want Detective-Sergeant Snyder passing judgment on my conduct.

"We're hoping to connect him to Walker's apartment building on the evening of the murder," said Scanlon. "When he was picked up, he was carrying one of Jordan Walker's credit cards. Said he found it in a trash can."

Sergeant Snyder snorted.

"You'll come down to the show-up," Scanlon said. It was not a question.

"Let's go," I said. "I'll call Jeffrey. We can pick him up along the way."

The show-up at headquarters was just about what I expected. Four fairly scruffy types, all of them white-faced and blinking in the strong fluorescent light, except for one black tossed in, I suppose, to make sure I wasn't color-blind. I looked at them carefully, one after the other. I didn't want to make a mistake, not at this stage. They were all dressed pretty much alike: jeans or army fatigue pants, short jackets, open shirts, a lot of jewelry and chest hair showing.

"Third from the left," I told Scanlon. "That's the one."

If it hadn't been for his complexion, I wouldn't have recognized him. It was the skin, covered with acne scars, that did it—that and the teeth, bunched together and tobacco stained. He'd shown them when he came at me in the park that night, knife in hand. For the rest, he looked like the others, like anybody else of his age and background. That nasty, feral smile set in his pitted face, however, was unmistakable.

How comforting when a criminal turns out to really *look* like a criminal, instead of like you and me.

Scanlon turned to Jeffrey. "How about you, Mr. Burgal?"

"Well ..." Burgal said. "It may be. ..."

"*What?*" said Scanlon.

"It may be the one," said Jeffrey, "but I can't be too sure. You know how dark it was, Nick, and I was out of commission, in a manner of speaking. ..." His voice trailed off in a sigh. "I guess Nick is right," he said. "Second from the left."

"Third from the left," I said.

145

"Oh, right,"

"I guess we have it, then," Scanlon said. "That's Salvatore Marco. Suspect numero uno."

"So what happens next?" I asked.

"We'll see what we can get out of him," the Lieutenant said. "We'll do our best to hang it on him. And we'll try to work the name of his buddy out of him while we're at it."

"Hang the assault charge on him, you mean?"

"Right around his neck," said Scanlon.

Sergeant Snyder growled something inaudible but undoubtedly profane.

"Incidentally," Scanlon said, as we were getting ready to leave, "have you had any more thoughts about Walker's pocket diary?"

"Nothing, I'm sorry to say."

"How about the location of his office?"

Again I shook my head. "But I'm working on it. I'll do my best to come up with something, Lieutenant."

"Thanks," Scanlon said. "All favors gratefully accepted."

"And you'll let me know what happens with your suspect?"

"Absolutely," he said. "If the doorman of Walker's building identifies him as our third visitor ... well, we'll see." And on that note we parted.

On our way uptown Jeffrey crouched down inside his Burberry, his lower lip out. I let him sulk, until finally he chose to break his silence.

"Jesus, Nick, how did we ever get mixed up in this ... this shit? Police lineups and grilling, for God's sake! I just hope it's all over, all of it. I have other things to do."

"So do I, Jeffrey, so do we all. What makes you think you're the only one? Even so, I think that finding Jordan's murderer and seeing him put behind bars is as important as anything we have to do."

"But—"

"He was one of ours, Jeffrey, one of *ours*."

"I don't know, I'm beginning to feel absolutely paranoid. When I talked to my shrink about it, he said ..."

I stopped listening for a while. I just couldn't bring myself to care what Jeffrey's shrink had to say.

I tuned in again in time to hear, "I must get out to the coast myself soon." He said this almost dreamily, as if California were some kind of anodyne, a haven for his troubled spirit if not a solution to all his problems. Nirvana, U.S.A.

"*Soon*," he said with a sigh. "Tomorrow." Whereupon he lapsed into a reverie that did not end until we reached our destination.

· · ·

If I had thought the surprises were all over for the day, I was proved wrong a short while later when Hannah came into my office with the day's mail. She looked shaken, as close to showing fear as I'd ever seen her. Without a word she handed over a letter she'd opened: a note printed with a child's set of letters—the rubber kind that come with an ink pad—on a paper obviously torn from a cheap tablet.

"THE PARK WAS JUST A WARNING. IF U PUBLIS THE GRAM FARRAR BUK, SOMBUDYS GOING 2 GET KILLED. WE MEAN IT."

It was signed: "A FRIEND."

"I don't like this," said Hannah. "Not at all."

"Neither do I."

"If it's a serious threat . . ." she said.

My, my, I thought. *This certainly makes the cheese more binding. Wait until Lieutenant Scanlon sees what the postman brought.*

17

Promptly at five-thirty the next day, Sidney Leopold and I presented ourselves at Ms. Dori Regan's apartment building, checkbook in hand.

She lived in a building without a doorman, in a slightly down-at-the-heels East Side neighborhood not too far from Jordan Walker's building. When we pressed the buzzer of her apartment, there was no answering buzz to admit us. I looked at Sidney.

"She does know we're coming?"

"Absolutely," he said. "She's in apartment three-C."

An elderly party with a beagle in tow opened the door and held it for us to pass through—apparently we looked trustworthy. I murmured my thanks, and we headed for the elevator, past a sad-looking plastic plant in the lobby and a dimly lit reproduction of a Maxfield Parrish painting: a young woman in a diaphanous gown flitting through a formal garden.

We stood in front of apartment 3C for several minutes, ringing the doorbell and then knocking. The door remained firmly closed. We rang again. Knocked again. Nobody came.

"Oh, shit, Nick."

"Are you sure she said five-thirty?"

"Quite sure."

"Well?"

Sidney squinted through the peephole in the door, then pressed his ear against the crack.

"Hey," he said.

"What?"

"Whatever it is, it sounds funny as hell. Here—you listen, Nick."

I took his place near the door and put my right ear—the best of the two—up to the crack. The noise coming from inside was odd, all right. At first I couldn't make out what it was, it was so muffled.

"Does Dori Regan have a cat?"

"She told me she's allergic to cats. Loves 'em but can't stand 'em."

It was a whimpering, mewling sound, building almost to a scream, then subsiding to a choking whine, like—then I got it.

"Jesus Christ! Get downstairs and find somebody with a key to this place. The super or whoever. And hurry, Sidney. I'll wait here for you."

He didn't ask for an explanation, just did as I told him.

While he was gone, I tried the bell again, then put my ear up to the door again. The sounds I'd heard before were still there but much fainter. And then, shortly before Sidney arrived with the superintendent, they ceased altogether.

"What's this?" Dori's super said. "Why don't she answer the door?"

"Just use your passkey, please," I said. "I think there's something very wrong in there."

The super fumbled with his key ring and, when he found the right key, fumbled with that too.

"God almighty," I said under my breath. "We're losing too much time."

The super finally got the door open.

"N-N-Nick," Sidney said, "you go fir . . . first, won't you?"

"I intend to."

For once I could understand why Sidney stammered; I nearly stammered myself.

The first thing I caught was the door. If you have ever once smelled blood—lots of blood—you won't forget the pungent, sickening stench.

"We're too late," I said. "We're too goddamn late."

"Oh, Nick," Sidney said. "Oh, *Nick*."

We found her in the living room, halfway between her bedroom door and the foyer. Obviously she had been trying to crawl to the front door. She'd left a trail of blood along her path, and I knew from the way she lay on the carpet, so still and white, knew even without taking her pulse, that she was dead.

She was naked, and she'd been bludgeoned. The force of the blows had left visible depressions on her right temple and splashes of blood all over her face and breasts. Her hair was matted in bright scarlet, and her eyes—which I doubt I will ever forget—were wide open, staring at nobody and nothing.

"Holy Mary Mother of God." That from the superintendent.

"If we'd only gotten in here a few minutes earlier," I said to the super. "She was still alive." Which meant that her murderer must have left not too long before we arrived.

But I knew, even as I spoke, that we couldn't possibly have been in time.

. . .

"So!" Lieutenant Scanlon said. "Here we are again." He did not sound at all happy to see me in Dori Regan's apartment. The late Ms. Regan had been removed, thank God, but the evidence of her rough passing remained. All that blood! And the murder weapon, the bronze statuette of a stallion, found in a corner of the bedroom. The bedroom itself, as I might have expected, was decorated mostly in pink chintz and carpeted in an off-white shag.

"People will talk," I said and tried to grin. "But let them, Lieutenant, you and I know that I'm just an innocent bystander in all this."

"That," he said, "remains to be seen."

"Lieutenant . . ."

"Anyhow, what exactly were you and your editor doing here?"

I told him. No point in lying, since I hadn't actually succeeded in breaking any laws.

"You know," he said when I'd finished, "the last thing we need is civilians going off on their own. You should have gotten in touch with my office first, and you know it."

"We were trying to be helpful, Lieutenant."

His expression softened somewhat. But not much.

"Lieutenant," I said, "are you suggesting I had anything do with this murder? I deplore it. Dori Regan may have been stupid and conniving, but she had every right to live out her life peacefully. And to die in bed, where I suspect she spent a good deal of her time anyway."

"Okay. Could it be that somebody knew about the talk you were planning to have and decided to muzzle her? You ought to have let me know about it in any case."

For the second time that day, I felt completely sickened. Could the lieutenant possibly be right? Had I been an unknowing accessory in Dori Regan's murder? I turned to Sidney, who looked as pale and wan as I felt, and swallowed hard. The taste of crow is never pleasant.

"Incidentally, we do have *some* good news," Scanlon said. "A break in this case, finally." He permitted himself a slight smile.

"Want to tell me what it is?"

"Actually, I'd rather not at the moment, but I don't have much choice. What the hell, I still do need your help. You're in the middle of all this mess."

"Not by choice, you realize," I said, crossing my fingers behind my back.

"All the same."

"So what is it you've learned?"

The lieutenant sat back on Dori Regan's love seat—the scene, I realized, of "The Seduction of Sidney Leopold" hardly two days earlier. Lighting a cigarette, Scanlon looked around vaguely for an ashtray. Sidney handed him one, then withdrew as far from the rising veils of smoke as he could get. I leaned forward. "What's the breakthrough?"

"We've traced your agent friend Jeffrey Burgal to Jordan Walker's apartment building on the afternoon of the murder."

"For sure?"

"Positive ID by the doorman and another occupant."

"You showed a picture around?"

"Of course. His picture, your picture, everybody's picture."

"*My* picture?" I said, in the how-dare-you tone I learned from my mother. "*Mine?*"

"I'm a policeman," Scanlon said. "In my job you can't trust anybody."

"Jeffrey, is it?" I said, eager to divert the conversation along other channels. "What do you plan to do?"

"Talk to him," said Scanlon. "By all means. Except . . ."

"Except what?"

"He's out of town at the moment. With Graham Farrar in California, according to his secretary, for a week or ten days. And we don't have enough reason—enough *evidence*, I should say—to bring him back against his will."

"So?"

"We wait," Scanlon said. "Sooner or later, he'll be back. Then we'll have a little talk. And there's more."

"Is Angela Farrar back?"

"No, but I did reach her attorney. You know, the guy who got in touch with you about the book."

"Yes?"

"And I told him to produce her as soon as she does reach New York, voluntarily, or else I'd swear out a warrant."

· · ·

Back to work—and believe me, the publishing business looked enticingly dull after the afternoon's events. Both Sidney and I plunged into our offices as though they were refuges. Which they were.

The first thing I did was shovel the mail off my desk into either the wastebasket or the Hold file—I've discovered over the years that, if you put all your correspondence into a manila folder, by the time you get around to looking at it again, most of it will not require any action. Then I called Jane Goodman into my office.

"I've been wondering when I'd hear from you," she said.

"Oh?"

"You said I might be working on the Graham Farrar manuscript, no?"

"Yes. I mean, that's right, I did say that."

"Well?"

"You may lower those eyebrows, Ms. Goodman."

"Jane, please."

"Jane. We don't *have* the Graham Farrar yet. Or still."

"What do you mean, Nick?"

"The police are seeking it, I'm seeking it—is it in heaven or is it in hell? That damned elusive manuscript!"

"Oh." Disappointment was writ large on her face. "Well, I do have other projects to work on, but I thought—"

"Don't worry," I said. "When we get the book, you'll be among the first to have a look at it." And we'd damn well better get it soon—I had heard again from my money man about those *unearned advances*, particularly *that one*, and I was getting increasingly apprehensive.

Not long after Jane left my office, Tim called.

"Nick," he said. "I've been giving some thought to your problem."

"Which problem?" I was losing track of them by now.

"That appointment book of Jordan's," Tim said. "The initials you found in it."

"What do you think?"

"FMS," he said. "The Graham Farrar manuscript, as you suspected and not the initials of a person. Someone must have met with Jordan to discuss the manuscript. And if the appointment wasn't with you— It wasn't, was it?"

"Don't be an ass, certainly not."

"Then it must have been with Jeffrey Burgal."

"Why not Angela Farrar," I said, "or Graham, for that matter? Both of them wanted to talk with him about the book."

"Yes, but what did they want to say about it? Angela already wanted herself cut out of it, probably upon threat of libel, possibly on threat of death. So her visit had to have been a surprise."

"Hang on, you've lost me."

"Elementary, my dear Nicholas. If she had called in advance, Jordan wouldn't have agreed to see her unless she'd said why. And if she'd threatened libel over the phone—"

"Jordan would have called me, and he didn't. But what if she'd lied about why she wanted the meeting?"

"Subtlety? Angela?"

"Point taken. What about Graham?"

Tim sighed. "All right, I'm on shakier ground there. But whenever Jordan had met with Graham before, he always referred to the meetings as 'GF.' I would think the force of habit alone would lead him to do it again."

"Sounds reasonable," I said.

"Besides, a meeting with Graham would have been about Graham. This meeting was about the manuscript. Jeffrey comes naturally to mind. What do you think?"

"I think you're brilliant, especially since you're right." I told him what Scanlon had said about the doorman's identification of Jeffrey as one of Jordan's visitors on the day of the murder.

"Well, all that's reassuring, but does it make sense?"

"Somebody had to get that murder weapon out of Jordan Walker's kitchen drawer," I said. "Somebody Jordan trusted, who could roam freely around the apartment. But Jeffrey a murderer? Is that possible?"

"You know him better than I do," Tim said. "You tell me."

I couldn't, of course. Jeffrey is a potential murderer, I suppose, as much as any of us. But if he did kill Jordan, why?

Too many questions, questions neither Lieutenant Scanlon nor my brother could answer.

"You think the lady is capable of murder?"

"First off, she's no lady. But yes, she could and would commit murder to save her forthcoming marriage and her rehabilitated reputation. She has every reason to want that manuscript suppressed—any way she can."

．　　．　　．

"We don't have any line on why Burgal might have done it," Scanlon said when I spoke with him shortly after my talk with Tim. "No motive whatsoever."

"About the mugging," I said, "any progress with your suspect?"

"Won't open up," he said. "Even Snyder can't get a peep out of him. I'm not saying I want us to go back to the days of the naked light bulb and the rubber hose, but still, if a suspect wants to keep his trap shut, there's absolutely nothing we can do about it. And if it were my decision, I'd keep this bird on Riker's until snow falls upward. As it is, he'll be out on bail by the end of the week unless we pick up some hard evidence."

"That's a goddamn shame," I said.

Scanlon said nothing for a long moment. Then: "He'll pull something else, I'm sure, and we'll haul him back in. But the hell of it is, somebody innocent is going to get hurt." Then Scanlon told me about a fifteen-year-old kid he'd arrested—a four-time killer. Since he was a juvenile offender all they could do was lock him up in a reformatory until he was twenty-one.

"Six years off the street, and he'll be back meaner and stronger than ever. But what can we do, put a permanent tail on him—a cop ready to shoot him down as soon as he pulls his own gun?"

"So much street crime," I said. "Why, do you suppose?"

"Because the people who commit it know there's only a slight chance of being caught and sent to prison. Suppose we catch a hard case like Marco—it could be years before he comes to trial, the courts are so damned clogged up, then he'll probably plea-bargain his way to a slap on the wrist." He sighed. "I guess I sound kind of bitter."

"No, just realistic. And you're certainly not ready to throw in the towel."

"No way," he said. "No goddamn way. I'll go after them with everything I've got, no matter how fouled up the courts are. By the way," he said, "do you think Burgal had something to do with setting up the mugging?"

155

"I'm beginning to," I said. "How about you?"

"How else would the muggers know you were at The Players together—and that the manuscript was there? Damn! It all comes back to that manuscript. Could it have been switched somewhere along the line?"

"Possibly. But why would Jeffrey *not* want to give me the manuscript? Without it he wouldn't get the rest of Jordan's advance."

"Rotten luck," he said. "That girl Dori was the link holding all this together, and now ..."

"We'll crack it somehow," I said. *We?* Who was we—Tim and me, Scanlon and me? Who did I think I was—Nick Barlow, boy detective? Maybe it was time to take a long walk and cool off.

18

Bingo!"

It was Lieutenant Scanlon on the phone, bright and early on the next morning, sounding as jubilant as the first cock to crow at break of day.

"Lieutenant?"

"Good news," he said. "We've located Jordan Walker's office."

"Congratulations," I said. "How did you manage that?"

"The phone numbers we located, remember? From Walker's diary? We traced them all backward through NYNEX and picked up a bunch of addresses. From there to the real estate offices until we finally found the right one."

"Good work," I said.

"We'll have a search warrant by this afternoon, and the key to the office. I'd like you to be there when we open up."

"Me? Why? I mean—of course I'll do whatever I can to help, but—"

"I know, I know. I climbed all over your back the other day because you're a civilian and you have meddled, and I ought to treat you like any other Joe as far as this case goes. But you've also been helpful, and maybe you can be helpful again, by spotting something I might overlook."

"I don't know."

"You're a publisher after all, and you're bound to know more about the way a writer's mind works than a nonpublisher."

Not for the first time, I detected a note in Scanlon's voice that led me to believe his invitation was not unconnected with a certain book he might or might not be writing. Was I being courted for myself or my publishing house? Did it matter?

*   *   *

Around three o'clock that day I met Scanlon on West Twenty-fourth Street, between Fifth and Sixth avenues, what I would describe as a grubby but respectable neighborhood. Sergeant Snyder was with him. The sergeant nodded at me with no particular show of bonhomie. I nodded back. Scanlon, for his part, favored me with a friendly smile. I smiled back.

"It's on the fourth floor," Scanlon said. "Let's get cracking."

The hallway of the building was clean, but badly in need of fresh paint, and the plaster had peeled in places. I looked at the directory; no sign of Jordan's name or office number.

"He remains anonymous," I said to no one in particular.

We ascended in an elevator that was surprisingly efficient; clearly the building hadn't been altogether neglected. At the fourth floor we went down a long hallway past the offices of THE NEW YORK DOLL HOUSE: NEW AND ANTIQUE DOLLS (I remembered that this was the toy district); THE MESA GROUP, an advertising agency; an accounting firm; a law office; and finally we came to room 404, which had nothing painted on the door at all. Jordan's lair, at last. Scanlon inserted the key and swung the door open.

What we saw was the absolute obverse of Jordan's apartment. Where that had been stylish, even spectacular, a statement of success, his office was dingy, cluttered, and obviously lived in. The furniture looked as though it had been bought secondhand: a cheap wooden desk, a bookcase whose shelves had splayed under the weight of the reference books Jordan had jammed into them, an old office chair whose cracked leather cushion still retained the impression of Jordan's ample rump. Here there were no pictures on the walls; only a calendar of New England scenes, and that a year old; no mirrors, either. All this suggested not the hugely successful writer, but the struggling young man who had come out of the West to make his fortune.

All but the computer, which sat in a work station in the corner of the room. The IBM PC was clearly not there for Jordan to play *Jeopardy*; it was there for him to process all those thousands of words he turned out weekly.

"Do you suppose . . . ?" Scanlon said.

"Jesus, I sure hope so."

I was already rummaging through the disks that were stacked beside the terminal. Where was the damn thing? Label after label, but no Graham Farrar biography. I was almost ready to despair.

"Do you know how to work this thing?"

I ought to have known better. Scanlon was already seated in front of the keyboard, and as I watched—I am a functional computer illiterate—he went to work. I wouldn't have been surprised if Snyder had been able to operate it, too.

The computer hummed, the screen brightened, and I waited hopefully for something interesting to appear. The silence in the room was tangible.

"What are you doing?"

"Checking out the directory on the hard drive," Scanlon said, as if I should have known. "Nothing here."

Then it occurred to him to look in the disk drive itself—and there it was.

"He must have been working on it the day he died," I said.

"Yeah, and forgot to take it out when he shut down the computer." Then, "*Shit*."

"What is it?" My voice sounded to me like a tenor, if not a falsetto.

"It's blank," Scanlon said.

"Blank? Completely?" That squeak again.

Scanlon sighed and leaned back, his shoulders sagging. "Yeah."

"But . . . why? How?"

"Well, somebody zapped whatever was on the disk," Scanlon said. "There's nothing there, nothing at all. They beat us to it again."

"Lieutenant," I said, "could I possibly have that disk?"

"I don't know . . . what for?"

"It just occurred to me," I said, "that I paid several hundred thousand dollars for what was on that blank disk. I intend to frame it and hang it in my office, as a reminder of my folly."

Scanlon rubbed his forehead for a moment. "I don't suppose it's really evidence. What do you think, Sergeant?"

Snyder shrugged and said, "Whatever you think, Lieutenant."

"OK, OK," Scanlon said. "What the fuck, take the goddamn thing. We can always get it back if we have to." He tossed it to me.

Scanlon and Snyder made a routine but thorough search of the office, hoping to turn up some hard copy. There wasn't any. I just watched until it was over, clutching my useless disk. Oh, well, no point in weeping. No point in laughing, either.

Just then Scanlon, who was rummaging in the back of a closet, made a find.

"Well now," he said, "what have we here?" He pulled out a leather shoulder case and unsnapped its catch.

"What is it?" I said.

"Looks like a mini-tape recorder," said Scanlon, "and a bunch of cassettes. Do you suppose?—"

"Interviews with Graham Farrar?" I said.

"Could be."

"I doubt it."

"Why?"

"You're forgetting how tight Jordan was with a buck. Once his tapes had been transcribed, I'm sure he'd tape right over them. Why buy new ones?"

"Oh." Scanlon's disappointment was palpable. "Well . . . it's worth a shot." He put the case over his shoulder and motioned to Snyder.

When the tapes were played back down at headquarters, it

turned out that I was right, unfortunately. The interviews on the cassettes were with Jordan Walker's next subject, the celebrity after Graham. The book Jordan would never write.

. . .

Back in my office, I gave Tim a call and told him about the afternoon's events.

"Nick," Tim said, "you still have that disk, don't you? Tell me you do."

"Well," I said, "I was about to chuck it in the wastebasket."

"Don't you dare!"

"Why not?"

"I want it."

"But why?"

"Don't be difficult, big brother, just get the damned thing to me *muy pronto*. All right?"

"All right, sure, I'll have it to you this very day. What are you planning to do with it?"

"You'll have the answer to that," he said, "if and when I'm successful with what I have in mind." And with that he rang off.

My brother, Tim, the family computer buff.

. . .

"It's like this," Tim said when I called him the next day. "Even though they erased the disk, Graham's biography is still in there."

"What's that?" I said. "Come again."

"Most people don't realize that when you erase a file from a disk, the file isn't really gone," Tim said. "You see, disks are divided into blocks of space called pages. It makes storage more efficient, for reasons I won't bore you with. Generally a page is long enough to store 512 characters, and each page has its own special address. When a computer stores a document on a disk, it doesn't store it all in the same place but breaks the document up into page-sized chunks and stores it in whatever pages are available on the disk. Clear, so far?"

"I suppose so. Go on."

161

"In order to keep track of which pages are used and which aren't, the computer keeps a special file on the disk—it's called the index—that contains a list of what documents are on the disk and which pages are available. OK?"

"Sounds like a table of contents."

"Exactly. Well, when you erase a document, the computer doesn't pick through the disk and wipe clean all the pages that contained the document, it just removes those pages into the 'available' list in the index. Then, when you write a new document on the disk, the new document is simply written over the top of the old one."

"Which means—"

"When you 'erase' a document from a disk, that document is still there until you write something on top of it. So if nothing else has been written over the Farrar bio ..."

"But how will you find it? How do you get it back again?"

"By writing a program that ignores the index and searches through the disk page by page. Eventually, I'll be able to piece Jordan's book back together."

"And can *you* do that, Tim?"

He snorted. "O ye of little faith. Give me a few days, and I ought to be able to produce a manuscript for you."

Scanlon was delighted when I called him. I thought of ringing up Jeffrey, too, but changed my mind. Suppose he *had* set up our mugging? I just couldn't trust him any longer. Moreover, Scanlon had told me he was in California.

I did call Graham, however, and told him the news.

"You really think your kid brother can bring this off?" Graham asked.

"If anybody can."

"Great," he said. "There'll be a book after all. I'm pleased."

Pleased? My own private accountant, Mortimer J. Mandelbaum, a man who almost never cracks a smile, will be turning handsprings.

19

Thursday: a welcome call from Lieutenant Scanlon to ask me if I'd be willing to appear at the Criminal Courts Building on Center Street for Salvatore Marco's hearing.

"The one we think mugged you and your agent friend on Gramercy Park," he said. As if I could possibly forget!

"Tomorrow morning? What's it all about, Lieutenant?"

"It's just a preliminary hearing. To ascertain whether a crime was actually committed, and if there's good reason to believe Marco might have done it. If so, the judge sets bail, then sets a date for the grand jury hearing."

"I see. And then?"

"If the grand jury indicts him, Marco comes to trial."

"You mean that ... that budding public enemy has been running loose around the streets of the city?"

"Would you want it any other way, Mr. Barlow? Sure we'd love to lock him up, but we have to give him his rights. It's the system."

"Lieutenant, you're altogether too much of a civil libertarian for your own good. I'd give him a dozen of the best with a cat-o'-nine-tails."

"No, you wouldn't. You may say you would, but you're too civilized for that."

"Don't be so sure."

"You'll have to admit there could be reasonable doubt."

"No, I don't."

"I hope you're right. Just stick to your guns when you're called to the stand, and we'll nail him."

I had to admit Scanlon was dogged. He really hoped, clearly against his own experience, that justice would be done.

As for me, when I went down to the Manhattan Criminal Courts Building the following morning, my doubts, if anything, were sharpened.

I found the courthouse ugly, narrow, and mean in its proportions. The epigraphs chiseled along its granite steps—"Only the just man enjoys peace of mind" and "Be just and fear not"—served only to raise my level of apprehension.

But once inside, I had to admit that the building did have its own powerful sense of community. It was a world within the city—vivid and loud, bursting with vitality. Dirty, unswept, the air heavy with stale cigarette smoke and the sweat of anxiety, its hallways crowded with people: policemen, clerks in shirtsleeves, guards in Sam Browne belts, lawyers clutching their briefcases or their clients, and most pitiful of all, the ranks of the indicted.

The hearing was scheduled in room 316, part C19C. Lieutenant Scanlon met me outside the door to the hearing room. When he saw me, he stubbed a cigarette out in an urn already overflowing with butts and crumpled packages and came toward me, hand outstretched.

"Glad to see you," he said.

"Did you think I wouldn't come?"

He shrugged. "You're a busy man, I know. We could have subpoenaed you, but I didn't want to do that. I'd rather this was voluntary."

"Surely you know, Lieutenant, that this is as important to me as it is to you."

"Good," he said, nodding his head. *"Good."*

"What do you want me to do?"

"Just answer the questions. The assistant D.A. will put you on the stand first. Marco's attorney will cross-examine."

"And then?"

"We'll see."

He smiled. I had no chance to ask him what he found so amusing, for just then the door opened and a guard beckoned us to enter.

Room 316, part C19C, was hardly overcrowded.

Presumably there were other trials going on that promised more drama. Moreover, the baseball season was under way, and after two weeks the Mets and the Yankees were both off to strong starts. Who'd want to sit in a courtroom on a gloriously sunny day in the spring?

The first row of seats in the courtroom was filled with bored-looking police officers. Through two doors at the front of the room a series of court attendants and policemen came and went. On one side of the room I saw Salvatore Marco, impassive and unnaturally rigid in his chair, wearing a tightly cut three-piece suit and a white linen tie on a blue silk shirt. His hands were folded in his lap and he stared straight ahead, his pitted face twitching occasionally when his attorney—a slick-looking party altogether—leaned over and whispered in his left ear.

The bench at the front of the room was empty. An American flag stood on a staff behind the judge's chair and off to one side. On the wall overhead, with one letter missing, was the inscription IN GOD WE RUST.

"Hear ye, hear ye," the bailiff called. "All persons having business before this court step forward and ye shall be heard. Part C19C now in session, Judge Emily Fein presiding."

Judge Fein, a slender, gray-haired woman with eyeglasses attached to a silver chain around her neck, was quite a contrast to the middle-aged lawyers sprinkled about the room. I heard her speak to one of them—she had a clear, melodious voice, pitched so softly that I could catch nothing of what she was saying. The bailiff, on the other hand, seemed to be using a microphone.

"Is Salvatore Marco in the courtroom? Salvatore Marco?"

"Here."

Marco rose slowly and swaggered forward. When he reached the dock, a brown oak lectern about the height of his waist, he leaned forward and rested both hands on it.

"Are you represented by counsel?" Fein asked.

"Yeah, sure. This is my lawyer."

Marco's attorney rose and walked over beside him. "Andrew Svenson, your honor."

The judge nodded curtly, but I could swear there was a glint of recognition in her eyes. Of course, I might have been imagining things. When I think of the number of courtroom cliff-hangers I've published . . .

"Be seated." And the hearing was under way.

The assistant district attorney presented the state's case, such as it was. It became evident quite early on that *I* was the state's case, more or less. There was no physical evidence— there was only identification of the suspect by the victim, me.

I was called to the stand. Sitting there, I could not help noticing how young and insecure the state's man appeared alongside Marco's. Svenson had the sleek appearance, burnished silver hair, and immaculate tailoring that suggest, to the layman's eyes, a largely unbroken string of courtroom triumphs. The people's man, on the other hand, seemed awed even by me. And I was *his* witness.

"Tell me, sir, is the man who attacked you here in the courtroom?"

"Yes, he is."

"Would you please point him out to us?"

I stepped down from the stand, walked over to Salvatore Marco.

"He's the one," I said.

Marco continued to stare into the middle distance, looking neither right nor left. But I caught a quiver in his right cheek, and he blinked, just barely. The air around him was heavy with the odor of cheap shaving lotion.

If that had been all . . . But now it was attorney Svenson's turn.

The Silver Fox rose majestically to his feet, a commanding

presence if I ever saw one, beautiful in his calm self-assurance. I was tempted to admire him myself until he began to work me over. All quite politely, you understand, but with a matter-of-factness more deadly than sarcasm.

"Mr. Barlow. You are a book publisher, I understand."

"Yes, sir." I knew from trial scenes I'd edited not to give him any more than I absolutely had to. Only yes or no.

He came closer to me, not in a threatening fashion, but as if we were sharing a secret, he and I, two men of the world.

"Mr. Barlow, you have identified my client as the man who attacked you in the Gramercy Park area on"—he consulted a slip of paper in his hand—"April twenty-fourth." Fat chance he didn't know the date.

"Yes."

"Let me reconstruct the situation, if I may, Your Honor," he added, bowing slightly in the judge's direction. Fein acknowledged the courtesy with a barely visible twitch of her lips. "Let me see. You had just had drinks and dinner"—he stressed the word "drinks"—"at your club, with a literary agent named Jeffrey Burgal. Is Burgal here in the courtroom by any chance? No? I see." At that point Jeffrey, four thousand miles away, became a witness for the defense. "After your drinks—"

"Object," the assistant D.A. said. "Mr. Barlow and Mr. Burgal were having dinner together. They weren't just sitting there drinking."

"Overruled," Judge Fein said. "The witness's consumption of alcohol is a valid indication of the accuracy of his recollection."

"Well," I said, "if my alcoholic consumption is the issue, let me tell you what I consumed that night. One vodka martini straight up, two glasses of wine, and a small glass of Remy Martin cognac."

I could have bitten my tongue out when I caught the look on Scanlon's and the young D.A.'s faces. The alcoholic intake I had described was for me an ordinary amount producing no impairment whatsoever—I could hardly have beaten the

167

whey out of that little bugger Marco if I'd been drunk. But I should have known it would be at least two drinks over the social limit of Scanlon or Svenson, or worse, Judge Fein.

Hastily I added: "You understand that we publishers are accustomed to drinking at our meals—all but breakfast, of course—though come to think of it, I have heard of champagne breakfasts served at sales conferences. At any rate, we do develop a certain tolerance—shall we say?—for *spiritus frumenti*. For alcoholic beverages of all kinds."

"M-m-m-m-m," said Svenson, with a world of innuendo in his murmur. "Moving on to the alleged mugging, Mr. Barlow ..." He then ran me through the attack in the park, step by step. Even as I described it, I began to feel vaguely foolish. Carrying a stick—"a rather fearsome weapon in its own right," as Svenson pointed out—hardly made me appear the hapless victim of a brutal attack.

"It was dark, of course, during the altercation?"

"Yes, it was past eleven o'clock."

"And if I'm not mistaken"—he consulted a slip of paper again—"on that night the sky was overcast. Given the ordinarily dim lighting of the streets around the park, and with no moon, visibility must have been limited, wouldn't you say, Mr. Barlow?"

"I could see well enough." So much for sticking to yes and no answers.

"You have extraordinarily sharp vision, then?"

"Sharp enough."

"Despite your occupation, which must—given the nature of the products that you manufacture—entail some eye strain?"

"I could see him." *Steady, Barlow. Don't get flustered, whatever you do.*

"What makes you so sure, Mr. Barlow, that my client was your assailant? He is, as you can see, a young man of medium height, normal coloring and hairstyle, and with no special physical deformities. How can you single him out from any number of young men of his age and background?"

"His skin," I said.

"I beg your pardon."

"The acne," I said. "He has one of the worst complexions I've ever seen. Terminal acne, you might say. His pallor—'like the belly of a fish,' I thought at the time—along with the acne scars, made his face unforgettable."

"I see," said Svenson. "Unmistakable, was it?"

"Unforgettable."

"You are absolutely sure? A young man's future is at stake here. I'd like to know you have no doubts whatsoever."

"I'm absolutely sure."

"Your honor," said Svenson, turning to the judge, "if we could have a short recess, and a word with you and the district attorney's representative?"

"Any special reason?" the judge asked.

"I believe so," Svenson said. "Surely none of us would wish to have an injustice done."

"Mr. Svenson—" Judge Fein said.

"Your honor," the defense attorney said, "bear with me, please. If the State has concluded its case, I am ready to call my first witness."

As he spoke, the door at the back of the courtroom opened, and a young man entered. A young man about Salvatore Marco's age and height, wearing a similar three-piece suit. And with the *second*-worst complexion I have ever seen.

•   •   •

"So that's it," I said to Scanlon afterward. "He gets off without even a reprimand."

"That's it," Scanlon said.

"Well, as for me, I found that business in the courtroom a farce. That kid who provided Marco with an alibi—he's probably as bad as Marco himself. I'm lucky the judge didn't charge *me* with assault and battery."

"You're embarrassed because Svenson bamboozled you on the stand," Scanlon said. "Not that I blame you. He's one of the sharpest lawyers in town."

"I believe that."

"He's an attorney for the mob." Scanlon dropped this one

on me so quietly I almost missed it. "To be specific, for the D'Angelo family."

"So?"

"He's also Jeffrey Burgal's attorney."

"What? *He is?*" Jeffrey again, it kept coming back to Jeffrey! At the very least he was going to have a lot of explaining to do.

"Mr. Barlow," Scanlon said.

"Yes?"

"Is there any chance, any chance at all, that you could have been mistaken? That Marco wasn't the one who jumped you in the park?"

"No, I don't think so," I said.

When Scanlon and I left the courthouse on Center Street, I offered to drop him off wherever he was heading. He declined with thanks, saying he had additional business downtown and wanted to walk. Walking helped him when he needed to think things over. As for me, I think better ensconced in the backseat of my Mercedes with Oscar at the wheel. Looking out the car window, I saw a city dappled with bright flashes of sunlight—not a cloud in the wind-washed sky.

For myself the clouds hung heavy and black indeed. Despite my confident answer to Scanlon's question, I could not escape a pervasive sense of doubt. *Could* I be mistaken about Marco? *Was* I infallible? I no longer felt quite so certain.

20

I won't say the outcome of the hearing spoiled my weekend completely; nothing and no one can ruin Connecticut for
me, not even the New York and New Jersey drivers who
occasionally clutter up our highways. All the same, the whole
business left me with a faint aftertaste of bile in my mouth.

As usual, Tim put the matter into perspective.

"You're still sure Marco was one of the muggers?" he said.

"Seventy-five percent sure," I said. "Down from one hundred."

"You do realize that the mugging is beside the point," he
said. "Its purpose, like that threatening note you got, was to
scare you off publishing Jordan's book."

"But why?"

"That's what we don't know yet. But the book is the only
thing linking Jordan's murder, the mugging, and Dori Regan's
murder."

"But we still don't have the book," I said.

"I'm making progress," Tim said. "I'll probably have it
pieced together for you before you head back to New York."

"I fervently hope so."

"Maybe Angela Farrar is involved," Tim said. "Clearly she
has a motive for suppressing the book. We'll see what comes
out when Scanlon questions her."

"I can hardly wait."

"By the way, Nick, what did Scanlon think of that warning note you got?"

"Same thing as you, that it's all part of the plot. We just don't know who sent it."

"So we stay tuned for future developments."

As usual, my mother had her own solution.

"Nicholas."

"Yes, Mother?"

"Have you considered the possibility that these murders are the work of a madman or madwoman? Somebody who wants to wreck Barlow and Company?"

"Come again?"

"Think about it. You've rejected hundreds of manuscripts over the years. What if someone whose book you turned down has been nursing a grudge against you all this time? Has decided to strike out against you?"

I decided to finesse this one rather than step on it.

"I suppose we *could* go back over our rejection letters for the past few years." The mere prospect of slogging through that graveyard of rejected manuscripts, each one a forlorn tombstone, made me quail.

"Exactly," my mother said triumphantly.

Of course an author *might* decide to kill a publisher, but since that would mean one fewer way to publish one's work, what would be achieved?

.   .   .

That Sunday night I turned in early, but I slept fitfully—until around three in the morning, when I heard a sharp noise that sounded like glass breaking. My eyes flew open, as if they could help out my ears. Somewhere in the house ... where?

Downstairs! I threw on a robe and went to the head of the stairs. I stood there for a moment, listening. Somebody was moving around down there—quietly, but not so softly I couldn't hear the footsteps. How many people, one or two? Maybe it was just Mother, unable to sleep. If it was an intruder, why hadn't the dogs barked? Bonnie and Zachary, like most

172

retrievers, wouldn't bite anything that didn't bite them first. But they made noise well enough.

It was too dark to see anything clearly, but I thought I could make out a figure moving around in the living room. Then a flashlight switched on, its beam directed toward the foot of the stairs.

I don't own a gun, never have. If I had my way, guns would be abolished altogether, but right then I wished I had one handy. Wait a sec—I *did* know where I could find a weapon of sorts. There was a baseball bat in Tim's room.

I moved down the hall as quietly as I could, eased opened the door and went into Tim's study. I pressed my ear against the bedroom door and could hear him snoring softly. I wasn't exactly sure where to look, but I thought the bat must be in the study closet. No luck; it had to be in his bedroom.

Hoping that Tim hadn't got rid of the damn thing, I tiptoed through the room and turned the knob of the closet door. I groped around in the closet, stumbling over a tennis racket and a bag full of balls, then closed my hand around the handle of the bat. I slowly pulled it away from the rest of the junk in the closet.

It occurred to me then that I ought to call for help, so I crept over to Tim's bedside table and picked up his phone.

There was no dial tone. Damnation!

I could already hear my own heart beating—a low, dull sound like a muffled drum. Now it was louder, a sharp, steady tattoo.

I went back into the study, closing the bedroom door softly behind me. Just then I heard a hoarse whisper at the doorway.

"This must be where the cripple sleeps."

Then the flashlight went on, catching me full in the face and blinding me.

"Jesus!" a voice said. There was a sickeningly sweet smell in the room—I couldn't identify it at first. I raised the bat and cocked it, ready to swing.

"Who the fuck are you," I shouted, "and what d'you want?"

Whoever was there didn't stick around to answer. There was a rush of footsteps, then the study door slammed. When

I pulled it open, I heard the sound of running feet on the stairs, and then the slam of the front door. By the time I got to the front entrance of the house, a car engine was roaring into life, and they—there was enough moonlight to see there were two of them in the car—sped off without even using their headlights.

By now, of course, the whole damned house was awake, lights on all over the place. Mother stood in the doorway of her room, clutching the collar of her bathrobe. Tim had wheeled himself into the study and was holding a washcloth in one hand.

Lola and Harry Dennehy appeared from their respective parts of the house, Lola gripping a carving knife she'd grabbed on her way through the kitchen. Harry, a World War II vet, had what looked like an army-issue .45 caliber pistol in his hand.

I turned first to Tim. "What have you got there in your hand—that rag?"

He raised the cloth to his nose, sniffed it.

"Unless I'm greatly mistaken," he said, "it's chloroform."

.   .   .

A short time later, after an obliging neighbor gave me the use of his telephone, the state troopers arrived.

"Was anything taken?" the taller and higher-ranking trooper asked.

"Not to my knowledge," I said.

"Good," he said. "You scared them off in time. In any event, this doesn't appear to be a burglary. We'll have to treat it as a break and entry for ... for reasons unknown?" Then he explained how the intruders had gotten in. They'd cut a pane of glass out of one of the French doors, carefully enough in all probability, but one of them had apparently dropped it by accident. That was the noise that woke me. They then had unlocked the front door from the inside so they could get away quickly if need be.

"Clever," I said.

"Could you give us a description of either man?"

I shook my head. "It was too dark to make out their faces, and I was momentarily blinded by the flash. The one with the flashlight was big, that's all I can say for sure. Built like a gorilla."

"Why didn't the dogs bark?" asked Tim.

"We found them outside, off the driveway near the road," said the other trooper. "They were put to sleep."

"Oh, my God!" I said, and Mother drew her breath in sharply.

"Not to worry," the tall one said. "They'll live. They weren't given enough chloroform to kill them. Apparently your intruders were dog lovers and perhaps would-be kidnappers."

Kidnappers? God in heaven! Then I had no doubt in the world they were after Tim. But why?

.   .   .

"Why indeed?" said Scanlon. "If I had to guess, I'd say it was because he was recovering the manuscript. Who did you tell about that?"

"Well, you and Graham. And my controller, and Sidney, and Jane Goodman. And it may have been noised about at the club. I wasn't trying to keep it a secret."

"Apparently not. This could have been another threat too, I suppose."

"Pretty damn rough way of doing it, if you ask me," I said. "Notes I don't mind, but when it comes to harming Tim, something's got to be done about it."

"We'll leave that up to the Connecticut police."

"If only I had seen their faces. Or caught the number on the license plate."

"Don't blame yourself, you did all you could. Some people would hide under the bed if they heard someone breaking in."

"I can't help it, I still feel inadequate." I caught a distinct note of self-pity in my voice; I don't believe I have ever sounded so small and pathetic.

"Look, Mr. Barlow—"

"Isn't it about time you started calling me Nick? I'm spending more time with you these days than with my staff."

175

"I'll do my best to get used to it, Nick."

"And I suppose you have a first name too?"

"Joseph. Joe."

"All right, Joe. If there's anything else I can do ..."

"I thought you said you wanted out of this business, Nick."

"I was wrong. I'm in it again, deeper than ever."

"Good," Scanlon said. "I can sure use help on this one." Then he sighed. "Maybe we ought to put one of your mystery writers to work on it."

.   .   .

Another week went by in which I did my work, much of it paperwork: reviewing contracts, profit and loss statements, and the like; saw a little of Margo; and heard regularly from Tim, who had been overoptimistic in promising me the book "before you head back to New York." He did say he was making progress.

On Friday morning Scanlon called.

"Good news," he said. There was even a faint touch of excitement in his voice. "Angela Farrar is back, and we're calling her in for questioning. We'll *bring* her in if she doesn't come voluntarily. She'll have her lawyer with her, of course."

"Of course."

"And I'd like you to be there, too."

"Won't I be a red flag waved in her face, Joe? Not to mention her lawyer's face?"

"We can work that out," Scanlon said.

.   .   .

As it turned out, neither Angela nor her lawyer ever laid eyes on me, though I saw them clearly enough. Scanlon installed me in a room adjoining the department conference room, where I watched the proceedings through a one-way mirror and listened to the interrogation through earphones.

Angela was as imperious as ever. "I don't see what *possible* right you have to call me down here."

"Mrs. Farrar wants to be cooperative," her attorney said. "But—"

176

"The hell I do."

"—she wants it understood that this is a voluntary appearance and that she resents the imposition."

"Sorry about that," Scanlon said. "But we believe she may have information about Jordan Walker's death that could be helpful."

"I don't know anything about Jordan Walker's murder," she said, hitting every word in the sentence hard, as if to punish the poor things being uttered.

"Mrs. Farrar," Scanlon said, "you called on Jordan Walker the afternoon of his murder. As far as we know, you were the last person to see him alive. Except of course for the murderer."

"So?"

"You knew him rather well?"

"No. I did not. I—" Her attorney stopped whatever verb she was about to use by raising a finger and wagging it at her.

"The doorman reports—and I think these were his exact words—you asked him to announce to Jordan Walker that 'Angela' was downstairs. On a first-name basis then, were you?"

"I did know him," she said, "and I called ahead of time and asked if I might drop by."

"Why, may I ask?" said Scanlon, who already knew the answer.

"I hoped to persuade the little—to leave me out of the book."

"The Graham Farrar biography?"

"Yes. That's why I met him in the first place."

"And were you successful in your errand?"

"No, goddamn it, I wasn't. He absolutely refused to delete the references to my marriage to Graham."

"And what did you do then?"

"I told him I'd sue him for libel if he didn't edit me out of the book."

"And win, too, there's no question about it." This from her attorney, who apparently didn't know truth is an effective defense against libel.

177

And that was about that. Angela said she had stayed only ten minutes or so, hadn't even taken off her coat, hadn't accepted a drink or anything else from Jordan, and had left—probably in the state of mind she was fast approaching now.

"I think we've taken enough of your time," Scanlon said.

"Damned right you have." She rose to her feet and glared at him.

"And thank you for coming," he said, and smiled ever so sweetly.

.   .   .

"What did you think?" he asked me afterward.

I shrugged. "It's hard to say. She's a practiced liar, but unless you can prove that Jordan was killed while she was still inside the building—"

"Which we can't."

"Or dig up some kind of evidence."

"We'll do our best."

"She had motive," I said, "and opportunity. She could have gotten the knife out of Jordan's kitchen. Wait a minute. Suppose she *wants* us to believe that she didn't want the book published."

"How do you mean?"

"If she killed Jordan," I said, "and then destroyed the manuscript, she'd be quite sure that nothing damaging about her past would ever be published."

"But why then would she want to kill Dori Regan?"

"For the same reason she might have wanted to kill Jordan—because as Jordan's typist, Dori would also know what was in the book. Anyway, how do we know there might not be two murderers involved, rather than just one. I remember one book we published—"

But I stopped short there, on that fine line between fiction and reality.

"Anyway, thanks for coming." He grinned. "This time I mean it."

21

To say that I couldn't wait for the weekend would be understating it by a country mile; I was mostly fidgets and tics until I could get out to Westport on Friday night and see what Tim had wrought with his trusty computer.

He had a manuscript, but . . .

"You'll be disappointed, old buddy," Tim said.

"Oh?"

"It's . . . well, I'll let you be the judge. You're the publisher, you have to decide whether you've got a hit or a flop. We'll talk again after you've read it."

So I took *Star Quality: The Life and Times of Graham Farrar* to bed with me, along with my after-dinner coffee and brandy, and the single cigar I permitted myself before bedtime. As the evening wore on into the witching hour and then the first rays of daybreak, the pile of printout paper on the floor grew ever higher, until it resembled a snowdrift.

Tim was right, I was disappointed. It was a strangely subdued book, even muted—certainly not up to Jordan Walker's usually breathless and scorching candor. What we had here was a life edited by its subject, a glossing over of everything that made Graham interesting and colorful.

Maybe my accountant wouldn't be so jubilant after all. But I wanted other opinions: Tim's first, and also an editorial view, either Sidney's or Jane Goodman's. And certainly Joe Scanlon's.

It was with a heavy heart that I headed back to the city on Sunday night, and the gloom was still with me when I arrived at the office. I called in Jane Goodman, who displayed the expected enthusiasm when I told her that we had a Farrar manuscript at last. She fairly beamed when I asked her to read it and report on it for me. She even thanked me for entrusting it to her. I had decided to let her play General Reader and not "sickly over" her mind with my own opinions—not yet.

By the end of the day, her report was on my desk. I was somewhat startled, not being used to such rapid turnovers. As a matter of fact, we publishers are notorious for our dilatory ways, keeping manuscripts around for weeks, even months, and occasionally losing them altogether.

"Why should you be surprised?" said Ms. Goodman. "It's important to the firm to have this book, isn't it?"

"Oh, quite."

"So I put everything aside to do this report, even lunch."

"I appreciate it," I said. "And will read your report first chance I get."

Reader's Report

To: Nicholas Barlow
From: Jane Goodman
RE: Graham Farrar: Manuscript
"And then I played Julius Caesar...." "And then I played Richard the Third...." "... Giles de Rais." "... Captain Eddie Rickenbacker."

Much of this biography is just such a recital of roles, producers, directors, supporting players, good notices, poor notices, Broadway and off-Broadway openings and closings, multimillion-dollar contracts—yes, the *deals*. Let's not forget the *deals*, most of them big, many of them described in eye-glazing detail.

I know Graham Farrar is your friend, and from the little I know about his personal life, I would expect him to have a far more interesting and dramatic story to tell than any four ordinary Hollywood stars. The truth is, in Mr. Walker's hands Graham Farrar comes out about as real, as human as ... well, a wooden Indian maybe. Even Charlton Heston would be a more likely candidate for a fun date. The chapter on his wife Angela stood my raven locks on end, it's true, and I gather from your penciled notes in the margins that you felt the same way. Allusions are made to his other wives—there were three of them, were there not? One of them he married *twice*, but what were they like, and why did the marriages break up?

And how about those infamous brawls of his or his drinking problem? You only find occasional reference to the short fuse on his temper. And far too much of the book is about one of his pet charities, the conservation of our natural resources—an important issue, certainly—but hardly the kind of thing that today's readers, particularly women, will want to balance on their tummies at the beach next summer.

Apart from the chapter on the beautiful harpy Angela, are there other good things to say about this manuscript? Yes, it does have its moments. The chapter about Farrar's boyhood in Nebraska has a kind of Huck Finn quality. And his theories of acting *are* interesting; they couldn't help but be, since he seems to have learned his craft as well as Pavarotti has learned singing. If only we had analyses of craft like that from Booth or Garrick or Barrymore!

But, on balance, the book is too often bland—which Farrar certainly is not. I'm sure the man wouldn't edit a film the way he's edited his own life in this manuscript. His most dramatic moments seem to have been left on the cutting-room floor.

I believe that Graham Farrar, along with Marlon Brando and George C. Scott, is one of the finest

American actors of our time. He deserves a better memoir.

Can anything be done about it? I say yes, the book can be saved. It needs more input from Farrar himself, certainly, and substantial rewriting. I'd throw out Chapter Four completely—it's anticlimactic—and start with Farrar's stint as a boxer and his military service. Chapters 14 and 15, the television and Broadway sequences, ought to be reversed. Pardon my red pencil, but I've already marked up the manuscript for cliché alerts and sentences that I think need to be rewritten for grace and clarity. One great editor I worked for at the beginning of my career told me I must never write on the manuscript itself, that it was "like writing on the author's skin." Well, in this instance, our author is in no position to complain. He's also not around to handle revisions, worse luck, but I'm sure you'll think of something.

Incidentally, the book doesn't seem to end as much as it peters out, just dribbles away into a few platitudes. What's he been up to lately? And what about the near future?

And if you're looking for a volunteer to take on this challenging assignment, it's just the kind of thing I enlisted with you to do. Try me. He may be a sexist, but Graham Farrar is also one hell of an actor!

By the way, couldn't we find a snappier title?

Do you agree?

JMG

When I arrived at my office the following morning, I had Jane Goodman's report tucked away in my briefcase. As soon as I was settled at my desk, a mug of steaming coffee close at hand, I sent for Jane. She entered my office bearing her own mug of coffee, a notebook, and a pencil.

"About your report," I said, before she could even sit down. "Was it all right?"

"It was fine, believe me," I said. "That's not what I wanted to talk about. I have a proposal for you."

She sat down in the guest chair and crossed her legs. I must admit they were lovely legs, long and tightly sheathed. Yes, she was attractive, I was beginning to appreciate that. Intelligence is best in a woman and in an editor, but nobody wants bright conversation *all* the time.

"Jane, how would you like to go out to California and work with Graham Farrar?"

She hesitated but only an instant. "Like it?" she said. "Are you sure you want me to?"

"And why not?"

"Well, after all, I am the new kid on the block."

"I know," I said. "Bur I can't spare the time just now, and I can't spare Sidney, either. I have a hunch—"

"I'd love to go." She said this as though fearing that I might change my mind.

"I have a feeling Graham might respond better to a woman editor. You're right—what you say in your report—Graham *is* sexist. Which could be the reason why the book is so weak, that he couldn't relate well to Jordan."

"What would you like me to do?"

"We'll fly out to the coast"—that word again—"together, and once you two are acquainted and at work, I'll fly back home. That shouldn't take more than a day or two. I'd like you to stay out there as long as necessary. As long as Graham is cooperative. You understand, he has a number of other things on his mind beside the book." And then I told her about his plans for the *Odyssey*.

"An ambitious project if I ever heard one," she said. "I know he's a great actor, but do you think he can pull it off?"

"My limited acquaintance with moviemaking suggests the contrary," I said. "However, Graham is both slightly mad and greatly gifted, so who knows? Now, Jane."

"Yes?"

"Be careful. He's an exceptionally attractive man, between wives at the moment. I'm only asking that you meet him and work with him on a professional level. Anything else is ..."

"My business."

"Exactly."

"Mr. Barlow," she said, "Nicholas, if you will let me call you that—I've never used sex before to advance my career, and I don't expect to start it now."

"Miss Goodman—Jane." I rose to indicate that the meeting was over. "I wouldn't ask you to go out there if I didn't believe you to be thoroughly professional. I want that book, and that's *all* I want. Just bring me back the book, the way you think it ought to be."

So far, so good. All I had to do now was persuade Graham that the book needed more work, and I thought I knew how to go about it. So as soon as the birds were busy out in California, I put a call through to his private number.

I must have gotten Graham out of bed, considering his manner on the phone.

"What is it?"

"Would you consider putting in another week or two on the book, working with an editor from my office this time?"

"Oh, *shit*, Nick. Is that really necessary? For Christ's sweet sake!"

Time for my best bedside manner. "I know you want this book to be a success," I said. "A best-seller for sure. It should be the only definitive statement you will ever make about yourself, your testimonial, in effect. Your legacy to your public and to the acting profession. Graham, we want that book to be not just good but fabulous."

"Well . . ."

"It doesn't need all that much work, I assure you. But we do need to add some of what I like to call 'music' to the manuscript."

"Music," he said. "Well, then . . . who'll be working on it?"

"A young editor I've just hired. Her name is Jane Goodman. A highly experienced editor, I assure you."

"Is she attractive?" Same old Graham.

"Tolerably," I said. "In fact, quite. Is it important?"

"Oh, I don't know," he said. "Right now I haven't been thinking much about women—too busy with the project.

And I'm batching it now, you know, Nick. . . ." His voice trailed off oddly, as though he had already rung off. Then he said, "All right—send your editor out, and I'll give her as much time as I can. That won't be a lot, but maybe it'll help."

"Whatever you can spare. And thanks."

"You're right, you know," he said. "My biography should be not only good, but . . ." He waited a long two beats. ". . . *sensational.*"

22

The first available flight to La La Land was at noon the following day.

I might as well admit that I hate flying. Air travel, even first-class air travel, is not much better in America these days than traveling by bus. Would that I had time to cross the continent at a leisurely pace by Amtrak. But I wanted to get this particular errand over quickly.

Fortified early on by a large vodka martini, with Jane Goodman close behind me, I boarded the plane. No sooner had I buckled my seat belt than I began to feel queasy, and we hadn't even started to taxi down the runway!

Jane, on the other hand, looked absolutely euphoric. It was her first trip west of the Mississippi, she told me, her eyes shining and that smile of hers brighter than ever. She was wearing a simply cut navy blue coat over a silk dress in a dusty rose. When I complimented her on the outfit, she beamed again.

"I've really looked forward to this trip," she said.

"That makes one of us."

"Why so glum, Nick?"

"I think I'm using up my lucky breaks too fast."

I have a theory, totally unsupported by statistics or the law of averages, that if you fly long enough, you're sure to be in an accident. When I began to fly years ago, I took to the air blithely. First class seemed like an epicurean banquet in the clouds, what with cozy wool slippers, endless glasses of champagne, and gourmet tidbits served on good china with gleaming silverware. By and by a certain anxiety began to blanket those innocent pleasures. Perhaps it was a rise in my blood pressure or a touch of airsickness; at any rate, with each succeeding flight this malaise heightened, until I became convinced that only my grip on the armrests was keeping the plane aloft.

And just then we started to take off. I gripped my armrests. We roared down the runway, then up, sweeping over the tract houses and swarming parkways of the borough of Queens. As we rose, I composed a silent prayer. No particular prayer to no particular god—just an earnest supplication that this one wouldn't be The One. *Please, Your Ineluctableness, please.*

A hostess materialized three seconds after the Fasten Seat Belts sign went off.

"Can I get you something, sir?"

They know, somehow they always *know* I'm in trouble. Maybe because I turn a light green and start to perspire heavily. Angels of mercy, that's what they are.

"Oh, yes, you can get me a double vodka martini," I said softly. Jane ordered a white wine. Sensible as well as intelligent.

Once my stomach stabilized, I asked her why she'd never gone West before.

"I don't know, I just never got around to it. My family wasn't much for long-distance travel. We spent summers in Maine and occasional winter vacations in Miami Beach. Most of the other girls I knew at Vassar went to Aruba or St. Vincent or Bermuda, but not me. I was sure that one day I'd get to San Francisco and fall in love with it, and of course, so many movies and television programs made me feel I'd be at home in California even though I'd never been there. Oh, God, those marvelous movies."

"Then you won't be disappointed," I said. "It's all much like the back lot of MGM. You'll have to see the Brown Derby and

187

the Polo Lounge and the Beverly Hilton ... Century Plaza and Pershing Square ... and maybe take the back-lot tour of Universal Studios. Once you've finished working with Graham, that is. Why don't you take a few extra days out there afterward?"

"I'd love that."

"And you'll have a golden opportunity to spend some time with one of America's most admired movie stars. Lucky you."

"Irony, Nick?"

"Perhaps. It's certainly not jealousy. Or envy."

"I don't see why you should feel either one. You're a successful, much-admired publisher."

"Anyone who says he never dreamed of becoming a movie star when he was growing up," I said, "is probably lying. Or has forgotten his childhood. But when I see what *being* a movie star can do to a person—well, I wouldn't want Graham Farrar's life for all those million-dollar-plus contracts. Did you know—I read it in *People*—that his price these days is around two hundred fifty thousand dollars a *day*? When he consents to work, that is. Most of the time, like Achilles, he sulks in that costly tent of his in Malibu."

"Tell me all about him," said Jane, star struck for sure. Not that I needed any prompting. Graham has always fascinated me. He didn't need a movie screen to be larger than life-size. All the movies ever did for him was to multiply his audience by geometric progression.

I began telling her what I knew of him from personal recollections, and what I'd been told by others who were closer to him than I had ever been. How he came to New York in the first place—*fled* to New York would be more accurate—leaving a wife and one child behind. He was about to start his first year in graduate school when he decided to chuck it all and become a professional actor. Some months later, two of his first wife's brothers showed up in Manhattan, traced Graham to his furnished room in the Village, and beat the bejesus out of him.

Graham himself is a regular gamecock when it comes to

punching people out. People and things. His nose was first busted in a golden gloves match. And rebusted a couple of times afterward.

Anyhow, he got divorced and remarried, produced another child. All this time he was practically destitute, making the rounds, knocking on doors, showing up for every open call in his one decent suit. Supported by his second wife, of course, who went out to work as a secretary despite the baby. And then Graham got his first break, as Iago in an off-Broadway production of *Othello*. He was brilliant, of course, completely dazzling. He made Iago convincing to me for the first time. Made him attractive and diabolical at once, a prince of duplicity. In fact, he stole the show from the Moor. Good reviews . . . rave reviews. It still took a long time for him to make it to Broadway, but make it he did.

My role in all this was to take him out now and then for extravagant meals, meals he couldn't have afforded himself. I would have given him money too, but he was too proud to take or ask for help. Odd, isn't it—he wouldn't take it from me, but he would from Virginia, his second wife? As well as from Kathleen, his first wife, and Orianna, the third wife. One fortunate thing: the women he married and abandoned, each one with a child to take care of, all ultimately remarried husbands who eventually adopted his various offspring. Graham was just too intent on his career to bother with them.

Have I made him sound like a monster? Well, the vanity and desperation of an actor struggling through repeated rejections *can* be monstrous. And all three women knew what they were getting. Graham had always had an inner fire—whether blazing or smoldering.

When he was finally cast in a Broadway play—with his name in lights—they posted a closing notice only a week after the opening. Graham went on a bender that lasted three days, slugged the producer of the show, and wound up in Bellevue. Most of this was the sauce, of course. When he stuck to beer and wine, he was perfectly pleasant, but with anything harder he was unmanageable. Yet he was always—what is that marvelous line of Yeats?—"a bright particular star." You loved him, were fascinated by him. You just learned to avoid him when he was drinking.

"You didn't, though?" Jane said.

"Avoid him? Not usually. Not while he was broke and unknown."

"But afterward?"

"I found his success harder to take than he did."

I thought about her question for a moment. Again, I didn't wish to appear jealous or envious. Jane Goodman hadn't worked for me long enough to realize that I'm almost constitutionally incapable of either of those two deadly sins.

"I suppose," I said finally, "the prosperity and recognition meant more to Graham than they did to me. I was born luckier than most, Jane. I didn't have to fight to get ahead the way Graham did, so I took success for granted. Nor was it necessary for me to keep proving myself."

The answer seemed to satisfy her, if not me. At any rate, she nodded agreeably, rewarded me with a small smile, settled back in her seat, and closed her eyes. In a moment she was fast asleep, breathing softly and steadily.

No, Graham was far more complicated than I'd made him out to be. And so was our friendship.

•　　•　　•

"Welcome to Mudville, U.S.A."

We were standing in the foyer of Graham Farrar's house in Pacific Palisades, the latest of his many residences. It had been raining for several days in Southern California, and by now the mire along the base of the palisades was several inches deep.

"At least," Graham said, "the woods aren't on fire. But wait until fall. They will be."

"I've sometimes wondered, Graham," I said, "why you go on living here. You're not a native Californian. Most of your movies are shot somewhere else, quite a few of them in New York. You could live anywhere."

"I know," he said. "I suppose ..."

"Yes?" Jane said. I felt proud of her. So far she had shown no signs of being overwhelmed by our star's presence; no openmouthed admiration, no dazed expression, no starlight in her eyes.

"I suppose it's because I like my privacy," Graham said. "And because I feel at home near the sea."

The sea. The wine-dark sea of Homer; Byron's deep and dark blue ocean, "dark-heaving—boundless, endless and sublime." Even as we spoke, we could hear the waves breaking against the cliff that fell away to the Pacific about fifty yards from Graham's redwood deck.

I recognized the house from the photographs I'd seen in an exhibition of Neutra's California architecture. To begin with, the place was round, so that no matter what time of day it was, you could find a room open to the sun. Graham's garage, where I'd parked a rented Datsun 280Z, was cut into the solid rock of the hillside. There was an underground passage between the garage and the house, as solid and secure as a bomb shelter.

Out by the road leading to Graham's property was a chain-metal fence that could be electrified and a guardhouse, complete with a well-armed and properly suspicious guard in uniform. Another ape, or maybe the same one I'd seen with Graham in New York. On our arrival I had stared at him a bit longer than might have seemed polite. He had received my inspection impassively, with eyes as pale and red rimmed as an albino's. Graham explained that both the fence and the guard had been added following a kidnapping threat directed against his family. No family was in evidence, of course, Graham being, as he told me in New York, a bachelor again.

"Sorry about the Berlin Wall out there, chum," he said. "Apparently I need protection from my adoring fans."

I made no comment. "The strongest guards," Scott Fitzgerald once wrote, "are posted at the gates of nothing."

We chatted for a while longer. About the weather, and about the hazards of life in southern California, which, we agreed, ranged from earthquakes to autograph hunters to tourists pointing cameras at everyone and everything in view.

Though we avoided mention of Jordan Walker, his murder seemed to hang heavily over our conversation. Jordan had spent weeks in this house, probing every aspect of Graham Farrar's life.

I asked about Jeffrey Burgal.

"Jeff?" Graham said. "You'll find him at the Beverly Hilton."

Finally we sat down, on one of those incredibly long, soft white couches that decorators love to put in front of window walls, under cathedral ceilings. Given my weight, I expected to sink into it up to my belly button, and I did. A Japanese manservant brought us drinks, and Graham talked about the only thing he wanted to discuss, his movie. *The* movie. Graham Farrar's *Odyssey*.

"We'll open it," he said, "on the plains of Troy." He raised his hand when I threatened to interrupt him.

"I know, I know," he said. "That's not how Homer started his version. But we'll have to take certain liberties. Cinematic truth is not the same as literary truth, as you well know."

"I want to film the sack of Troy, the end of a glorious civilization, the Trojan horse episode, the deaths of Hector and Achilles. Wonderful action scenes. *Then* we dissolve into Odysseus and his wanderings."

He could bring it off, I thought, if anyone could. I glanced over at Jane, sitting some yards away from me on the couch, metaphorically at Graham's knees.

"And I plan to end it," he said, skipping over years and years of Odyssean exile and adventure, "with the death of Odysseus."

"His death?" I asked. "Surely, Graham—"

"How do you think he did die?" said Jane. "Since Homer never told us, I mean."

"On his last adventure," Graham said. "You don't suppose he could be satisfied with life on Ithaca. Not after the war. Not after Calypso and Nausicaa. No, following a few years of happiness with Penelope, he feels restless again. So he and his son Telemachus travel to Phaecia, which is now being attacked by a neighboring city-state. Odysseus remembers his debt of gratitude to the king of Phaecia, Alcinous. So he buckles on the old sword and sets out. And there—"

Graham suddenly jumped to his feet and strode over to a bookcase—jammed, I was pleased to see, with real books, books that looked read. Returning with his dog-eared copy of the *Odyssey* clutched in both hands, Graham thumbed through its pages until he found the passage he wanted.

" 'As for my end,' " he read aloud in a voice darkened with intensity, " 'Death would come to me in his gentlest form out of the sea.' " He put the book down and stared at me: Graham Farrar, district attorney. "What do you suppose that meant, Nick, death out of the sea? A great fish? A shark? Drowning, perhaps. Shipwreck, I think. A great storm at sea, with the wily Ulysses fighting against overpowering waves, rallying his sailors for one last effort." His voice trailed off. I looked again at Jane, who now appeared to be, like me, quite at sea. Only Graham was now under Graham's spell.

We were spared any further news of Odysseus's fate just then, for the telephone rang. Graham excused himself and went into the next room to take the call. As with so many southern California houses, there were no doors in the open areas, and few interior walls, so we could easily overhear Graham's side of the conversation.

"I see. . . . Yes, of course. . . . He has? Well, we'll have to do something about that, won't we? . . . All right. If you insist. . . . You *do* insist? . . . I understand. . . . Of course."

When he returned, Graham wore the strangest expression on his face: a combination of anger in check and extreme impatience. He began to tap his hand against the arm of his chair, as though he couldn't wait for us to get up and go. I got up.

"Well, Graham," I said, "I'm going to borrow Ms. Goodman here for a while."

"Oh?" He looked at Jane as though he were seeing her for the first time. "You'll be coming back, Miss Goodman?" I was startled. The Graham I knew usually moved from formality to intimacy with a woman in a matter of minutes.

Jane looked at me.

"Tomorrow morning," I said.

"I'll look forward to it." Graham bowed in a mock-formal way. "My amanuensis."

"*My* editor," I said. "Remember, Graham—I want that book."

"All right, you piratical old bastard," he said. "You'll have your damn book, you can be sure of that."

Before we left Graham's windswept promontory for our hotel, I suggested to Jane that we take a look at my friend's portion of the Pacific. There was no front yard properly speaking, only a winding path bordered by railroad ties sunk into the rocky earth. Sedge grass, wild grapevines, heaps of stones on all sides. Not far from the house a hot tub steamed away, rimmed by dark slabs of slate. Just before the end of this rough path, we were stopped by a split rail fence about three feet high. Past the fence the path ended. A yard or so beyond that, the land fell off sharply into a rock cliff, and a hundred feet below that, the ocean hammered relentlessly against the shore.

"Not exactly an inviting place to swim," Jane said.

The late afternoon sky was slate gray and clung about us like a shroud. There was no horizon to speak of; sea seemed to merge into clouds in one continuous tone.

"Californians swim in pools," I said. "Though I think I see steps down to the water's edge about a quarter of a mile from here. Want to go look?"

"I don't think so." Jane pulled up the collar of her coat. "No—let's leave."

"Gladly." I'd begun to shiver myself, whether because of a chill in that onshore breeze or an atavistic fear of heights, I'd find it hard to say.

When we passed Graham's house on our way to the Datsun, we could see Graham through his glass wall. The lamp on his desk was on, and he was sitting with his head in his hands, elbows on the desktop.

"He looks so terribly alone," Jane said.

He looked, I thought, as though he were grieving.

· · ·

Back in what passes for civilization in the foothills of the Sierra Nevadas, we drove down Laurel Canyon past Hollywood to Beverly Hills. According to the brochures it's one of the world's richest communities, and I could easily believe it. The houses all look like money—old money, new money, borrowed money, and stolen money. If I were to move to *southern* California, a most unlikely prospect, that's probably where I'd wind up.

A light rain had now begun to fall, more a mist at the start, but within a few minutes the drops were spattering loudly against the windshield. I turned on the wipers, and we drove silently through the rain-washed twilight. Lights were coming on in the windows of houses. It was the advent of the cocktail hour.

I had reserved two rooms at the Beverly Hilton. Jane's was actually a suite, bed and sitting rooms.

Jane stopped in the center of the living room, drew her breath in sharply. "Oh, my God," she said.

"Like it?"

"It's ... it's ... I hardly know what to say, Nick—it's, God, picture perfect. Like a movie set."

"You'll be here for a while," I said, "so you might as well be comfortable." My own room, I discovered shortly afterward, was considerably more modest. Noblesse oblige.

Jane toured the entire suite, exclaiming over everything she saw or touched. Even the painting over her bed, she marveled, was not a reproduction.

"It's a lithograph," I said, feeling like a proper pedant, "but it's a Rauschenberg, and a damned good one."

When it came to the bed itself, of a size that might justifiably be called "emperor," Jane contented herself with bouncing up and down once or twice while murmuring contentedly.

"Wait till you get between the sheets," I said.

"Oh?"

"They're satin."

"And there's a balcony overlooking the pool."

We stepped outside and looked down. Some of the gaily striped umbrellas turned slowly around and around as the wind caught them widdershins. Raindrops stippled the green surface of the pool, and puddles had formed on the tiles. The reclining chairs were empty, except for one small child sitting with his hands thrust in the pockets of a slicker, kicking his feet up now and then or opening his mouth wide to drink in the rain.

I stayed a few moments longer, and when Jane invited me to sit down while she fixed me a drink in a minibar tucked away in an alcove, I refused. I felt uncomfortable. I wasn't sure what, if anything, was expected of me. Nor was I sure what I expected of Jane—nothing, really, I suppose—or what I expected Jane to expect. Long ago I learned that when you are undecided whether to go or stay, you'd better go. So I went in search of Jeffrey Burgal.

I found the Wizard of Clauses in his room, two floors below mine. When he answered the door, Jeffrey looked as though he'd just risen from a nap; he was still pulling his sleeves down and buttoning them. He led me into the room, pausing to shut the door to the bathroom (or what I presumed was the bathroom). The door refused to cooperate and swung back open again, just a few inches.

Burgal sank down in an armchair and stared gloomily out at the rain.

"Hateful weather," he said.

"I don't know," I said. "Probably makes it a lot easier to tee off early."

"Very funny, Nick. Got any others?"

"Yes." I made myself at home on Jeffrey's studio couch. "How many WASPs does it take to murder a biographer?"

"What's that you said? *What?*"

"Lieutenant Scanlon wants to have a talk with you. Any chance of your coming back to New York soon, Jeff?"

He glanced over at the partly open bathroom door, then back at me.

"Why would Scanlon want to question me?" His voice rose slightly on the last word.

"I didn't say he wanted to question you. He just wants to have a talk with you. He suspects that the last person to see Jordan alive was connected with the manuscript. That would make it me, Dori the typist, or yourself. Or—and let's not forget him—the third mysterious visitor."

"Well, it wasn't me," he said. "By the way, Nick, I am sorry about Dori."

"You read about it out here?"

"My secretary sent me the clippings. You're getting to be a regular, aren't you? Scene of the crime and all that."

"Had you seen Dori before you came out here?"

"Not since Jordan's funeral services."

"She told Sidney you were taking her into the agency as a partner."

He snorted. "You met her, Nick, you know what she was like. How could I possibly do something like that?"

"I've seen worse in your business," I said. "At least she was easy to look at."

"Tell me, Nick," he said, "if Lieutenant Scanlon doesn't want to 'question' me, why are you?"

"Just curious," I said. "You don't think you have anything to offer Scanlon, then? That's not a question, Jeffrey, despite the way I framed it—just a statement."

"Nothing I haven't already told him."

I could swear he was lying or covering up something, and I was dying to get a peek into that room whose door he'd been so damned anxious to close when I came in. From where I sat I couldn't get even a glimpse inside.

"But I'll be back East in a couple of weeks," he said, "and I'll be glad to talk with Scanlon then. Just as soon as I have a couple of deals worked out here."

"Fine." I yawned and stretched—then, before Jeffrey could get up to stop me, moved across to the bathroom.

"This your john?" I said.

Jeffrey was there instantly, standing right beside me.

"Let me tidy the place up before you use it," he said.

"Tidy it up?" I said. "Whatever for? Looks fine to me."

"Be right back." He popped inside the bathroom, closing

the door behind him. But not before I spotted what he was so anxious to keep hidden.

A hypodermic needle lying on top of the toilet tank.

I shouldn't have been surprised, I suppose. After all, this was Hollywood. At any rate, it explained why Jeffrey wasn't drinking. I did hope, for his sake, that he wasn't using strange needles.

In a moment or two he emerged, looking composed, and I went in. The needle, as I expected, was gone. I flushed the toilet for show and ran some water over my hands in the sink.

When I reappeared, Jeffrey had put on his St. Laurent cashmere sport jacket and one of those string ties favored by Texans and Nebraska wheat farmers. He was sipping a Perrier and lime.

"Fix you a drink, Nick?"

"No, thanks," I said. "I'm going to have a drink with Jane, dinner, and then an early bedtime. My body clock says it's time for the eleven o'clock news."

"Jane? Who is Jane? Another conquest, Nick?"

"Jane Goodman," I said. "Ms. Goodman is a new editor I've hired. She's going to work on rewrites with Graham."

I explained the nature of our mission. He nodded, without any apparent enthusiasm. "If you think more work is needed—"

"I do indeed."

"Well, you're the publisher. Do you think this Jane Goodman is up to it?"

"Yes, I do. She's experienced and she came highly recommended."

"Well, let's hope she brings it off."

"I feel quite confident she can."

"When are you heading back?" he said. When I told him I was leaving on Sunday, he didn't seem at all disappointed. "See you back in New York," he said as he was showing me out.

"Jeffrey. You know . . . if you need—"

"Need what?"

I don't know if I was going to say "need medical help" or

198

"need a lawyer." I just shrugged and said: "Nothing, Jeff . . . never mind."

· · ·

Dinner with Jane was pleasant if unexciting. Although I was wearying fast, she was still ebullient. I could tell that the day had been a heady one for her—like one's first glimpse of Paris or the Grand Canyon. Graham Farrar, after all. And Los Angeles.

"There's so much of it," she said. "And so many people."

"It hardly matters," I said, "since everyone drives anyhow. As one commentator put it, the New York equivalent of a typical California evening would be if I called you in Manhattan and said, 'Let's go out to Long Island. We'll stop in Mineola for drinks, we'll hit a movie in Massapequa, and then we'll drive out to Center Moriches for a party.' " I also told her to remind me not to do any more business with Jeffrey Burgal, no matter who the client was. "Not ever."

"But why?"

"I'll tell you later," I said with a yawn I could not and would not suppress. "When you get back."

"Nick," she said. "I don't want you to worry."

"About what?"

"Graham Farrar. I can handle him."

"Well," I said, yawning again, "if you can't, you won't be the first who couldn't."

23

When I got back to New York I discovered, rather to my chagrin, that Barlow & Company had not suffered at all during my absence. No one had even missed me apparently—not even the receptionist, who greeted me as though I had just been out to lunch. Even Hannah received me matter-of-factly. So much for the hunter home from the hill.

"Mortimer Mandelbaum wishes to see you as soon as possible," said Hannah.

"Send him right in."

I have mentioned that Return on Investment and Profit and Loss are Mortimer's daily bread. I must not forget the other sacred figure in our controller's trinity: Cash Flow. Dreaded or welcomed, depending on which direction the cash is flowing.

"Morty," I said when he appeared, downcast in mien as usual, " 'Oh, tell me not in mournful numbers.' "

Mortimer was not in a literary frame of mind, but then, he seldom is. "Nick," he said. "The April figures."

"Oh? I thought we had rather better sales in April than usual. Better than last year, certainly."

Mortimer's face always brought to mind a basset hound I once owned. Now more than ever the resemblance was compelling; his eyes in particular were doglike, open wide and trusting.

"I meant the returns, Nick. Do you know what percentage we're running?"

"Offhand, no. I haven't had the chance to review them. I've been in California."

"Forty-one point two percent, Nick, *forty-one point two*."

"Pretty bad, I admit, Morty."

"Even the Prudence Henderson Harte is returning."

"But it was only shipped to the stores a month ago."

"The cookbooks and diet books, too."

"Well, as we know, April is the cruelest month."

Returns are Cash Flow, right enough, negative cash flow. Unsold books coming home, not only in cartons but sometimes on skids. All because our books are sold fully returnable, which is to say, on consignment. As Alfred Knopf once put it, in a widely quoted publishing chestnut: "My inventory is gone today and here tomorrow." Bookstores, alas, sometimes return them for credit because they cannot pay their bills, and then order them all over again. A most peculiar business, but our very own.

"Any good news, Morty?"

"Let me see." He scratched his head industriously. "Well, Nick, Harry Bunter tells me that the Literary Guild might have a slot for the Jordan Walker bio."

Harry Bunter is our subsidiary rights director, a man who can squeeze revenue out of even the deadest turkey. Give him a live one and he's unstoppable.

"Really?" I said. "That's great news." Unlike movie deals, where the publisher has no rights and earns nothing, book club sales are split fifty-fifty between author and publisher— and are always profitable.

"As soon as they can see a finished manuscript," said Mandelbaum.

"Great," I said. Just bloody damn *great*. A finished manuscript. Hah.

"We will have a finished manuscript soon, won't we, Nick?"

I might have known that Morty's exit line would be on the downbeat.

Sidney Leopold told a different story. "We even have a new best-seller on the lists," he said.

"How nice. The Prudence Henderson Harte?"

"N-not yet," he said, and named a young first novelist who had written a horror story about an American dybbuk—a Jewish actor possessed by a demon while performing as Channon in a production of *The Dybbuk*. The novel was called *The Demon Within*. Because it was a first book and by a complete unknown, we'd paid the author a ridiculously low advance.

"And now he's about to become rich," I said.

"It isn't exactly hurting our c-cash flow either," Sidney said. We both knew well that having a best-seller can be like printing money—provided the publisher doesn't spend too much on advertising or on an author's tour. In this case the author wasn't touring, being both inarticulate and unphotogenic.

"Sidney," I said, "we've probably created another monster of ingratitude. Overnight successes have a way of becoming overnight prima donnas."

"Maybe this t-time it will be . . . different," Sidney said. "He seems the grateful young author."

"Give him time, Sidney, just give him time. Let him split a six-figure paperback sale and make his own movie deal, and then watch what happens. We'll be lucky if he doesn't auction his next book off to the highest bidder."

"You're probably right," Sidney said. "we have an option on his next n-novel, but—"

"There's no loyalty in this business anymore, Sidney. And you know what? I like it better that way."

"You do?"

"I can't stand sentimentality. Grateful authors slobbering all over me, taking cuts in royalty when my company has a bad year. My staff telling me they don't deserve a bonus this year—"

Sidney raised his hand. "All right, Nick, p-please."

He went on to tell me of a new book he'd just signed up. "The ultimate d-disaster novel," he said. It seems that as the year 2000 approaches, anxieties about global disaster are rife. Martin Luther expected the world to end in the year 2000. This particular apocalyptic novelist predicts a nuclear conflagration in the Middle East, followed by earthquakes, floods, and the second coming of Jesus Christ. To me this sounded more like the ultimate California novel. I had heard that out there they were using crystals to repair their cars.

"Fine, Sidney, fine. If the world is going to come to an end, we might as well get a book club selection out of it."

It was good to be back.

24

Good to visit my mother and brother in Connecticut. Good to experience Pepita's cooking and Oscar's driving. Just good to spend a weekend at home, sleeping off my jet lag.

And it remained good—until the phone call I got on Monday afternoon, about five-thirty or so, after Hannah had left for the day.

"Meester Barlow?" A man's voice, muffled, as though the caller were holding a handkerchief over his mouth.

"Speaking."

"I got som'ting you want—" he said, or at least that's what it sounded like to me. "I try call man' times."

"I've been out of town," I said. "Who is this?"

"Don' matter."

I was about to hang up when I caught the name "Walker" in the man's next remark, which was otherwise unintelligible.

"What about Walker?" I said quickly.

"I got d'papers you lookin' for."

"The papers?" Was it possible that someone had found Jordan's original manuscript? "Keep talking," I said. "Don't hang up, whoever you are."

"Very valu'ble," he was saying now, "I hear police asking about it, no?"

"Hold it," I said. "Listen carefully. Is it a manuscript you have? The manuscript of a book?"

"Wha'?"

"A bunch of paper with typing on it—is that what you have?"

"Yah," he said. "You wanna buy, huh?"

"I want to buy, hell yes! How much do you want?"

"Fitty thous'n dollar."

"You've got to be kidding." I said. "No manuscript in the world is worth that kind of money."

"You no want?"

"Yes, of course I want it. It's of no use to you or anybody else except me."

"Wha' you pay then?"

I thought for a moment. How could anybody put a price on what might after all turn out to be the same anemic manuscript Tim had reconstructed? On the other hand, I figured it was worth a chance.

"One thousand dollars," I said.

A long pause. "Twenny-five."

We continued in that vein for some time, until I began to feel I was dealing with a rug merchant in a Middle Eastern bazaar—or a stereo dealer on Canal Street. But we finally settled on three thousand in twenty-dollar bills. Tired of both the haggling and my struggle to understand the man's English, I agreed to his terms with the condition that he would show me some of the manuscript before I gave him the money.

"Wha'? How I do that?"

"Put some of it in an envelope and leave it at my office." I gave him the address.

"No come your office," he said. "Subway station, Ninety-six Street, Lexin'ton Ave, ten 'clock tonight. Bring money, you get it all. Twenty dolla bills."

"Hold on—where in the subway station?"

"Uptown side. You come alone. No cops."

"That doesn't give me much time to get the money ready," I said. "The banks are closed."

"You get," he said. "Tonight. Alone. *No cops.*" And then I was listening to a dial tone.

Three thousand bucks, on top of the money I'd already invested in this book! This was going to end up being the most expensive biography I'd ever published.

Scanlon had thoughtfully supplied me with his home phone number, and luckily I found him in his apartment. When I told him about the call, he spoke with more excitement in his voice than I had ever heard before.

"Listen," he said, "you can't pull this one off alone. I'm going with you."

"He said no cops."

"The hell with what he said. I'll stay out of sight until the contact has been made, just to cover you. And then I want to pick this bozo up, whoever he is."

"Whatever you think is best."

"The Ninety-sixth Street IRT station." He clucked his tongue, "The pits. So badly lit you're lucky you don't fall down the goddamn stairs on your way to the platform."

"But it's a break, isn't it?"

"You bet your tushie it is. Now here's what I want you to do. Meet me at ten to ten at the entrance to the Ninety-sixth Street Station—"

"Hang on."

"What?"

"Shouldn't we get there earlier—to check the place out?"

"Trust me. I'll have two backup men there ahead of us, undercover. Just stay in the light, clearly visible, until I get there."

.   .   .

Ninety-sixth Street to me is No-Man's-Land, a kind of raffish combat zone between a thriving middle-class residential and commercial neighborhood called Carnegie Hill and Spanish Harlem. The street's most striking landmark is a Muslim mosque, the city's first, a bizarre touch of the Arabian Nights in Manhattan.

When Scanlon and I arrived at the entrance to the Lexington Avenue IRT, the sidewalks were virtually deserted, although a long line of cars still flowed down the street, heading for the FDR Drive and the distant suburbs.

"We'll split up here," Scanlon said at the subway entrance. "You go first—I'll follow." One of his backup men was posted near the station turnstiles, and the other, I assumed, was somewhere down on the platform.

He was right about the lighting; the station was about as cheerful as the catacombs of Rome or Paris, or any other sewer you might chance to visit. First I had to thread my way past a homeless couple lying in a welter of blankets, loose clothing, and two overstuffed shopping carts. Then I had to pass a gaunt unshaven panhandler, with a sign around his neck: "Jobless Desert Storm vet needing food." He cursed me under his breath when I ignored his outstretched Styrofoam cup. I was tempted to curse him back—one entrepreneur greeting another in my wealth-laden yet poverty-ridden city—but I thought better of it.

Thanks to the miracle of automatic cash machines and several credit cards, I was supplied with three thousand dollars in twenty-dollar bills, now tightly wrapped and sealed in a manila envelope. But when I reached the uptown subway platform, I saw no sign of anyone with a briefcase. There were only two other people on the platform—a short, stocky black man in a neatly pressed business suit, and a rather plump woman, also black, in a pair of extremely tight red slacks and an electric-blue jacket.

Could the black man be Scanlon's backup? Possibly. He carried only a *New York Post*; she was holding a bulging Macy's shopping bag. I strolled past them to the end of the platform and stood with my back solidly braced against the wall. Not long afterward, Scanlon appeared and took a seat on a bench some hundred feet away. He opened a newspaper and held it up in front of his face. I had expected greater subtlety but what the hell—I was relieved just to see him there.

It was damp and sultry below ground. I could hear the far-off rumble of trains and, from above, other noises: the murmur of automobile engines, the shrill grinding of brakes.

Ten-fifteen, and our mysterious caller still had not appeared. Then a swarthy man in work clothing came down the stairs slowly, looking around him as he descended, and yes, he was holding a thick parcel tied with string in one hand and several loose sheets of paper in the other. Our man for certain! I felt a surge of adrenaline along with wild hope that we might at last be on the verge of a solution to Jordan's murder. At the very least I might gain possession of Jordan's original manuscript.

Now there were five of us on the platform and no sign of an approaching train. The man with the parcel looked first toward Scanlon. Apparently he didn't like what he saw, for he drew back toward the foot of the stairs and beckoned me. I came toward him.

"Meester Barlow?" A low growl.

"Yes."

"You got d'money?"

"Right here. Show me what you have."

He thrust several pages of the manuscript into my hand. They were slightly soiled and rumpled, but they were the distinctive ivory-colored bond that, I knew, Jordan favored, and the name "Walker" and a number at the top left corner of each page. I decided they looked authentic. I held out my hand with the packet in it and reached for the parcel.

He took a step back. "Show me money."

I ripped open one corner of my envelope and riffled through the bills.

"All twenties," I said, "as you asked. Now, let me have the manuscript."

What took place then happened so swiftly that I could not really recall it in any detail. I had to depend on Scanlon to fill me in.

As I handed over the money and took hold of the parcel, Scanlon put down his newspaper and stood up. The moment he did, our shady friend made an attempt to bolt.

"¡Mierda! ¡Policía!" he cried out. *"¡Carajo!"*

He couldn't go back up the stairs because I had spun around and blocked him, so instead he broke away and darted down the platform, now holding both his parcel and the money. First he collided with the shopping bag woman, who screamed at him. Then he ricocheted off the wall and headed for the man in the business suit, who looked up from his newspaper in alarm. Our fugitive wrapped his arms around him from behind, using him as a shield.

At this point Scanlon drew his gun and shouted: "Hold it— you're under arrest!" or words to that effect.

They certainly had an effect on the burly black man, who broke free, shoving his adversary over the edge of the platform in the process.

And then all hell broke loose. The black woman screamed again, the man down on the tracks got to his feet and ran up the uptown tunnel. It was then that I saw a light in the tunnel—not a welcome sight. I shouted a warning to the man, but he must have already seen the approaching train himself, because he turned and ran back toward us.

I thought sure he would make it in time. Scanlon holstered his gun, and we both went to the edge of the platform, ready to help pull him back up.

He tripped and fell flat on his face just before he reached us. By now the train was bearing down on him, its horn blaring a futile warning. He made one last effort to get under the edge of the platform, but the parcel and the money— he was still clutching both of them—apparently slowed him down just that fraction of a second he needed.

The sounds that followed—first his, then the train's—were indescribable. Scanlon instinctively made the sign of the cross. I groaned, mourning both the manuscript and the poor bastard who hoped to sell it to me. Both were gone now. The wheels of a subway train make a most effective paper shredder. Not to mention what they do to human flesh. As for the package of money, it alone survived the carnage. My three thousand was found lying in the center of the track after the body had been removed and the train had traveled on. A handful of manuscript pages had also survived the carnage—all of them, without exception, blank.

"He was pulling a scam," I said. "Selling me blank pages, for God's sake."

"Sure looks like it," Scanlon said. "The sad son of a bitch. He couldn't even pull off his stupid con. Hell of a wind-up, isn't it?" He shook his head, but I had a feeling he was hardened to this kind of slaughter. I, on the other hand, am not used to real blood; I barely controlled my nausea.

The two of us made our way back above ground, and I wondered aloud what had happened to spoil the transaction.

"He *made* me, damn it," Scanlon said. "And I recognized him at the same time. It was Angel Cordoba, of course."

"Who?"

"The porter at Walker's apartment building. I told you about him way back when. A druggie—and I grilled him myself. I should have guessed. No, for Christ's sake, I should have *known*. And he's the baby who saw the third visitor and could identify him for us. Shit!" He shook his head. "Maybe there wasn't a third man at all."

"But the doorman got a name," I said. "Spelvin, wasn't it?"

"Only the porter could swear the man was in Walker's apartment," Scanlon said. "He's the only one who saw him leave."

"No reason to blame yourself for what happened. It was a break all right—just a tough one."

"What about those pages he gave you?"

I had shoved the three or four pages in my pocket when the excitement started. Now I pulled them out and took a closer look at them.

"They're from *My Life on the Casting Couch*, Jordan's last book," I said. "He must have dug them out of the trash."

"Or typed them himself," Scanlon said. "Jordan didn't work at home, remember? Anyway, it's history now."

"What next?"

"I've read the manuscript your brother pieced together," he said, "and so have two other smart men in my department. All three of us came up empty. There's nothing there that gives anybody a motive. If only there'd been something in the book that someone could have used for blackmail."

"Nothing about Angela Farrar that would even raise her ire," I said. "That too has been sanitized."

"Well, better luck next time."

And that was that.

25

Another week went by in which I did my work, spoke occasionally on the phone with Margo, and heard regularly from Jane in California. Yes, the book was going well. She wasn't sure how long she'd be out there, but Graham had been "most cooperative"—her exact words. I whistled softly when I heard that one. She must have won Graham over fast. Anyhow, *that*—whatever it was and if indeed it was anything at all—was none of my business.

Came the weekend and once again I was closeted with my brother, Tim.

"I've been playing around with the manuscript," he said.

"And?"

"I've read it three times now, and I've noticed some very odd things."

"Like what?"

"Specifically? Well, some of the chapters—Farrar's early career for one—seem to be building toward something and then fall flat at the end. There are paragraphs summarizing or glossing over certain episodes in Graham's life that don't have the same tone as the rest of the book. His brawls, his sexual escapades, especially. And I'd bet any amount of money that the last chapter was written by somebody other than Jordan."

"How so?"

"I don't know, it just doesn't feel right. Besides, I did a sentence word count on it with the computer, and the numbers didn't match up. I also ran a style analysis. No, I think another hand has been at work here—and not a fine Italian hand, if I may say so. The additions and changes are inferior to the underlying style of the book."

"You mean somebody else has been tinkering with that disk?"

"Just so," Tim said. "It's as though there were fingerprints all over it. But ..."

"What?"

"There's no way of knowing whose prints they are."

"I ought to have spotted that change in writing style," I said, "but I suppose I was in too much of a hurry to read the manuscript and too damned eager to find it publishable."

Tim smiled forgivingly. "We all nod from time to time, good brother," he said. Myself more often than himself, be it said.

·   ·   ·

After what seemed like a month—and actually it was only two days short of a month—Margo and I finally got together for dinner. Our restaurant of choice that Monday evening was Fortunato, a high-tech feeding trough on Park Avenue South whose prices are haute even if the cuisine is not.

We stood in the foyer and looked over the scene, taking in the flora (enormous plants reflected in long glittering mirrors) and fauna (stylishly dressed young things right out of *Vanity Fair* and *GQ*, being served by equally young things in equally stylish uniforms).

"A trendy spot," Margo said

"Nobody here over thirty-five but us."

"You're just grumbling because you're too old or too out of shape to play racquetball."

"Humph," I said. "I'm grumbling because we're standing here in line when we have a reservation."

We were finally seated, served a cocktail, and given the obligatory rambling recitation of the evening's specials by a sparkling young waitress who sounded as though she was auditioning for a part in an Andrew Lloyd Webber musical. After we ordered, Margo asked—nay, demanded—to be brought up to date. My account of recent events carried us all the way through *scampi, zabaglione*, and *caffe amaretto*.

"Well," she said when I'd finished, "you've been a busy boy, haven't you?"

"Not entirely by design."

"Oh, come on," she said. "You know you love being caught up in all this hugger-mugger. Admit it, Nick."

"Well . . ." Any more sheepish and I'd have been bleating. "I won't say it isn't more fun—or at least more interesting— than reading balance sheets."

"Except when Tim is threatened."

"Then it's no fun, you're right."

"So what d'you think?"

"Meaning?"

"Whodunit?"

"I can't be sure yet," I said. "All the signs point to Jeffrey, but I don't see any reason for him to do it. Why kill one of your best meal tickets?"

Margo sat for a moment, rubbing her lovely chin with a long vermilion fingernail.

"Are you sure there's *nothing* in the manuscript? No clue at all?"

"Nothing I could find on first reading." I had brought her up to date on Tim's suppositions that somebody else had been at work on the disk.

"What about *your* second reading?"

I just sat there for a moment, pondering the depth of my own stupidity. As a point of comparison, I felt about as stupid as I did the time I turned down the chance to publish Stephen King's first novel.

"Actually . . ."

"You mean *you* haven't gone over it again?"

I cleared my throat. "In a word, no."

"Why not?"

"I've been rather busy," I said. "One of my editors has read it."

"So what?"

"Lieutenant Scanlon and two of his sleuths have read it."

"And?"

"Tim has the electronic aspects under control. And ... ah ..."

"I see. Where is it now?"

"The manuscript? In the office, I suppose."

"Well, Nick?"

"Well what?"

"Why don't we go take a look at it?"

"Now? The office is closed."

"So open it. Have we got anything else planned for the rest of the evening?"

"Well, now, I *had* hoped—"

"Oh, Nick, let's not get on that topic again."

"If you say so, *dear*."

"Don't pout, Nicky. Wouldn't it be more fun to go up to your office and do some detecting—together, just the two of us?"

So there we were shortly afterward, under the lamplight, combing the manuscript of Jordan Walker's biography of Graham for a clue, any kind of a clue. "Detecting," as we were practicing it, was hardly distinguishable from browsing.

"There may be something in Graham's early years in the theater," I said. "Let's look at the chapter on Princeton."

"I know," she said. "You want to see what he may have said about you."

"I *know* what he said, darling. 'Nick Barlow, the publisher, son of the founders of Barlow and Company, was one of my classmates. Somehow we all knew he had a bright future.' "

"Is that all?"

"He gives me credit for being a good poker player. And for being a hell of a good host, especially when it came to popping champagne corks."

"I like the part about your bright future."

"All right, have your little joke. So I'm a son of a somebody. May I remind you that two of my predecessors at Princeton, many classes ahead of me, were named Harold McGraw, Junior, and Nelson Doubleday, also Junior?"

"Distinguished company."

"Back to business. Here—I'll read a page and then pass it on to you. If you spot something—"

"I'll yell."

Some time went by, I'm not sure how much. We were absorbed in reading through Jordan's book, page by page.

"How about this?" Margo said at one point. "The part about the guy he lived with on the Lower East Side when he was trying to break into the theater?"

I looked again at the paragraph in question. Graham spoke of another young actor, like him a beginner, like him struggling to establish a career.

" 'Tom Jefferson and I were both students at the Neighborhood Playhouse,' " I read aloud, " 'and for almost a year we shared a two-bedroom tenement apartment on Monroe Street. John Cage, the composer, also lived in the building, and we sometimes pooled our resources—which in my case meant an unemployment insurance check or a loan from my family—and feasted on squab and wild rice. We could sometimes even afford wine.' Why should that mean anything?"

"Do you suppose Graham's roommate was really named Thomas Jefferson?"

"Could have been a stage name," I said, "or he might have changed it. You know, there may be something there. We ought to check Equity and find out if he was a member, and what his real name was, if it wasn't that of our third president."

"Ah—Nick?" Margo's voice was soft but urgent.

"Yes?"

"I think we have company," she said. "Don't look now, but—well, maybe you'd better look."

I looked up from the manuscript, squinting a bit because the room was so dimly lit outside the range of the lamp on my desk. But even the half-light was enough to make it clear that Margo and I were no longer alone in the room.

There, standing in the doorway of the office, was Salvatore Marco. And this time he was wielding not a knife but a pistol.

"How the hell did you get in," I said, "and what do you want?"

"Fuck you, Barlow." His speech was slurred, and he shifted unsteadily back and forth on his heels.

"Marco, why don't you turn around and get out of here before that thing goes off and somebody gets hurt?"

"You fucking bastard, you . . . you tried to get me sent up, didn't you?"

So much for sweet reason. What now? Stalling for time? Prayer? I seriously considered the latter—the gun was pointed, quite accurately, at my chest. I could hear the blood in my ears, and my lips suddenly got puffy.

"If you've got a gripe with me," I said, "OK, fine. But leave the lady out of it."

He stared at Margo as though he hadn't realized she was in the room at all. Then back at me.

"You goddamn rich guys think you can get away with anything."

"What has that got to do with it?" *Stall for time, Barlow*, I told myself. *Keep him talking*. As Winston Churchill once remarked, "Jaw-jaw is better than war-war."

"You sound like you've got some kind of resentment," I said.

"You're damn right I do," Marco said. "Nobody sent me to college or handed a business to me on a silver platter. When did you ever have to worry about where your next meal was coming from? If you'd ever been in reform school instead of one of those fancy private schools you people go to, or even public school, you might feel differently about the rest of us."

I could not deny he had a point. One thing I would never, ever know—how successful I might have been on my own, by my own efforts and abilities. True, I had not wasted or shamed my inheritance, but there were times when I almost envied the self-made men and women of this world.

217

"So what do you expect *me* to do about your problems?"

"Cut the bullshit, Barlow. You don't give a fuck one way or the other. For you it's all fun and games." The very words I have sometimes used to describe my view of life and work.

Just then I saw, or rather glimpsed, Sidney Leopold. He was standing in the doorway behind Marco, a file folder in his hand, and gaping at us, mouth open like a fish. *God is with us after all!*

As quickly as he had appeared, Sidney vanished, an instant before Marco glanced back over his shoulder.

"Ah, shit," he said. "What am I wasting time for?"

What indeed?

Then a number of things happened. Just as Marco fired, I lunged to the right, swept my arm around and knocked Margo to the floor. I felt a sharp pain on my left side. Marco raised the gun to fire again, but before he got the chance, my lionhearted editor-in-chief rushed back into the room, clutching a heavy portfolio in his hands—a manuscript, in fact. With this he smote Salvatore Marco on the top of his skull with all his bantam strength. Marco swayed briefly like a wounded brute and then collapsed to the floor.

Margo got to her feet and took in the scene.

"Why did you knock me down, Nick?" she said. "I missed the whole damn thing."

"Lucky you, dear," I said. "Sidney?"

"Yes?" No stammering this time. Sidney Leopold, mild-mannered Sidney, was in command of the situation. "We'd better call the police, Nick."

"First we'll have to deal with this outlaw," I said. To make sure Marco didn't stir again, I went over and sat down on him, giving him the full benefit of my two hundred and forty-odd pounds. "We need something to tie him up with."

"I know what," said Sidney, and hurried off in the direction of the mailroom.

Margo picked up Marco's gun.

"What about this?"

"Just hold it in the well-known threatening position," I said. "In other words, keep him covered."

Now Sidney returned, with a roll of the wrapping tape reinforced with wire that we use to seal book packages.

"Just the thing, Sidney." I wound a generous yard of tape around Marco's wrists. "I defy anyone born of woman to break loose from this stuff." Certainly the publishing folk we sent our review copies to struggled with it.

Marco moaned softly underneath me. I leaned over and whispered "Shut up, *paisan*," into his ear.

"Nick, you're . . . there's blood on your shirt!"

So there was. Not a lot of it, but enough to get me a fair amount of sympathy from Margo. "Nicky, poor boy," she said, stroking my cheek. "You're *hurt*."

"Nothing serious," I said, and indeed, when I pulled out my shirttail, the wound turned out to be no more than an ugly laceration.

Sidney crossed the room to my desk and picked up the phone. "I'll c-call n-n-nine-one-one."

The two police officers who showed up in my office to haul Marco away looked familiar, as well they might. They were Artie, the black patrolman, and Buster, his young woman partner—the same dynamic duo who had responded to my call after the mugging. I shook both their hands warmly.

"Am I glad to see you two," I said.

"One for Riker's Island." Artie nudged the prostrate Salvatore Marco with his foot. Not a kick, exactly, just a prod. "You have the right to remain silent, asshole," he said to his prisoner, now securely handcuffed. "I would suggest you do."

"And one for the hospital." Buster pointed to the blood on my shirt.

"Nonsense," I said. "Iodine and a Band-Aid will do just fine."

"Don't worry," Margo said. "I'll take care of him." To me she whispered, "My *hero*."

I snorted. "Sidney is the real hero of this episode."

"W-well," our hero said, "I happened to b-be working late, and . . ."

The truth of the matter is, if Sidney were a nine-to-five man, both Margo and I—well, I don't want to think about what might have happened. Nothing, as far as I was concerned, was too good for Sidney.

.   .   .

"So you got Marco," Scanlon said. It was the following day, and he had come to my office "to pay a courtesy call."

"Sidney did, that's the truth of it."

"You're living dangerously, aren't you, Nick?"

"Still counting my blessings, Joe, that's all."

"I'm beginning to think the publishing business is almost as hazardous as police work."

I smiled but said nothing.

"At any rate," he said, "our little friend Salvatore won't get off so easily this time. Not even attorney Svenson can talk him out of this rap."

"I'm delighted," I said. "It may even be worth a bullet wound. Maybe."

Scanlon rose.

"You know, we'll just have to say that Sidney Leopold threw the book at him."

.   .   .

I was out most of the following morning, since Margo insisted on my seeing a doctor. My regular internist disinfected the wound—the scratch, rather—and bandaged it again. Feeling no worse than usual, I took lunch at home, caught up on my reading and mail, then headed in a leisurely fashion for the office. No appointments had been scheduled, and Hannah and Sidney both expressed a gratifying concern for my well-being, but it was otherwise business as usual.

I found a message on my desk from Tim.

"A real breakthrough!" he said, when I returned the call. "This is it. I found a chapter in the disk that wasn't in the Farrar bio I printed out for you. It looks like part of an earlier draft that had been rewritten. Anyway, there's quite a bit in it about this roommate of Graham's when he was a student at the Neighborhood Playhouse. If you recall, there's only a brief mention of Jefferson in the draft I gave you."

"As it happens," I said, "I just reread that section of the manuscript." And I told him what had happened to Margo and me in the office.

"You are having an adventurous time of it, aren't you?" he said.

"More than I bargained for. But go on, tell me what you think about the material you found."

"It's only a hunch," said Tim, "but I get the impression that this early relationship Graham had with Tom Jefferson may have been romantic."

Graham, the quintessential he-man involved in a homosexual affair? I found it hard to believe. But if Graham was bisexual . . .

"Tim," I said, "it may only be coincidence that we both picked up on this, but I know you don't believe in coincidence. I think we should track this Jefferson down."

Joe Scanlon agreed with me when I told him it was clear this section of Graham's life had been extensively cut from the original manuscript.

"I'll look into Jefferson through Actor's Equity," he said, "also the Screen Actors Guild, and get back to you."

It didn't take him long to find out what I'd already begun to suspect, that Thomas Jefferson was a stage name.

The actor's real name was Jeffrey Burgal.

26

By the next evening I was in Los Angeles. I drove in a rented Nissan from LAX to the Beverly Hilton, turned the car over to a valet, and headed straight for a house phone before I even checked in.

"Jeffrey?"

"Yes. Who is it?"

"Nick. Are you free?"

"Oh, Nick—Nick Barlow, I assume. How are things back East?"

"I'm not back East, Jeff, I'm—"

"I've meant to get in touch, but . . . you know how it is."

"Well, now, I know how it is back East, but I don't know how it is out West, so I decided to come and see."

"You mean . . . you're here?"

"Downstairs."

"So come up, by all means."

I checked in, dumped my overnight bag on the bed of my room, and took the elevator to Jeffrey's floor.

He greeted me in slacks, an open shirt, and slippers. Judging by the stubble on his chin and the condition of his hair, he'd just gotten out of bed. At this late hour? It wasn't like Jeffrey Burgal to let himself look disheveled. His handshake was effusive, almost as though he was glad to see me. I didn't buy it.

"You could have phoned, Nick."

"In too much of a hurry."

"So what's the big rush?" He plopped himself down on his living room couch and motioned me to the armchair. "Drink?"

"Thanks, no."

"You're sure?" He gestured toward his minibar.

"I'm sure. Jeffrey . . ."

"What is it, Nick?"

Not knowing how to begin this particular colloquy, I took a deep breath and plunged right in. "Jeffrey—or should I say 'Tom'?"

"Tom?" His eyes widened. "What's this?"

"Tom Jefferson."

He broke into laughter, a rising tide of mirth that started out strong and threatened to send him into a racking convulsion of laughter. I feared for his heart but couldn't help chuckling myself and then guffawing along with him. I suppose there is nothing in this world quite as contagious as laughter. At the same time I was quite aware that merriment is one of the easiest emotions for any actor to counterfeit.

When our mutual hilarity finally subsided, I managed to say, "So what's so funny?"

"Well, Nick, you must realize"—he wiped his eyes with a pocket handkerchief, then blew his nose loudly—"I haven't been Tom Jefferson for a long time. And anyway, what's that got to do with the price of potatoes?"

"I'm talking about Graham's biography," I said. "It would appear you played a rather more important role in his life than I realized."

"A much more important role than any I played on the stage," he said. "But so what?"

"Jeff." I was still uncertain quite how to proceed. "I wish you'd come back to New York." Scanlon had told me that he had insufficient evidence to extradite Burgal but hoped I might talk him into coming back. I said I would do my best.

"Why? Why should I come back now? I have work to do out here. I'm also helping your Jane Goodman with Graham's manuscript."

"We want you to help us clear up Jordan Walker's murder—and the murder of Dori Regan."

"We?"

"Lieutenant Scanlon and myself."

"Wouldn't you say that the book is considerably more important to us than any murder?"

Ordinarily I would have agreed with him, especially with all the money I had riding on Graham's life story, but now I remembered what Tim had said early along: "The murder case is the book."

"So you won't come back? You're under some suspicion, you know."

"For what? Changing my name years ago? Since when is that a criminal offense?"

"You *seem* to be implicated in the case and would surely be able to clear yourself *if* you came back and talked to the police."

Burgal thought this over, then frowned. "I think we've had this conversation once before," he said. "And my answer is still the same."

"So you won't help. You won't come back."

He shrugged. "Ultimately I'll have to be back. As soon as my work is done."

It seemed fruitless to attempt any further persuasion, so I rose, nodded, and left without shaking hands, without a word of farewell. Nor did Jeffrey speak to me. What was there to say?

Jane was not in her hotel room, nor was she at Graham's home. His Japanese manservant told me when I phoned that she "not here ahr day."

I found her by the Hilton pool lying on a chaise, brown and slender in her bikini, sporting turquoise shades and a wide-brimmed floppy panama hat. Altogether a pleasant sight, like an advertisement for an expensive perfume or an elegant cigarette. "Hello, Jane," I said. "Enjoying L.A., are you?"

"Nick!" She sat up and pulled off her shades. "I didn't expect you. What brings you here?"

"Just checking on the progress of the book. You're not working with Graham today?"

"He's on location," she replied. "Not a big part, just a cameo in a big picture."

"Getting his usual million or two."

"I suppose so," she said. "I didn't ask. We've been working just about every day, for hours. I haven't had much pool time."

The color of her body rather belied this last remark, but I made no comment. I pulled up a chair, sat down, and stared intently at her for a moment, looking to see if she had gone native yet. Going Hollywood: a certain blasé attitude toward large sums of money. The stars dim in one's eyes—or are extinguished altogether. I decided that she had not yet succumbed to the perfume of the lotus. Almost, but not quite.

"How's it going, really?"

"Quite well, I think." Her voice was animated, musical. "And Jeffrey agrees."

"Good. May I see what you've got so far?"

"By all means, Nick." She gathered up her towel and slipped into a robe. "Come up to my room. I have the first part of the manuscript there, all retyped."

Back in my own room, I took off the rubber band, opened the folder Jane had given me, and took out the hundred or so sheets of paper. The text was single-spaced, but the type was reasonably large. I put on my reading glasses and set to it.

An hour later I put the manuscript back in the folder and reattached the rubber band. I was debating whether or not to call Jeffrey and give him my opinion of the material, when the phone rang. It was Jane.

"Well?"

I could sense the eagerness but decided not to spare her feelings. This was a strictly professional situation.

"Well," I said, "it many be better than it was, but it's still not good enough."

"Oh." A silence. "Do you want to be more specific?"

"I've marked places where it needs attention."

"But overall?"

"Overall it's still too ... well, *bland*, damn it. There's still not enough juice in the writing, and not enough of Graham's early years." And certainly nothing about a liaison with one Jeffrey Burgal, aka Thomas Jefferson.

"What do you suggest I do, Nick?"

"Get back to it," I said. "Pump Graham dry if you have to." I was beginning to believe this book was another lost cause, a promising project that somehow misfired, got lost on its way to the best-seller list. "Hang in, Jane. Persist."

"Maybe if you stayed for a while and spoke to Graham—"

"No," I said. "Not this time. I'm on my way back as soon as I can get a return flight."

And so I was, so quickly I had no time to suffer from jet lag—and empty-handed at that. Joe Scanlon would have to wait for Jeffrey to show up in his own sweet time.

27

It was back to the hum and the drum. Scanlon had nothing to report; Tim had found nothing else on the disk that might prove helpful. As a detective, I considered myself a total flop. As a publisher, not much better. Here I was sitting on what was supposed to be the lead title on my fall list, and it read like a *Reader's Digest* article.

It was status quo ante until three days later, when I found a message on my desk that Jane had phoned from California. I was in no hurry to return her call—I assumed it was her regular report—so I busied myself with other matters, and inevitably Jane's message got buried under manuscripts and correspondence. I forgot all about it until Hannah told me that Jane was on the phone, calling from Los Angeles. *Oops.*

I was going to apologize, but she didn't give me time, opening the conversation on a pitch just short of hysteria.

"Is it in the New York papers yet?"

"Is what in the papers, Jane?"

"Jeffrey Burgal, Nick. He's dead."

"Oh, my God! Are you sure?"

"Well, I haven't seen the body, but they say he drowned in a hot tub."

I sat for a moment in silence, until I recovered the power of speech enough to whisper, "When did it happen?"

"Yesterday," Jane said. "And there's bound to be a perfect circus about it—reporters, TV cameramen, gossip columnists, the works—because it was Graham's hot tub that he drowned in."

"Oh my. My oh my."

"They're calling it an accident, Nick."

"Thank God for small favors. Exactly how did it happen?"

"They won't know until the autopsy, but they suspect he fell asleep in the tub. And that was it."

I didn't know whether to feel relieved or upset. At this point I had become disenchanted by his evasiveness, his lack of cooperation in the investigation. Some of his authors might miss him, I suppose, but few if any publishers would. And his death certainly eliminated the possibility of questioning him further about the Walker case. Whatever he might have been hiding had gone down the drain of Graham Farrar's hot tub.

"Where are you now, Jane?"

"In Graham's study."

"May I talk to him?"

"He's too upset to talk now, Nick. This has hit him really hard, and . . ."

"And what? Come *on*, Jane."

"All right, he's lying low for a while, to avoid the press."

"OK, Jane—thanks for letting me know. Keep in touch, will you?"

"Sure, Nick."

I couldn't reach Scanlon until the following day. I didn't have to tell him the bad news—he'd already heard it.

"We're not having a whole lot of luck with this business, are we?" he said. Then he told me he would call an acquaintance of his on the LAPD to find out as much as he could about Jeffrey's death, after which he'd call me back.

It was almost four hours later when I finally heard from him. The M.E. had reported in by then. Burgal had a count of seven milligrams of alcohol in his bloodstream, much more than enough to have him charged with drunk driving if he'd been on the freeway instead of dunking himself. And he hadn't drowned. What had happened, Scanlon explained, was that the poor sap fell asleep and just stayed in the tub too long. A human being can endure a water temperature of 117 degrees for only a half-hour or so. After that—well, there is no after that.

"In other words, Joe," I said, "alcohol and boiling water don't mix."

"Something like that, Mr. Barlow—I mean, Nick."

Something about Jeffrey's death bothered me, some nagging little detail. What was it? Oh, yes.

"Incidentally," I said, "did your friend in L.A. say the medical examiner's report showed Jeffrey to be a drug addict?"

"No, he didn't," Scanlon said. "Why?"

I told him what I had seen in Jeffrey's hotel bathroom.

"And he didn't want you to see the needle? Interesting. I'll look into that."

That evening I headed for The Players, still troubled by some elusive aspect of Jeffrey Burgal's death, an irritating question I couldn't quite put into words.

Whatever I thought of Jeffrey Burgal the man, or the literary agent, I lifted my first glass in the Grill Room to him, toasting Jeffrey silently. Every dead Player deserves some final recognition at 16 Gramercy Park.

In one corner of the grill a bridge game was in progress; another member, his right foot planted on the brass rail, was playing chess with the barman, who had to abandon the board—reluctantly, for apparently he was winning—whenever someone called for a refill. In the background I could hear the soft hiss and click of pool balls colliding, and all around me the soothing hum of conversation wafted my way through a cloud of cigarette smoke.

I had sat in this room not too long ago with Jeffrey, on the night of the mugging. I had ordered a vodka martini, like the one I held in my hand now, stirred not shaken, cold and clear, and he ...

He had *not* ordered a drink. Doctor's orders, he'd said.

Then why had he had been drinking in California—enough to pass out in a hot tub?

If he had stopped drinking because of his health, then why had he fallen off the wagon so suddenly?

And what about the evidence—the possibility at least—of drugs?

I drained my glass and slammed it down on the table. Heads turned in my direction. Even the barman put down the chesspiece he was about to move and stared at me. I couldn't have cared less. Had I been a cartoon character, as I sometimes fantasize myself to be (black and white during the week, four color on Sundays), a light bulb would have flashed above my head.

I had an idea. But there was only one way to find out for sure—and I'd have to wait until the next morning to do it.

· · ·

"Dr. Cook's office." The nurse who answered my phone call had a pleasant, matronly voice. I pictured her in her late forties or early fifties, efficient and organized, watchdog of the doctor's time. And I had to break through that protective screen.

"This is Nicholas Barlow speaking."

"Yes, Mr. Barlow?"

"You may have heard of me—the book publisher?"

"Oh, yes, Mr. Barlow. I've read books published by your firm, I remember them well. Yes, indeed." An improbable reply—who remembers a book's publisher?—but gratifying all the same.

"And you're?"

"Miss Vane. What can I do for you, Mr. Barlow?"

"A patient of yours, Mr. Jeffrey Burgal, recommended Dr. Cook to me." This at least was the truth. "You know Mr. Burgal?"

"Oh, yes, Mr. *Burgal*." Recognition in her voice, but no sign that she knew of Jeffrey's death. Could that be possible? The story, complete with pictures of Graham's hot tub, had appeared on page 3 of the *Daily News* (and on page 28 of *The New York Times*, sans photos). Perhaps she wasn't a newspaper reader.

"I'd like to make an appointment with Dr. Cook," I said.

"I'm sorry, but I'm afraid he's quite booked up for the whole of next week. And the week after. He's not eager to take on new patients, you know. Perhaps I can recommend someone. What seems to be your problem?"

I was desperate enough to invent any ailment that sounded reasonable. "I think it may be a kidney problem." A wild stab. I didn't even know what Cook's specialty might be. "Pain . . . severe pain in the area of the kidneys."

"Both kidneys?"

"Well, only one. At a time."

"Discoloration of the urine?"

"Oh, yes, absolutely."

"Well . . ."

"Couldn't you possibly squeeze me in? Today . . . somehow? Any time at all?" By now I was so determined to get an appointment no matter what that I might almost have convinced myself that I was in pain.

"Well, if you could come promptly at twelve."

"I'll be there at a quarter to."

And so I was, looking as woebegone as a man in the pink of health and the prime of life can look. Pain, albeit counterfeit pain, blatantly evident in my demeanor, especially in the way I occasionally clutched my side whenever Miss Vane glanced in my direction. Only one other sufferer was with me in Dr. Cook's anteroom, an elderly man with a few tufts of white hair jutting out wildly on an otherwise starkly bald skull, his complexion the shade of saffron rice. From time to time I leafed desperately through copies of *National Geographic* and the *Harvard Medical Letter*.

Miss Vane was solicitous.

"Mr. Burgal is quite a nice man," she said. So she still hadn't heard the sad news. "Do you work with him, Mr. Barlow?"

"Oh, yes, I have, many times," I said. "Prudence Henderson Harte was among the authors he represented." Not for me the present tense.

"Um," she said. Just "um."

After two minutes of filling out a short form and half an hour's wait, I was ushered into Dr. Cook's private office. He was on the phone, so I had a few moments to look at his diplomas, photos of his family, certifications of his membership in various societies, and a parchment naming him the Best Dressed Man in Palm Springs, California, 1983.

And the doctor himself. Tall, lanky, with a full shock of pale red hair, turning white around the temples. He spoke with a pronounced Yankee twang, saying into the phone such dismaying things as "If the patient goes into coma, administer dexaphalin intravenously. . . . And call me if you see signs of [medical term, medical term], though I think it likely to be irreversible. . . . Just can't offer much hope. . . . Good-bye."

"Nicholas Barlow." He hung up the phone and studied my form. "Recommended by Jeffrey Burgal." He raised his bony face and gazed at me with a pair of unblinking gray eyes. "A friend?"

"Yes, in a way, Doctor. Business associate, actually. Sad, wasn't it?" I gestured toward the copy of the *Times* that lay folded up on his file cabinet.

Cook nodded.

"In fact," I said, "an absurd way for someone like Jeffrey to die. He was absolutely the last person to be caught dead in a trend."

"I suppose you might say that, Mr. Barlow. But what"— he cleared his throat sharply—"seems to be your problem?"

"Jeffrey Burgal," I said, "is the problem."

"I beg your pardon?"

"To be specific, Doctor, I'm really here for information about Jeffrey—important information."

"Mr. Barlow"—the doctor rose to his full height, which I judged to be about six feet seven inches—"I'm extremely busy. There are people out in the other room waiting to see me, people in genuine need of medical attention. You have finagled your way in here under, I would say, false pretenses, and now you tell me you want information about a patient—"

"A dead patient, Dr. Cook. Please hear me out or at least give me a moment or two. It may save you another, less agreeable interview with the police later on."

"No innuendos, Mr. Barlow. Just what do you mean? And by what right do you presume to question me? Are you a member of the police force?"

"No, certainly not."

"Then why should I talk to you? If the police want to talk to me, why not send a policeman? Are you by chance a private detective?" He let me know by the tone of his voice what he thought of gumshoes.

"I'm a book publisher. Actually—well, actually—I mean I'm *assisting* the police in a murder case and—well ..." I could see clearly that I was getting nowhere rapidly with the good doctor. So I smiled my most disingenuous smile, hoping somehow to disarm him.

Cook lifted his copy of the *Times* as though it were a specimen of diseased tissue. "Mr. Burgal's death was an accident. It says so right here in the paper."

"Mr. Burgal was a suspect in the murder of one of my authors, Dr. Cook. You've heard of the Jordan Walker case?"

"I don't follow the crime news, Mr. Barlow. Accounts of random violence do not interest me."

"Be that as it may, the police were quite anxious—eager, in fact—to talk to Jeffrey. As was I."

He spread his hands. "I don't see how *I* can help you."

"But you can—by giving me medical information about him."

"You know that our relationship, like all doctor-patient relationships, is privileged."

I sighed. "All right, it's privileged. However, let me remind you once more, if you're summoned to testify in a murder trial—which I certainly hope would not be necessary ... And I can assure you that I have Mr. Burgal's interest at heart."

"All right, Mr. Barlow." He frowned, sat down again. Drummed on the desk with the fingertips of his right hand.

Reached for the phone and then changed his mind. His attorney, perhaps? I would never know.

"What is it you wish to learn?" he said at last. "Mind you, I can't promise to answer your questions. It will . . . well, it will depend on the questions."

"Fair enough. First, was Jeffrey an alcoholic?"

"He was not."

"Was he a drug addict?"

Cook snorted. "Most certainly not."

"Then what was his medical problem? Why did he have to stop drinking?"

"I should think that would be obvious, even to a layman like yourself. He ought never to have drunk alcohol in the first place. Jeffrey Burgal was a diabetic."

"And so drinking—"

"Was potentially fatal to him," Cook said. "I warned him off liquor early on. He knew the dangers of drinking. But—"

"Then why would he suddenly start drinking—and to excess, at that?"

The doctor shrugged his shoulders. In that gesture I saw all his compassion for human weakness revealed, along with all his contempt for human folly.

"Who knows?" he said. "He may have been tired of life. The drinking was a form of suicide, perhaps. Whoever knows?"

I thanked him for his help and rose to leave.

"Mr. Barlow," he said.

I stopped and turned. "Yes?"

"May I assume that I will not see you again? Unless, of course, genuine illness brings you here?"

"You may."

He smiled wanly. "Then I wish you many long years of robust health."

· · ·

Back in my office, I called Scanlon.

"Hello?"

"Lieutenant Scanlon? Joe?"

"That you, Nick? What's up?"

234

I told him about my talk with Dr. Cook and gave him the big news. Jeffrey Burgal was *not* a drug addict.

"I could have told you that, Nick."

"Oh?"

"Sure. The M.E. in L.A. told me there were indications Burgal had been using a hypodermic needle, but that the punctures were subcutaneous. Junkies go for a vein, diabetics usually inject in the hip or the thigh, so they can use either hand. And that's what Burgal did."

"Oh," was all I could say.

"Or so I was told." He hesitated, listening to my silence. "Never mind, Nick. It was a very good shot. You did fine with the doc. We'll make a cop out of you yet."

And that was that. Next stop, Connecticut—and Tim.

.   .   .

We began by playing chess. I know of no better way of focusing the mind, clearing it both of distractions and preoccupations.

At chess Tim is the master and I the pupil. He plays three or four moves ahead of my two. I felt lucky to come out with one draw against a pair of losses, one of them mate in seven moves. I cursed him for that—affectionately, of course.

"All right," Tim said as I turned my king on its side. "Tell me what you've found out."

"Before we move on to that subject," I said, "have the state police made any progress tracking down our intruders?"

"Negative."

"That's what I was afraid of."

"So it goes," said Tim. "Next."

I related it all to him, right through my interview with Dr. Cook.

"I have all the pieces in hand now," I said. "At least I think I have most of them—all I'm probably going to get. And Scanlon has some of them. But they just don't fit together."

"So give me your summation of the business."

"We have—I mean *had*—four suspects," I said. "Five, if you count Graham himself. One—the porter at Jordan's apartment building. A man with an expensive habit and access to Jordan's apartment. Building supers always have passkeys, and the porter might have lifted or copied it. Let's suppose that Jordan surprises him during a break-in. The guy grabs the first weapon he can find, a knife, and does Jordan in. Two— Salvatore Marco. Scanlon and Snyder liked Marco at first, but I'm not so sure about it. And he came after me, bear that in mind."

"You can't blame him for being ticked off."

"Oh, *can't* I just."

"But why would either of them want the manuscript sanitized?"

"Well, if it was one of them, the murders would have to be unrelated to the editing job. Or maybe Marco was working for somebody."

"Fair enough. Next?"

"Jeffrey Burgal makes three," I said. "Evasive, elusive—and now dead. If he did it, that's an end of it all."

"But you don't figure him for it."

"I can't see his motive. I mean, he may have wanted to stay in the closet, but that's not enough to kill for, not nowadays. Besides, I can't imagine Jeff bludgeoning Dori Regan to death, can you?"

"Well, you know him better than I, and even you didn't know him that well. Who's to say what he was capable of? What about Graham?"

"What about him? He had the temper to commit the murders, but what was his motive?"

"To cover his affair with Jeffrey. That sort of thing can still hurt a career in Hollywood, even today. Especially the career of a leading man. Remember Rock Hudson."

"Graham's leading stud days are just about over. Besides, Graham *commissioned* the biography. Why would he do that if he had something to hide? For that matter, how did Jordan learn about the affair if not from Graham or Jeff?"

"All right, all right. What about Angela?"

"Angela Farrar. Every motive, every opportunity, and yet . . ."

"What?"

"It's too simple. I don't like things to be quite so uncomplicated."

Tim shrugged. "Typical publisher's mentality."

"I suppose you're right."

"Too bad we can't do it by the book," he said. "Get all these people into the same room, stage a reenactment of the murder, and expose the killer, who panics and promptly confesses."

"Shades of Ellery Queen—"

"And Nero Wolfe—"

"Well, he had a good excuse. He never left West 35th Street."

"But you and I," I said, "wouldn't give houseroom to an author who fell back on that tired old device, would we?"

"Why don't you go pay a visit to Mother?" Tim said. "Or walk the dogs, whatever appeals to you. I want to give this a lot of serious thought."

"I feel—" I spread my hands helplessly.

"Go ahead," said Tim.

"I feel the whole thing is about to bust loose on us. Damn it, Tim, *something's* got to give, or I'll go off my trolley. D'you know what I mean?"

Tim nodded. He knew.

•　　•　　•

It was Sunday afternoon, the following day, before Tim brought the subject up again.

"I have a theory," he said, "which you'll have to prove or disprove. In person."

"All right."

"It means going out to California again."

I sighed. "Okay, Tim."

"Now then," he said. "Listen carefully. This is what I want you to do. . . ."

28

Jane met me at the airport in the Datsun. We joined the passing parade on the freeway, saying little to each other at first, isolated from exhaust fumes and traffic noises by tightly closed windows, air-conditioning, and the radio. After a while, tiring of billboards, shopping centers, and housing developments, I turned to Jane.

"How's it going? Your collaboration with Graham?"

"Fine," she said. "Making progress."

Which meant what? Her lips had tightened at the word *collaboration*.

"You haven't said what brings you out to California this time," she said.

"That's right. I haven't said." My reply just lay there between us, the victim of my uncertainty as to how much Jane should be told.

"Graham is waiting for us at the house," she said.

"Good."

"I hope you're not going to press him in any way."

"What do you mean, press him? Is there some problem?"

"It's just that he's been under quite a bit of pressure lately, with his *Odyssey* project mostly, and ... and I don't think he has much resilience at the moment. I thought perhaps you've come out here to push the book along faster."

"Why should I do that? You've just told me you're making progress."

"So I did. And so we are."

"Jane, you're being awfully vague."

"And what are you being, Nick? Open?"

"Hell, I don't think I have to be. My business with Graham today is personal."

"I see."

"And private."

"Whatever you say."

She was silent until we got to Pacific Palisades, and then made only the most perfunctory comments. As we wound through the hills, passing acres of scrub pine forest, much of it burned out or second growth, I decided I really should make some effort to bring her into the picture.

"Where were you when Jeffrey Burgal had his accident?" I asked her.

"In my room at the Beverly Hilton,"

"Do you happen to know why Jeffrey was out at Graham's house, Jane?"

"No, I don't. Jeffrey came and went frequently. Sometimes he stayed over, other times he drove back to the Hilton the same night."

So Graham had been alone with Jeffrey. No one else around to pull him out of the tub before it was too late. No witnesses. Here I was, not even at his doorstep, already charging Graham with, at the best, negligence. And the worst?

Once on Farrar property, we fell silent again and just drove through Graham's Ithaca, acres of rock and sand and beach grass. At the gatehouse we were stopped and questioned by the same gorilla who had greeted us before. This time he positively radiated hostility and suspicion, glaring at me and not even returning Jane's fetching, dimpled smile. I'd seen this goon at least twice now, and I liked him less each time.

"We can't all have the advantage of a liberal education," I said when we were through the gate and on our way up to the house.

"He's that way with everybody," Jane said.

We found Graham sitting out on his terrace, looking at the sea and nursing a Bloody Mary. He offered to pour one for each of us from a pitcher on a nearby serving table. I nodded yes. Jane shook her head no.

When I asked how his movie plans were coming, he grimaced. "Those *people*," he used a harsh snarl that left no doubt as to which people he meant. "All they do is 'take' meetings. One goddamn meeting after another."

"Sounds like the publishing business."

"Only worse," he said. "So little gets accomplished—except frustration. *Hollywood.*" The word sounded like a Baptist preacher's reference to Sodom or Gomorrah.

"Hollywood." When Jane said it there was an almost reverential note in her voice. The silver screen obviously had its magnetism for her, although I expected she'd grown up dreaming of rock stars rather than movie stars. Still, whatever else may be said of the movie business, it still manufactures America's most resonant myths.

"Actually," Graham said, reading her mind if not mine, "the Hollywood that meant so much to all of us is dead. Long gone. Preserved for posterity in the film library of the Museum of Modern Art or in the revival houses. Go see Selznick's *The Prisoner of Zenda*—glamour and romance and pure escapism in glorious black and white. Or *The Trail of the Lonesome Pine*, Henry Fonda and Fred MacMurray—both so incredibly young. And Spanky McFarland, for Christ's sake!" He rolled his eyes, silent-comedy style, at which point both Jane and I burst out laughing.

Graham's own laughter quickly shifted into a prolonged sigh. He shook his head as though to clear it of whatever memories were pressing to be given audience.

"Graham," I said after a silence, "I know you probably hate talking about Jeffrey's death—"

"Goddamn right I do."

Jane got up to go. "I have things to do," she said. "If you two will excuse—"

"I want you to stay, Jane," Graham said.

It was a command, not a request. She sat down. He turned to me and said, "So what's on your mind?"

I remembered Tim's instructions. I had to get to the bar. Alone.

"Let's have another drink first," I said.

Graham gestured toward the pitcher on the glass table.

"No, something a little stronger," I said. "Don't bother to get up, Graham, I know where the bar is. I'll fix it myself."

He shrugged, and I went through the sliding glass doors to Graham's living room. So far so good. At the bar I fixed myself an extremely dry vodka martini, straight up, cutting off a thin slice of lemon peel and rubbing it on the edge of the glass with elaborate care. Meanwhile I opened the drawers of Graham's bar one by one. In the second drawer, along with corkscrews, stirrers, the little fork you use to stab olives out of their jar, and lots of coasters and bar napkins, I found what I was looking for: a long, thin tube made out of red rubber.

Right on the money, Tim!

He hadn't even bothered to dispose of it—probably thought no one would know what it was or what it had been used for. And he had come damn close to being right. I slipped the tube into my pocket and returned to the terrace.

"You look mighty pleased with yourself, chum," Graham said. "That's what we call a shit-eating grin out here."

So much for being evasive. I raised my glass.

"I do make a helluva good martini, if I say so myself."

"How can anybody make a bad one?" Graham said. "It's just straight booze, right?"

I sipped my drink in what I hoped was a nonchalant fashion. Graham stared at me, unblinking, tapping his fingers lightly on the arm of his chair.

"Isn't it?" he said.

I nodded, then looked over at Jane, who was shifting uncomfortably in her chair. Then she glanced at her watch and started to her feet again.

"I really must—"

This time I stopped her by leaning over and resting my hand on her arm.

"Not yet," I said.

"Don't linger on my account," Graham said.

"No rush."

"If you still have problems with the book—" he started.

"None," I said.

"Then what the hell brought you here? I don't mean to sound inhospitable, but *I'm* busy, I'm sure *you're* busy—so just what's on your mind, Nick?"

"Well, Graham," I said, "we do have a problem, and I not only don't know how to solve it, I'm not even sure how to articulate it." I paused. "I was going to put it to you as a possible screenplay a writer I know is doing, or as a detective story where the sleuth is stuck for a solution to the crime, but since you asked, I'll give it to you straight. Graham, I think you murdered Jeffrey Burgal. You, or somebody working for you."

I have no powers of description sufficiently eloquent to render the expression on Jane's face, but her hands opened and closed convulsively.

Graham, on the other hand, decided to treat it as a joke. He opened his mouth wide and went "Haw-haw." *Okay, Graham*, I thought, *now I've got your attention. Here goes.*

"I don't know why," I said, "but I do know *how.*"

"And what makes you think you know anything?" Graham used his patented screen sneer.

"My conscience," I replied.

"Oh bullshit." He raised his glass to his mouth, drained it down to the pink-tinged ice cubes. These he ostentatiously rattled around in the glass.

"My conscience lives in the family seat in Connecticut," I said. "He doesn't get around much, so he has plenty of time to read and think. If it hadn't been for him, I could never have put together what went on here. But he sketched the outline clearly enough for me to fill in the picture."

"Crystal-ball crap," Graham said.

"This isn't funny, Nick," Jane said.

"Tell your writer his plot is—"

"Graham, goddamn it, stop interrupting me. I realize this is

242

your house and I'm a guest in it, but I mean to finish what I came here to say, one way or another, whether you like it or not. And if you won't listen to me, I'll go to the police and tell them. Is that what you'd prefer?"

"I should think you'd have gone there first."

"No, as a matter of fact, I still hold you in some esteem. I even have a feeling of friendship—"

"Hell, I don't know who would believe you anyhow."

"It's quite a clever scheme, you know, and virtually unde-tectable." I was speaking to Jane now; Graham was glaring silently into his empty cocktail glass. "Jeffrey was a diabetic and obviously needed regular shots of insulin, which he was trained to give himself. Somebody—and I'm thinking of you, Graham—substituted vials of plain tap water for Jeffrey's insu-lin. There's no way you could tell them apart. When Jeffrey injected himself with one of the ineffectual vials, he went into a diabetic coma. While he was out of commission, I surmise that you, Graham, stuck a Levine tube down his esophagus into his stomach. You then poured a hell of a lot of alcohol down a funnel through that tube. An easy matter to stick Jeffrey in your hot tub and let nature do the rest. The medical examiner's verdict—accidental death."

"What's a Levine tube?" This from Jane.

For my answer I reached into my pocket.

"Found in the drawer of Graham's bar." I withdrew the tube. Nor could I help but feel exultant. *Gotcha!*

"Bastard." Graham shook his head in mock admiration. "You sneaky bastard. Remind me never to invite you out here again. So that's your story, Nick?"

"That's it."

"It'll never sell," Graham said. "Never, no way, no how. Not even a publisher as slick as you are can put that one across."

"We'll see," I said.

"That's my property there." He pointed to the Levine tube, still dangling from my hand. "Stolen from me by your own admission."

I put it back in my pocket.

"I'll just hang on to it for a while, Graham, if you don't

mind. After you've cleared yourself, at least to my satisfaction, I'll let you have it back."

"You call that evidence?"

"There may still be a couple of those fake insulin vials around in Jeffrey's effects," I said. "You could have been careless about that, too."

Graham chuckled. "Oh my," he said, "this is a friend indeed. Ill met, old man. I hope you're on your way."

"You bet I am."

"And don't come back. Understand?"

"All right, Graham. Though I'm sorry it has to be this way, I really am. Coming, Jane?"

She raised her hands in a mute appeal for help. She looked first at me and then at Graham. He remained impassive.

"I guess I'm going with you, Nick. But, Graham, please try to understand—"

"Fuck off," he said.

"Oh, Christ, Graham," Jane said, "you know I'll be back."

He turned away from both of us, staring out toward the ocean again. We let ourselves out, headed for the car.

"Nick . . ." said Jane.

"Don't do it," I said.

"I think I'd better go back. He needs me."

"Not now."

"But what will he do?"

"That," I said, "is up to Graham. He's the director of our little drama. And the producer." I knew that I probably sounded histrionic, but I didn't bother to apologize. Graham, after all, wasn't the only actor around. I felt as though I had just gone through an opening night myself: heart pumping away like 60, damp palms. Anyway, I'd brought it off. Your cue, Graham.

The sky was aboil with great darkening clouds when we escaped from Graham's house—the ideal setting for my present mood. In part because of the storm ahead, in part because I no longer felt comfortable on Graham's property, I hurried Jane to the car with almost indecent haste.

"I just can't . . . walk . . . that fast," she said.

244

"We're not welcome here," I said. "At least I'm not."

"Oh, Nick," she said, "do you think he'll forgive me for running out on him?"

"You aren't running out, for God's sake. We're being kicked out."

We said no more to each other until we were inside our car. Sporadic drops of rain had begun to splatter on the windshield. I turned the ignition key, gunned the engine, then turned on the wipers.

"What will happen to Graham?" Jane asked, an unspoken plea for mercy implicit in her anguish.

"He'll undoubtedly think of something," I said. "He can afford the best lawyers in the country. And when did you last hear of a multimillion-dollar movie star going to jail?"

"You sound so cynical, Nick. So bitter."

"I am. And disillusioned as well, though I thought I'd lost all my illusions long ago. I admired Graham. I won't say I liked him, though maybe once . . . well, I respected him. What he stood for. You know what I mean. *Shit.*"

As we moved down the winding driveway toward the highway, the rain mounted in intensity, until it streamed off the hood and fenders. When we approached the gatehouse, the guard stepped out in the road, one meaty hand on the pistol hanging from his belt. He was wearing an old rubber rainhat that only deflected the rain from his head to his shoulders and arms. I felt rather than saw him stare impassively at us. As we neared him, speeding up, the car skidded on the wet drive and turned broadside. When I tried to get the car moving again, the wheels kept spinning and hissing in the mud. Out of the corner of my eye, I saw the guard reach inside the gatehouse and pick up a phone. I threw the car into reverse, then into forward—reverse, forward, reverse—the wheels kept spinning and hissing. Suddenly the car began moving backward down the drive.

And then, a second or two later, a hole big enough to let in the rain opened in the windshield, a sunburst of cracked glass spreading out all around it, and I heard a dull *boom!* close after.

245

"Get down, Jane, for God's sake. Down!"

A stifled scream, then she ducked down under the dashboard, huddling in a fetal crouch. The fear I saw in her eyes was nothing to the paralyzing terror I felt in my stomach.

Another bullet buried itself in the back of her seat with a *chung* ... the son of a bitch had the range. If he got his aim right ...

We skidded again, heading now for the woods, still within range of the gatehouse, targets in a shooting gallery. More by instinct than anything else, I spun the wheel, shoved the stick shift into reverse, and floored the gas pedal. We barreled straight backward, heading right toward the gatehouse. In the rearview mirror I saw the goon, his gun pointed at us—then the mirror, too, exploded.

I heard his scream when the car carried the gatehouse, with him in it, back off the road and into a clump of trees. It was a sound I won't forget—ever.

When the car finally came to a halt, listing about fifteen degrees to starboard and trailing broken branches, I hauled Jane off the floor and inspected us both for damages. She was trembling uncontrollably but was unharmed except for a few superficial cuts from flying glass. I wasn't so rock-steady myself, and I looked as though I'd been in a catfight. When we got out of the car—battered, punctured, ready for the automobile graveyard—Jane held her scarf out in the rain until it was soaked through, then sponged the blood off my face.

I limped over to what was left of the gatehouse. In the midst of it, crumpled up in a bloody twisted heap of clothing, lay the guard.

"A hit," I murmured, feeling nauseated. "A palpable hit."

"Nick," I heard Jane cry out, "are we safe now?"

"Safe as houses." I held an arm out to keep her from coming any closer to the wreckage. "You don't want to look, Jane."

On the side of the road a few feet from the gatehouse, I found the gun that had almost done us in. A .357 Magnum. I felt a sudden, perverse surge of anger directed at this piece of deadly blue steel and drew back my arm to hurl it into the woods. Then, without really knowing why, I stuck it in my pocket.

"Let's get the hell out of here," I said.

"No."

"What d'you mean 'no,' Jane? For Christ's sake!" We were both soaked by now, blood still trickling from our scratches—and she wanted to stick around?

"I'm going back to the house," she said.

"But that's crazy! Look—what the hell! Graham just tried to have us killed."

"The man's in trouble, can't you see that? The man needs help. He trusts me, Nick. I'm the only one he can trust now."

I put my hand on her arm to hold her back, but she pulled away from me violently.

"No, Jane, please—I'm asking you as a friend."

She started to run back up the driveway.

"All right, I'm ordering you to stay here. As your boss, goddamn it!"

She stopped and turned toward me. "Whether you go with me or not, I'm going."

What could I do? I had no choice, really. I couldn't let her go by herself, stupid as it was. So against my better judgment—hell, against my worst judgment—I started after her.

"Okay!" I called out to her. "Okay! Wait up for me, will you?" Puffing a bit from the effort, I caught up with Jane and took her by the arm.

"But this time," I told her, "Graham is going to have to give us *all* the answers."

29

We found him sitting in his living room, a drink clutched in his hand. He hadn't turned on the lights, although the storm had brought on an early twilight. When I flipped on the switch by the door, he looked up at us with a puzzled half-smile. I kept my hand in my coat pocket, firmly on the butt of the gun.

"Ah," he said. "Back so soon."

"Not according to plan, I know," I said.

"It happens." He sighed heavily. "Things don't always work out ... as planned. Scenarios have to be rewritten, do they not?"

"Graham, *I* intend to rewrite this one."

"Do you now? Well, then." He put down his drink, letting his right hand fall from the arm of the chair.

"At least," I said, "you might have had the guts to kill me yourself."

"Quite so," he said. "I should have." He gestured toward a pistol lying on the endtable. "Shall I do it now? It's rather late for that, Nick."

I felt the Magnum heavy and reassuring in my pocket. Graham's eyes were slits, and he sighed, a deep, desolate sigh.

"So suppose you have me killed or kill me yourself," I said. "How do you explain it away?"

"You were trespassing," he said. "I heard you come in the door—how did I know it was you and not an intruder?"

"You thought it was your goon, didn't you?"

He nodded. "How did you get away from him?"

"We used him for a parking space."

"That's very good." Graham smiled again. "I like that. You've always been witty, Nick."

"I don't need anybody to write my one-liners, if that's what you mean."

"I suppose so. Anyhow—I'll miss you." He turned his head away for an instant but, when I edged forward a step, snapped it back again. "Don't worry, Nick. You won't have to shoot me. Unless you want to."

"What were you thinking, Graham? Just then?"

"That it's all so sad."

"I'm thinking the same thing. And what did you intend to do about Jane, here? Would you have killed her too? She might have been as dead out there as me."

He looked up at Jane as though he had been completely unaware of her presence.

"How about it, Jane?" he said softly. "Can you keep a secret?" Then he shrugged. "No, you're in the communications business, aren't you? Both of you. Anyhow—"

"Graham," Jane said, "please. It doesn't have to be this way. I'll take care of you, I promise. I won't leave you again."

"Ha," he said. "And 'ha' again. You've already done what you could to be helpful, haven't you?"

"Graham, I love you. *Please.*"

"That only makes you my number one fan," he said.

I could see tears start in Jane's eyes, and she slumped back on the couch, struggling to keep from sobbing. So much for soothing the savage beast. My turn now.

I was beginning to feel a strange exhilaration. At long last— the real thing! This wasn't like any of the mystery novels I'd ever read or edited. The suspects weren't all lined up in chairs, waiting for me to play *Name That Killer!* No cop was cached in the next room, ready to charge in and put the cuffs on the culprit. And Graham wasn't cooperating at all! Didn't he know he was supposed to panic, break down, confess, and then bolt before being shot or shooting himself or jumping out the goddamn window, assuming there was one and it wasn't the first floor? But he isn't doing any of these things. Instead, he's just ... just sitting there impassively.

I took a deep breath.

"Graham, whatever else you are, you're not a damn fool. Killing us wouldn't get you off the hook. Scanlon knows I'm out here now and why. And it was my brother Tim who sent me here. Who figured out how you killed Jeffrey."

"Smart mother," Graham murmured. "We had a feeling we ought to get rid of him."

"We?"

"You don't think I was alone in this, do you?"

"You mean Jeffrey, I suppose."

"Among others."

"So that was why our house in Connecticut was broken into," I said. Graham just stared at me.

"And how did brother Tim figure it out?" he said.

"Well, once he knew Jeffrey was a diabetic ..." I hesitated. How *had* Tim figured it out? "He ... he just figured it out."

"I see." He made a noise that sounded like a chuckle.

"What he couldn't figure out is why you did it. Nor can I. Why did all those people have to die? Jordan? The typist? Jeffrey? What was the point?"

"The *Odyssey*," he said. "Graham Farrar's *Odyssey*. I would do anything to get that movie made, you have to understand that. Anything. And anybody who stands in the way of it—"

"But you aren't going to get it made now, are you?"

"What makes you say that? You do *know*, Nick?"

"Know what?

"What I have," he said. "My death sentence."

Silence seemed my safest bet.

"Jane knows." He turned to her. "Don't you, Jane?"

Eyes bright with tears, she nodded.

"So tell me too," I said.

"Why should I, pallie?"

"I'd rather have it straight from you. You owe me that much, Graham, for what you've just put us through."

"I'll tell you, Nick," Graham said. "It's called a carotic aneurism. An enlargement of one of the arteries leading from the neck to the brain. I know it's there because of the headaches." He rested the long, slender fingers of his left hand against his forehead. I remembered the way he looked the last time we left him here. As though he were grieving.

"Incredible headaches," he said. "That's how I found out. I had an angiogram done and it showed up there—a tiny bubble in the artery. Tiny now, but slowly getting bigger. A swollen bud, preparing to burst at any time. No way of knowing when. No way of stopping it—that's why I called it a death sentence. The doctor told me it could happen at any moment."

I didn't know what to say.

"Pop!" said the actor. "Just one *pop*, and I'm dead. As quickly as that. Well ..." He rolled his eyes. "Ain't nobody gonna give me no ten-million-dollar insurance policy if I've got me one of those aneurisms, now is they? And you can't make a movie as expensive as mine without a whole shitpot full of insurance on the star. Because without me, there'd be no production. No understudies need apply."

"So?"

"So you turn to less conventional sources for your financing."

"The sharks?"

"They're here, old buddy, just as surely as they're on Wall Street or in Washington. Maybe Spielberg or Lucas don't need them, but Randall did."

Richard Randall was a producer who had won at least one Academy Award. I found it hard to believe.

"There are others I could tell you about too. Look, I didn't want to go that route, but there wasn't much choice. And once I was into them, once I had the money, it was still risky. I was only safe so long as nobody knew about my aneurism. And nobody did know—until your Jordan Walker got nosy and found out. He would have put it in that godamn book too, Nick."

"Couldn't you keep him from doing that without *murdering* him?"

"I tried to buy him off, but he wouldn't sell. Still ... he knew. I figured sooner or later it would come to blackmail. It wasn't safe for him to know. Jeffrey knew too, and that dimwitted typist.

"Actually, Jeffrey was the one who made the connections for me. He was in on the *Odyssey* production for everything he had too. Then he got scared—he thought the cops were after him—and he was ready to spill. Yellow bastard! If he'd hung tight, he'd still be alive. Then ... then ... how many people have the guts, Nick, right? You do, maybe—you're a helluva poker player. And Jane here is savvy too ..." His voice trailed off into a slow, deep respiration, as rhythmic as the surf outside.

"Graham," I said. I would have thought him asleep except that his eyes were open, staring at nothing.

"Graham," I repeated. Finally he raised his head.

"It's a wrap, isn't it?" he said in a whisper.

"Yes," I said, "it's a wrap. Graham, I'm leaving now. Jane is coming with me. We're going to have to go to the police, sooner or later. Sooner rather than later."

He nodded, the only sign that he had heard me.

"Good-bye, Graham."

Still no reply.

Jane and I left without a word or a backward glance. This time she didn't hesitate. I could tell she was stricken; at one point she stopped and leaned against me, shaking. I put my arm around her and drew her along. The rain had stopped, but the air was still thick with moisture, and thunder rumbled overhead.

"We'll have to walk," I said. "To the highway, at least."

"That's all right."

"No car." I sighed. "I could always steal one of Graham's, I suppose."

"No."

"Right. Jane . . . ?"

"Yes?"

"You did know about Graham's aneurism?"

"Yes. Once, while I was with him, he had an attack—so severe he fainted. I called the doctor, and when he came, I overheard him talking to Graham. Graham swore me to secrecy. I'm sorry, Nick—I ought to have told you, anyway."

"I know, I know. It's all right, Jane. It's quite all right."

Then it all came out, as we walked to the highway.

"From the beginning," she said, "I had meant to be completely businesslike, no fooling around. I was also kind of in awe of Graham, frightened in a way because of his reputation, his charm, the aura of supreme assurance he wears like his sunshades—that old movie cliché!—both to attract attention and to repel intimacy. By and by, he relaxed with me, though, and I with him. We started having drinks together every evening and an occasional meal.

"And then one day he invited me for a swim after our work session. He had a considerable supply of women's tank suits and bikinis, I discovered. It was a hot day, and he suggested I'd better use a sunscreen, which he rubbed on my back.

"What I remember most clearly from that afternoon was the smell of the suntan oil, and his hands. Virtually every other man I've ever known has done his best to *talk* me into bed, has so *intellectualized* the foreplay that what happened afterward was always anticlimactic. Graham never said a word, his hands and his body said it all."

"I see."

"He's beautiful in his way," said Jane.

"You're right, he is." I remembered from somewhere—was it in the Bible or in *Paradise Lost*?—that of all God's angels, the most beautiful was Lucifer.

Just then—rather inappropriately, it seemed to me—Jane giggled.

"I suppose you think it's silly, my falling in love with a movie star." It struck me that there was a tiny note of insincerity in her voice, vainglory perhaps, or excessive pride. *I fucked a movie star, after all.*

253

"Silly? Not at all. There may be folly in passion, but certainly no silliness." And what has passion to do with reason, or intelligence? Even self-interest and greed seem to falter when the heart acts out its obsessions.

Still, there was something wrong with this conversation. But what?

"What are you going to do, Nick? Will you really turn him in to the police?"

I nodded.

"But what will he do now?" Jane asked, despair in her voice.

I told her that I had always thought of Graham as an antique Roman, though I assumed he wouldn't fall on his sword, if in fact he owned one.

"It would be more in character for the man who starred in the most recent remake of *A Star Is Born*," I said, "to take a long walk into the surf."

30

Yet that wasn't what happened after all.

Between the time Jane and I left his house and got back to New York, the fragile, swollen membrane in Graham's carotid artery, the perilous bubble in his brain, burst at last. He was found lying beside his pool, a broken wineglass near his body. About the carnage at his gatehouse, the newspapers were juicily graphic but unenlightening. The headlines, the articles that went along with them, were eulogistic, as might be expected. Graham always did get good press.

As for me, I made my confession to Lieutenant Scanlon, who read me a severe indictment of my negligence out in Los Angeles. Number one, I had failed to report a homicide, the death of Graham's guard.

"Accident," I said. "He got in the way of my car. And besides, he was shooting at me."

"All right," said Scanlon, "we can call that justifiable vehicular homicide, and I'm sure I can get you out of it."

"You must have killed in the line of duty, Joe."

He frowned but remained silent.

"Well, haven't you?"

"One probable," he said finally.

"What do you mean?"

"My partner and I were both shooting. It would be hard to say which bullet killed the guy."

"Who was it?"

"A crack dealer who had just murdered an old Jewish storekeeper and his wife with a shotgun. Which was then pointed at us, my partner and me."

"Did you regret it?"

"Are you kidding?" He looked at me as though I had said something monumentally simpleminded.

"We were trained in the air force," I said, "never to take a piece out of its holster without shooting."

Scanlon smiled. "I prefer 'Hands up!' or 'Freeze!'"

"I feel exactly the same way."

"But you also totaled a rental car, and didn't report that either."

I tried to explain that, in the circumstances, I just wanted to put as much distance between Graham and me as I could.

"You ought to have known better," he said. "You might've gotten yourself killed out there."

"That's for sure."

"After all," he said, "you're the only publisher I know. I'd hate to lose you."

"All right, Joe," I said. "You can bring in the manuscript anytime. Nonfiction, is it?"

"A novel, actually."

"Hmmm," I said. Well, why not? Police stories are in demand right now, judging by the new movie releases and the television sitcoms. One year it's the cops, the next year the robbers. Or first it's the cowboys and then it's the Indians—it hardly matters which.

There were still a few loose ends to be tied up, and Scanlon filled me in. It was a shocker. Graham himself had killed Jordan Walker, using Walker's own knife. Naturally, there was a lot of blood, and a good deal of it got on Graham's clothes. So he phoned his buddy Jeffrey Burgal. Burgal disguised himself with a mustache and beard, put a change of clothes for Graham in his attaché case, and trotted over to Jordan's apartment building. He was our third visitor. I snickered.

256

"So what's funny?" Scanlon said.

"I just remembered," I said. "The doorman said he gave his name as George Spelvin."

"So?"

"George Spelvin is the name an actor uses when he's playing two parts in a play. Spelvin is listed in the program for the second, smaller part."

"Clever," said Scanlon.

"No, cute."

"Anyway," Scanlon said, "we figure they then roughed the place up to make it *look* like a robbery."

I felt slightly ill. "And Dori Regan?"

"Burgal and Farrar knew that Jordan had written the book on a word processor. It wasn't enough just to destroy the hard copy of the book, they had to find and erase the original disk. That meant locating Walker's office, which they did, through Dori Regan. The poor damn fool probably tried to blackmail them."

"Jesus! And the mugging?"

"Jeffrey set that up," Scanlon said. "I always thought it was sort of funny the attacker went after Burgal with only his fists, but after you with a knife. Obviously Jeffrey wasn't meant to be hurt."

"But I was."

"They probably intended to scare you off publishing the book altogether."

"Or kill me."

Scanlon shrugged. "Same result, probably. Incidentally, while you were occupied with the muggers, Jeffrey shoved the so-called manuscript he had brought you through the railings of the fence around Gramercy Park into the bushes. He came back later and retrieved it."

"Using The Players' key to the park," I said, "which every member has access to."

"Exactly. I sent a man there yesterday. He found one page of the manuscript that Burgal had overlooked tucked away in the shrubbery."

"And I suppose the break-in at Jeffrey's office, when

the other copy of the manuscript was swiped, was also staged."

"Correct."

"I still can't figure out why. Jeffrey was Jordan's agent, he'd lose a lot of money if the book wasn't published."

"There was more money at stake than the book," said Scanlon. "There was the movie and what they had both tied up in it."

"It's the odd couple, you know, Jeffrey and Graham. They must have been a lot closer than I thought."

"They were," said Scanlon. "A lot closer, and a long time ago. It was pretty much as your brother called it. We picked up some old gossip about Farrar's early days in the theater, when he and Burgal were both struggling young actors." He hesitated. Perhaps he too was reluctant to paint Graham gay or bisexual. "Well, anyway, that's about all we do know for sure. For the rest . . ."

"We speculate."

"Yeah."

"Such *waste!*" I said. "Four people dead—five, counting Graham. But Graham was bound to die anyway. And all for a movie! A movie, for God's sake! One that probably never had a chance of being made. One that wasn't even *worth* making. It was an absurd monomaniacal obsession of Graham's, that's all."

"I've seen people killed for less. A lot less."

And on this note we parted.

• • •

"Well, Nick, are you through playing detective for a while?"

Margo and I were at 2 Gramercy Park. We had just finished the first relaxing meal I'd had in weeks. We had eaten asparagus tips in puff pastry with lemon butter, a casserole roast of veal with carrots and celery hearts, sautéed grated zucchini and fresh spinach. The first course was washed down with a Chardonnay, the veal and vegetables with Cabernet Sauvignon. Then we had *île flottante*, a giant meringue soufflé floating on a sea of custard. Nothing would do for the floating island but Dom Perignon, which we were now sipping. Pepita had quietly cleared away the dishes, and she and Oscar had retired to their rooms. I had just finished unfolding the whole sad, squalid story of the peculiar odyssey of Graham Farrar.

"I'm glad you're back."

"So am I."

Margo leaned back, smiled benignly at me, and said: "I'm also glad to be here with you tonight."

"I'll drink to that," I said, and promptly did.

We were standing on my terrace, looking out over Gramercy Park. The trees were in full leaf now, and although we could not see them in the darkness, I knew that the park's beds were bright with spring flowers. Edwin Booth, head slightly bowed, looked as princely as ever in the moonlight, the perfect Melancholy Dane.

"Such a nice night," I said.

"Yes."

"Shall we take a walk in the park?" I suggested.

"No." Margo hesitated. "Why don't we just take a walk into the next room?"

"Do you really mean that?" I said. "After all this time?"

"Don't be silly. You know I never say anything I don't mean. We'll call it . . ."

"Yes?"

"Our nightcap."

A Victorian novelist would draw the curtain on the next scene. And so we did draw the curtains. Put out the lights, all but a single candle. And drew back the bed covers.

Suffice it to say that love between old friends is as good as love gets. The joy and the satisfaction of desire are enhanced by familiarity, by the memory of past gratifications. There are no fears, no hesitations, no restraints. Just pleasure, long sighs, confidences murmured in the darkness, and, sweet and most welcome, sleep.

· · ·

Back in my office the next day, I found a few things to tidy up. And there was still a doubt nagging me. Something was wrong with that neat little package Scanlon had given me. What was it? It had to do with the altered manuscript, and with that business out in California between Jane and Graham. And there was something I didn't like about Jeffrey's death, too. But what?

Well, perhaps it made no difference. I console myself sometimes that not every problem needs to be solved. Some just work themselves out, others are swept up in the Great-Mystery-of-It-All.

But I couldn't let this one alone. I had to call Tim and ask.

"How did you figure out the way Graham killed Jeffrey? As far as I know, you never studied medicine—and neither did Graham."

"Don't you know?" said my brother. "You're a mystery buff. You don't remember?"

I searched my memory, in vain. I knew it would come to me ultimately—maybe even tomorrow, but not now.

"I admit it was a few years back," Tim said. "And it was just another mystery novel, I suppose, but the murders were ingenious. The first one was done by rubbing a few drops of liquid nicotine on the victim's back, surreptitiously. Dry ice was the weapon for the second murder. A pound and a half of it put in a closed bedroom while the intended victim slept. The result—suffocation. And finally, the murderer—a doctor, of course—used the Levine tube on his own wife, who happened to be a diabetic."

"Now I remember!" I said. "It was called *A Guilty Thing*."

"Precisely," said Tim. "You read a great many more books than you remember."

"I'll see you this weekend," I said before ringing off, "with a bottle of champagne and a bundle of manuscripts."

So that was it. *A Guilty Thing!* Now I remembered. And now I knew, goddamn it, I *knew!*

I buzzed Hannah on the intercom.

"Yes, Nick?"

"Send in Jane Goodman, please, Hannah."

When she came in, Jane was carrying a notebook in one hand and a pencil in the other.

"Yes?" she said.

I fussed with some papers on my desk for a minute or two; I really didn't want to look at her. When I finally did, I thought: *She* is *beautiful, and she gets more beautiful every time I look at her*. Meanwhile she was staring at me.

"What is it, Nick?"

"I was thinking of giving you another manuscript to work on," I said, "but something's bothering me about Graham."

"His biography?" Jane said. "I thought we did as much as we could to get it ready for publication before ... well, as much as we could."

"It's not his biography that's bothering me."

"Then what is it?" Jane said. "He's dead and buried. Can't we just—can't we just leave it at that and get on with our lives?"

"You're right," I said. "That's what we should do. But there's something else I can't get out of my mind."

"Well, what is it, for God's sake?" She rose to her feet and started to pace back and forth in front of my desk.

"*A Guilty Thing*," I said softly, so softly she barely heard me.

"What? What did you say, Nick?"

"Graham committed three murders," I said. "Two of them were particularly violent—vicious, in fact. That's not surprising—Graham in a temper, or when he was drinking, was a violent man. He would use maximum force, no doubt about it. But the third murder was much more subtle, not Graham's style at all. He'd be inclined to bash Jeffrey on the head or push him underwater and hold him there until he drowned."

"So?"

"Someone must have directed this murder for Graham ... or supplied him with the *modus vivendi*, as they call it."

"And you think it was me? Why?"

"That particular kind of murder appeared in a book called *A Guilty Thing*, Jane. It was published by Doubleday, around the time you worked for them. For all I know, you edited it— at least you were probably familiar with it. Also, one other thing."

"What?"

"You were in love with the guy. You wanted to help him, that's all. In fact—" I rose from my chair and slapped my hand on my desk, hard. "In fact, you knew him before, didn't you? That missing year on your résumé was Graham. It wasn't love at first sight at all."

I wish I could say she caved in and asked for . . . what? Forgiveness? Understanding? She just looked me straight in the eyes and said: "Do you blame me?"

"No," I said. "No blame. But I'm curious to know just how deeply you were mixed up in this business. You used a brief acquaintance with Margo to get to me, but you were really sent here by Graham and Jeffrey, weren't you? Planted in my office so Graham would have somebody to keep an eye on the book."

She said nothing, made no attempt at denial, just stared at me.

"Maybe," I said, "you were the one who worked on Jordan's disk, trying to rewrite the book so it would pass muster without incriminating Graham? Were yours the fingerprints Tim found on the computer disk? Well?"

She nodded. Now there were tears in her eyes.

"I just couldn't bring it off," she said. "Graham and Jeffrey couldn't write for beans, and I couldn't write in Jordan's style. So we erased it."

"The three of you?"

"Yes."

"Then what?"

"You sent me out to California to help Graham bring the book up to speed. I'd already done my best to do just that, so I didn't have much hope. But I couldn't tell you that, so I went."

"And Jeffrey?"

"He panicked, so Graham said he'd have to be"—she hesitated, trembling—"removed."

"With your guidance."

She bit her lip and nodded again, then said, "And what are you going to do about it? Call the police?"

I sighed. "You were, after all, an accessory to a murder. I'll

262

tell Joe Scanlon about your role in this mess and let him decide what to do. I expect he'll play it by the book, no pun intended. It's up to him. You'll have to take your chances, Jane. Also—"

"What?"

"I don't want you working for me any longer."

"So I'm fired."

"That's right, you're fired."

I could think of all sorts of reasons for keeping her on, including my own libido. She herself supplied the best one.

"But I'm a damn good editor."

"I know."

"The loss will be yours, Nick."

Didn't I know that? Still, as my father taught me long ago, you can't have anyone working for you that you don't trust. You wouldn't be able to turn your back on him—or her.

"Good-bye, Jane. I'll miss you, I really will."

She walked out without a word or a backward look.

.   .   .

Murder is fascinating, but publishing is my business, and it must be attended to. The loosest of my loose ends at Barlow & Company appeared, brand-new hat in hand, the week after I got back to New York. It was Warren Dallas, looking somewhat crestfallen though sounding as cocky as ever.

"Nick," he announced once my office door had closed behind him, "I think we ought to talk business again."

"No hard feelings?" I gestured toward his hat.

"None. Hey, this hat is even better than the one you threw out the window."

"Bygones are bygones?"

"Right."

"But I thought"—and here I lit a cigar, offering one to my ex-author—"that you'd signed with Simon and Schuster."

"No, we couldn't come to terms. And anyway, it was Random House, Nick."

"I see." I did see. *They wouldn't meet his price.* "But you'd rather be back with me again."

"We understand each other," he said. "Yeah, I would like to be back with you, Nick. Provided we can work out a few details. Dot a few *i*'s, cross a few *t*'s." He began by crossing his legs and settling back in the visitor's chair with a profound sigh.

"It's just not the same business it used to be, Nick. Not the way you and I have always known it. The good old days, don't you think? It's no longer man to man, gentleman to gentleman."

I suggested that it had never been a gentleman's business, at least not the way my father and his colleagues had conducted it. It was a business begun in the nineteenth century in an atmosphere of piracy and carried on in cutthroat fashion. On a small scale, America's first publishers were robber barons.

Warren, however, was off in his own private fantasy. "You know something, Nick? You go out with these young editors for a meal these days, and they order an omelet or a chef's salad, for Chrissake, and wash it down with mineral water. Mineral water! Rabbit food!"

Warren somehow made these wholesome dishes sound vile and disgusting. Fleetingly, I pictured him trussed to his chair, being force-fed a diet of yogurt and raw vegetables.

"Pipsqueaks," he muttered.

"Have you heard the definition of an editor that's making the rounds, Warren?" I said. "Somebody who knows what he wants, but doesn't know what it is."

"When I think of the great meals you and I used to have. [*At my expense, Warren.*] All those martinis we could put away and still get back to work. [*Speak for yourself, Dallas.*] There are so many accountants and lawyers and M.B.A.'s mixed up in this business now that a simple country boy is in danger of being screwed six ways from Sunday."

Not in as great danger as I felt at that moment. Whenever a man like Warren Dallas refers to himself as a "simple country boy," I pat my hip to make sure my wallet is secure.

"Now, Warren, about those *t*'s we going to cross, after we've dotted all the *i*'s—"

"All in good time, Nick, all in good time. I have a strong

264

feeling that we're going to come to some kind of fair, gentlemanly agreement, a truly honest contract—if that's not a contradiction in terms."

"I'd like to have your next book, Warren, if that's what you mean. Provided I don't have to give away the store to get it."

Warren laughed, slapping his thigh as though that was the funniest thing he'd heard all day. Hilarious!

"*No* problem," he said. "So . . . what do you say we start the negotiations by having a drink?"

"Followed by dinner?" I said.

"If you insist."

"Oh, I do, I *do*. I wouldn't have it otherwise."

Check—and mate.

·   ·   ·

Publishing people, I firmly believe, are eternal optimists, individuals strong in what F. Scott Fitzgerald called "an extraordinary gift for hope, a romantic readiness." No doubt it comes with the territory. Why else would we send so many books out into the marketplace, with all their imperfections on their heads, knowing that only a relative handful of them will flourish, or even survive?

Two days after Warren Dallas returned to the fold, the newest Barlow & Company hopeful arrived, a neatly wrapped package under his arm. It was Lieutenant Joseph Scanlon, off-duty. He dropped his package on my desk.

"Here it is, Nick," he said.

"I'll take good care of it, Joe."

"I know you will. I just hope you like it, that's all."

"I'm predisposed to like it."

He grinned. "Well, I guess I'd better be getting back to the precinct."

"Not just yet."

"What do you mean, Nick?

"I'm going to take you out to lunch first. A true publisher-author lunch. What do you prefer—the Four Seasons? 'Twenty-one'? The Rose Room of the Algonquin? Or maybe the Century?"

"I wouldn't know," he said. "I'm too new to your part of the world. Why don't you decide?"

"I know the perfect place, Joe. The Players."

"Oh, yeah," he said. "The building down in Gramercy Park. The one with the gas lamps."

"You got it, Joe. Let's go."

As we walked through the foyer toward the elevator, it occurred to me that Scanlon and I had shared an adventure, old news to him but exciting to me—and that we were now about to share another adventure, this one of a quite different nature: the making of a book. Here I would be the mentor, and he the protégé. Was it not also possible that a real friendship had been forged between us? Ah, forever the optimist. And why not?

Just then the elevator doors opened, and I took Joseph Scanlon, author, to lunch.